ETHIC V

BY

ASHLEY ANTOINETTE

Ashley Antoinette Inc.
P.O. Box 181048
Utica, MI 48318

ISBN: 978-1-7328313-5-3

Trade Paperback Printing October 2018
Printed in the United States of America

Distributed by Ashley Antoinette Inc.
Submit Wholesale Orders to:
owl.aac@gmail.com

LETTER TO THE FANS

Ash Army!!!! We're so deep into this thing I can no longer discern between Ethic Land and reality. Thank you, guys. This entire series has been such an honor to pen. I have tapped into a level of creativity that many artists never see, and you guys are right there with me. You have allowed me to drown you in the pain of this story. There is such sorrow on these pages and you're feeling it, you're going there with me. You trust me with your emotions and there is no greater connection between author and reader than that. Before you start this one I need you to think about all the pieces of this puzzle I've put before you. You put them in place perfectly inside your mind in one some ways. In other ways, you haven't even scratched the surface. This one will hurt. Badly. Why? Because life is unfair at times and the perfection these characters are hoping for rarely exists. They are just people trying to figure it out along a road of pitfalls and potholes. These characters…hmm…it feels a little disrespectful to even call them that at this point because they're real. These people…are trying their hardest to love through the odds…to fight for one another. There is no doubt that between these two couples there is love but is love enough? You be the judge. When it hurts…cry! When it feels good…smile! When you feel like laughing…please do. Feel it all, while you can, because it's almost over. I'm an artist. I'm not writing what you want to read. So, if it doesn't end the way you want, I need you to understand that these people have told their own story. Their fates were sealed by the pen, not my heart. Allow the story to evolve naturally. Don't force your own preferences. If you love these characters love the experience of them. Love the time you have left, before it ends. Thank you for believing in me. Y'all have no idea how you have inspired me to write what I feel instead of what I'm branded to be. Ashley Antoinette books have changed, have grown. A style of writing has come from me that is so heartfelt I don't think I'll ever let it go. Thank you for appreciating my vision for this story. I saw these words in color on the page. I stopped writing this story a long time ago. I'm painting on these pages. The picture might not always be clear. Sometimes you might have to turn your head to the side to see the canvas from a different angle to try to understand the art. But it's beautiful to me. I hope you open your hearts and put down your judgements. E&A and M&M are going through enough. They don't need judgement, they need empathy. Give them that. Step outside yourself and put away the "I could never do this, or I would never do that." This isn't about you. Or I. Or the real world. It's about Ethic Land and in Ethic Land, love is a high stakes game that requires sacrifice and a lot of forgiveness. So, you know the routine! Grab your wine, maybe something a little stronger, put the rug rats to bed, put the significant other on pause because Ethic and Messiah need you for a little while. They always return who doesn't belong to them in the end.

-xoxo-
Ashley Antoinette

ACKNOWLEDGEMENTS

To Ashley Jackson, my goodness the ways you let me use your brain! Thank you, Ash. You have been stuck on this emotional rollercoaster with me the entire way. Your discretion, commitment, and understanding of these characters is incomparable. You know them as well, if not better than me. I could not have done this without you. You listened, you test-read, and you invested yourself in this world…trapped yourself in it and I appreciate you. We have had hours of conversation about this series and those notes/convos have given me clarity and insight into a reader's mind. You are the best love! My absolute fav!

To the fans. I owe you everything. Thank you will never be enough. I am so grateful for you.

WARNING

This series has been known to cause *The Ethic Effect*. If you experience shortness of breath, palpitations of the heart, day dreaming, overactive emotions, out of body episodes, lustful thinking, or inexplicable yearning for an imaginary man/woman...find your book bestie and discuss immediately!

Happy Reading!

ETHIC V PLAYLIST

Treat Me Like Somebody, Tink
Unfair, 6lack
Where'd You Go, Destiny's Child
Almost Doesn't Count, Brandy
End of the Road, Boyz II Men
Fuckin' Wit Me, Tank
Cursed, Vivian Green
You Mean the World to Me, Mackenzie Capri
Never Say Never, Brandy
I Wish You Loved Me, Tynisha Keli
Without a Woman, Trey Songz
Nobody's Supposed to Be Here, Deborah Cox
Angel in Disguise, Brandy
Diggin' on You, TLC
Just Be a Man About It, Toni Braxton
Love and War, Tamar Braxton
It Kills Me, Melanie Fiona
Gut Feeling, Ella Mai featuring H.E.R.
Backin' It Up, Pardison Fontaine featuring Cardi B
Angel, Amanda Perez
I Nominate U, Fantasia
Close, Ella Mai
Waves, Normani featuring 6lack
I'll Find a Way, Blu Cantrell
Myself, Layton Greene
Loved by You, Mali Music featuring Jazmine Sullivan
I Wanna Be Down, Brandy
Me & U, Cassie

Lead, Asiahn
Learn the Hard Way, Brandy
Session 32, Summer Walker
Worst Luck, 6lack
Sweet Lady, Tyrese
All the Way Home, Tamar Braxton
Would You Mind, Janet Jackson
Love Train, Asiahn
The Truth, India.Arie
One Sweet Day, Mariah Carey

CHAPTER 1

Have you heard anything, Nannie?" Bella asked, as she entered the kitchen.

"You say good morning when you wake up and join the rest of us, little girl," Nannie said, as she turned from the stove with a plate in her hand.

"Yes, ma'am," Bella answered. "Good morning." She took a seat in the chair across from Eazy.

"Good morning, baby," Nannie answered, kissing the top of Bella's head. "And no, I haven't heard anything new. She hasn't opened her eyes yet, but we just going to keep praying."

Nannie placed the home-cooked breakfast in front of Bella. Grits, homemade biscuits, bacon and eggs. A plate full of effort, especially from Nannie's old bones…it all took so much effort, which equated to love.

"When you're done, I want you to go down to the corner store and put my numbers in. I'ma send you with a note and the money. Jimmy knows me down there. All you got to do is give it to him and he'll do the rest," Nannie said.

"Yes, ma'am," Bella said.

"Nannie, what if Mo doesn't wake up? Is a comma the same as dying?" Eazy asked.

"It's a coma, idiot," Bella snapped.

"Don't talk to your brother like that," Nannie said. "Ever," she reinforced. "You speak out of love, or not at all, when you're talking to family."

Bella's head hung low, as she played in her food, unable to stomach much because she was wound so tightly with anxiety. "Yes, ma'am."

"Will they have to like put her in the ground like my mom?" Eazy pressed. He just wanted information. Bella too. They were in anguish over the uncertainty of Morgan's condition.

"We're not there yet, baby. God sits a person down sometimes when they need to rest. When you're doing too much...God will come and take your legs right from under you and give you a little nap. She's resting. We're going to pray really hard because she still has a lot of life to live and a lot of people who love her. Don't you worry. God is in the miracle-granting business," Nannie said.

Bella picked up her fork and Nannie cleared her throat. "Bless your food," Nannie reminded.

Bella lowered her head.

God, please...this isn't about the food. I mean, yeah, bless the food and the hands that prepared it, but please don't let Mo die. God, please. Pleasse. I'm begging you. Take a little life away from me and just give it to her. Just let her wake uppp.

She lifted her head. "Amen."

Bella picked at her plate, and when she was done, she washed the dishes - a rule at Nannie's and Alani's - before grabbing the note and heading out the door. Her heart was so heavy that her legs almost couldn't carry it. She felt an unbelievable burden on her soul and her chest ached. As soon as she was up the block, her tears came. She tried not to cry in front of Eazy because she didn't want to scare him. She had held these tears in for days. The waiting was unbearable. If Morgan died, Bella would be crushed. Morgan was her sister. She had shared moments with Mo that no one else knew about. They had secrets between them that they had shared, under the same cover with a flashlight, in the middle of the night. They had argued and made up a thousand times over the years. Bella looked up to Morgan. She had never seen anyone prettier, never met anyone smarter. She used to love when they would be in a room full of people and sign the entire time. They had their own bond, their own understanding, and they had never let anyone else in. Sisters by love, not blood…it still counted; and if Morgan died, Bella would never forgive her.

Bella made it to the corner store. It was graffiti-covered and had bars on the windows. The glass door was so dirty it was no longer see-through. She walked inside and headed straight for the counter.

"What can I do for you, darling?" the Chaldean man asked, as he stood behind the counter.

"Ms. Pat sent me," she said. She handed him the handwritten note.

He opened the paper and read it. "Coming right up." He typed the numbers into the machine and then handed her a stack of tickets. "That'll be twenty-eight bucks."

Bella handed him two twenties, and then accepted her change.

"Do you have seltzer water and veggie straws?" she asked.

He snickered. "Nah, li'l mama. I ain't got that. I got quarter waters in the back. Faygo pops and Hot Cheetos and shit over there."

Bella grimaced, sticking out her tongue in disgust, as she shook her head.

"You too good for Hot Cheetos, Pretty Girl?"

She turned toward the voice…turned too quickly to play it cool…and Hendrix scoffed in amusement, smiling at her eagerness. He stepped up and tossed five dollars on the counter. "Two Hot Cheetos, a pickle, and a rillo," he said. "Gimme two quarter waters too, and some Now and Laters." Hendrix pulled off another five and then turned to Bella.

"You're going to eat all that?" she asked, frowning.

"Nah, you're going to help me," he said. "You gotta act like you from the hood, if you gon' be parlaying in the hood." He licked his lips and she shook her head.

"You got it, G," Jimmy said, as he slid a brown paper bag across the counter. Hendrix grabbed it and walked out the store. He let the door swing closed and Bella stopped walking. He turned back, noticing she was still inside the store. His brow dipped low, in confusion, and he pulled the door open.

"What's wrong?" he asked.

"When you're walking with me, I don't open my own doors," she said.

He stared at her for a beat, then pulled his bottom lip between his teeth. He opened the door wider and extended his hand. "A'ight. I hear you. Now a nigga know better, I'll do better," he said.

Bella eased out in front of him.

"I'll take you back to Ms. Pat's," he said, nodding toward the car parked in front of them. It was an old-school, boxed-style car from the 80's. It reminded her of the ones Ethic would buy from the junkyard and rehab. It was rusted in places where the winter had eaten away at the body, and in bad shape. "This is your car?" she asked.

"Yeah. You too good to ride in my Chevy? I know you used to Teslas and all. I'ma grind up one day. I'ma get that too; but you got to be willing to ride in this to sit in that with me one day. From the bottom, feel me?" he asked.

"Who said I wanted to sit next to you at all?" Bella asked.

Hendrix smiled and nodded his head. "Just let me take you back," he said. "Please?"

"I can't pull up with you to Nannie's. She'd kill me. Then, my dad would kill me. Then, Alani would bury my body because she doesn't play at all," Bella said, only half joking. "Are you even old enough to be driving?"

"I don't follow rules too good." He smirked, looking off down the block, before rolling charming eyes back at her. He was so damn cute. Gorgeous, in fact. Bella tore her gaze from his and forced it to her feet, as she shuffled from side to side. "I'll drop you off at the corner. Get in," he said.

Bella knew better than to follow him, but her feet moved anyway.

They hopped in the car and he dumped the junk from the paper bag. He popped open a bag of Hot Cheetos. "Veggie straws," he snickered. "This is real nigga food." She jerked her neck back, as he held the bag up to her face.

"It smells like feet a little bit," she said, with a chuckle.

"Come on, man. Get your G up," he said. "Taste one." He stuck his hand inside the bag and popped a handful in his mouth. "They good as fuck, no lie," he said.

Bella stuck her pinky out and dipped two, dainty fingers inside the bag. She pulled out one Cheeto and put it in her mouth. Her eyebrows lifted, in surprise, as she chewed slow.

"Aghh!" He teased. "Good as fuck, right?"

She smiled and snatched the bag. "Give me those," she said.

"Pretty Girl ain't that bougie, huh?"

She stuck out her tongue. "They're hot."

He passed her a quarter water and she popped her thumb through the aluminum and drank a sip.

"Look at you, looking like a regular around the way girl," he teased. He grabbed the cigarillo and opened the package before gutting it. He pulled out a small bag of weed.

"Can you not do that with me in your car?" she asked.

"You don't smoke, my bad," he said. "Good girl shit. . . I forgot."

"I mean, I have before. . . I don't often, but I just don't want to go back smelling like it," she said.

"I got you," he said. He started the car and drove the short distance to Nannie's block. He pulled over at the end of the block, as promised, then cut off the engine.

"How old are you, Hendrix?" she asked.

"Fourteen," he said. "And you're thirteen in three months," he added.

She nodded.

"Who made you cry?" he asked.

Bella looked at him, in stun, thrown off by his question.

"Your eyes are red and glossy, a little puffy. Who I got to fuck up?"

"Why would you mess up anyone just because they made me cry?" she countered.

He shrugged. "That's just how I'm cut. Fuck shit up over what I feel like fucking shit up over. Over you, it feel like I'ma be fucking a lot of shit up."

She looked out the window, fighting an unexpected smile. Her chest went warm, like it did when she swallowed hot chocolate, and then it faded. "My sister's in the hospital. She tried to kill herself and I don't know if she's going to be okay," Bella admitted.

"That's messed up," he said, a heavy tone in his voice, as he stared out the window. He rolled sympathetic eyes back to her.

"I've got to go," she said. "Thanks for the snacks." She smiled, and he opened his car door.

"Where are you going?" she asked.

"You said you don't touch doors when you with me. Car doors count, right?" he asked.

Bella smiled. "Yeah, they count." She waited in the passenger seat until he got to her door and opened it.

She stood and looked at him. He stood in front of her, trapping her between his body and his raggedy car.

"Thirteen in three months..."

“Why do you keep bringing that up?” she asked.

“Because that’s when I’ma kiss you. On your birthday. When you’re thirteen,” he said.

Suddenly, it was scorching outside, and Bella’s stomach went missing. Her phone rang, and Bella answered it, immediately, when she saw her father’s face on the screen.

“Daddy…”

She paused, and then her eyes widened, before she pushed past Hendrix and took off running, full speed, towards Nannie’s house.

CHAPTER 2

"Where the hell is this girl?" Aria whispered. She glanced at her phone screen, briefly, snatching eyes from the road ahead, as she tried to dial Morgan and drive simultaneously.

"Hi, you've reached Morgan Atkins. Leave a message that will make me smile!"

BEEP!

"Mooooooooooooooo," Aria shouted in the phone. "You know I thrive off attention, sis. Where's my attention? It's been two days since I've heard your voice. You know I'm not the one to be ignored. I stopped by your place, you're not home, so I'm taking that as a reason to slide by your fine-ass daddy house to see if you're there. Whew, chile, that man is fine…I just want to be your step-mama, Mo! My godddddd, why is he so fine?" Aria snickered into the phone, as she maneuvered onto the highway. "Okay…I know you're probably disgusted at this point. You better be there, got me wasting my gas, driving all the way to Grand Blanc cuz you don't want to answer your phone. I'll be there soon. Love you. Bye."

Aria hung up, and as soon as she sat her phone down, it rang loudly through her speakers.

Mo Money aka Main Thang aka My Bitch

The name popped up on the screen in her car. Aria pressed answer. "About time you answered!"

"Hello, Aria. This is Alani, Morgan's..." There was a pause and Aria frowned. "I'm a friend of her father. Morgan is hurt. She's..." Aria heard the emotion stuck in Alani's throat, the hint of a sob was leaking through the speakers. "She's in the hospital. Hurley Medical Center. You should come here."

Aria's heart obliterated in her chest. The sinking feeling that consumed her was so overwhelming that she had to pull over. Her foot shook against the accelerator and tears filled her eyes. She didn't even need to hear more. She recognized the anguish in Alani's voice. She could hear the worry, the fear. She had no inclination of what had occurred, but she knew it was bad.

"What happened?" she asked. "Is she okay?"

"We don't know yet, hun, but you should get here. Ethic said she would want you here," Alani said. "We're on the 7th floor, room ten."

"I'm on my way," Aria answered.

"Aria?" Alani called. There was a pause, and then the sound of a cry that sent a pang of fear through Aria's belly. "Hurry."

The line went dead, and Aria's eyes prickled. Her lip quivered, and she gripped her steering wheel so tightly that the pads of her fingers hurt. Her mind flashed to the last time she'd seen Morgan. The dance studio. The practice.

"You make sure Messiah knows that this is all his fault..."

Morgan's words played through Aria's head, as she pressed her foot to the gas, all the way to the floor, causing her to spin out a bit, as she maneuvered back onto the road. She knew. She hadn't known before that moment, but after this phone call from Alani, she was sure. Morgan had hurt herself. Morgan had put all her value in the basket of Messiah and the bottom had fallen out of it.

"Fucking Messiah," she whispered. Her eyes clouded the entire way down the highway, but she kept driving. She might as well have been flying, she was driving so fast. Aria picked up her phone, struggling to keep her sights on the road, and dial Isa at the same time.

"The number you've dialed is no longer in service."

Aria's heart plummeted. She tossed the phone in her handbag and hightailed it to Flint.

Aria wasn't a girl who made friends easily. She didn't trust women. She didn't love women, but Morgan was her sister. They developed such a strong bond, in such a short period of time, that it felt like her own flesh and blood was hurting. Aria could feel it in her soul. She was such an empath that she had tossed and turned all night. Something in her had been unsettled, and now she knew why. She couldn't get to her fast enough; and when she pulled into the hospital, she didn't even park her car. She hopped out right at the entrance.

"Ma'am, you can't park there..."

The words were spoken to her back because she was already

inside. Everything seemed to take forever. The security guard checking her bag, the elevator descending slowly from the top floor. It was torture. Aria just wanted to get to her. She just wanted to see her. When she made it to the 7th floor, she had to brace herself. She had to clench her stomach to stop the sob from bursting through her trembling lips. She could see Eazy and Bella sitting on the floor at the far end of the hall. She could see a beautiful woman, whom she assumed to be Alani, pacing around them. Aria's steps quickened. She was counting them, she was so anxious. When she got to the trio, she stopped. She gulped in air, not realizing she had been holding her breath until that very moment.

"Aria?"

She nodded.

"Come on," Alani said. She placed a soft hand to Aria's shoulder and led her inside the room.

"Oh no," Aria said, turning around, right into Alani, collapsing into her as she clenched her eyes tight. "Nooooo. Why would he do this to her? How could he do this to her?" Aria, who prided herself in never letting anyone see her sweat, folded under pressure…under the pressure of possibly losing the only friend she had ever had.

"I know," Alani whispered. "I know."

Aria didn't even know Alani, but this embrace was the only thing keeping her standing. This hug felt like it came from a woman who cared, and she clung to her until she gained her composure. She turned to the bed where Ethic was sitting, head bowed over intertwined fists. Aria couldn't even admire Mo's *fine-ass daddy,* or the fine-ass man sitting on the other side of Morgan, head bowed in prayer also, because she was focused on the tube running out of Morgan's parted lips.

Her face was swollen, her throat bloated, and her skin so pale that it looked blue.

"I'm going to BEAT MESSIAH'S ASS!"

She walked to Morgan's bedside. "What happened to her? What did she do?"

Ethic lifted a penetrating stare to Aria.

"What do you mean, 'what did she do'? What makes you think she did this?" Ethic asked. She knew he was upset. She knew he was looking for someone to blame. She knew that her implying that Mo did it meant she had prior knowledge of the possibility of her doing exactly this. Ethic was looking for explanation, reaching for someone to blame, searching for someone to punish.

"The last time I saw her," Aria stammered. "She was upset. She was emotional. She said to tell Messiah it was on him. I had no idea she would do something this stupid. Why would she do this? Mo, how could you do this to yourself?"

Ethic stood and allowed Aria to sit beside Morgan.

Aria reached for her hand.

"Is she going to be okay?" She looked back at Ethic who stood behind Alani, with his arms draping over her, leaning on her, as his red eyes stared at Morgan.

"We don't know," Alani answered.

"We're praying hard."

Aria turned to the man across from her. Gold chain on his neck, fitted 'D' cap on his head, dimples in his cheeks that she wanted to stick her tongue in.

"This is Nyair, our pastor, and a friend," Alani introduced.

"You're a pastor? Like a pastor, pastor?" Aria asked, lifting eyes of surprise. "Like, bless the food, take my tithes, preach a Word, type of pastor?"

Nyair gave a half smirk and a nod of confirmation. "I do all of the above," he said.

"Where the fuck they make you at?" Aria asked. "Nigga, I'll lay all this on your altar."

Alani hollered. Ethic too. It was the first laugh that had infiltrated the somber hospital room in days.

Nyair licked his lips and smiled, while shaking his head. He was used to this type of response...no one had ever been this blatant, but it wasn't foreign.

Aria couldn't help but chuckle. "Sorry, Pastor. I'm just saying. I'm a sinner. I'm in need of prayer. Closed door confession, sir."

Nyair lifted from his seat. "On that note, I think I'ma slide, G," he said.

"Mmm hmm... you better," Aria mumbled.

Nyair showed Ethic love, hands clasped, a quick hug, a gangster's handshake, before kissing Alani's cheek, and then making his exit.

Aria sighed. "See, Mo, you got me out here talking crazy to men of God. Wake up, sis. You're the calm to my crazy. Wake your ass up before I fuck your pastor."

Her jokes were only her way of distracting herself from the seriousness of the situation. It was easier to laugh than to cry; but as a tear slid down her face and she reached for Mo's cold hand, she knew that this was one time she wouldn't be able to play tough. Her heart was on her sleeve and would remain there until Morgan opened her eyes. "Wake up, Mo. Please, God, let her wake up."

The darkness of night cloaked the block, as Messiah sat on the front porch of the old, one-story house. The idea of knocking on the front door and stepping foot inside made his heart riot inside his chest. Messiah didn't fear much. He had been through hell. After the things he had endured, every other threat held no power over him. These four walls. The memories that dwell inside. The ghosts he had run from... they terrified him. They paralyzed him right on the stoop. He couldn't take a step further. It was taking everything inside him to be there.

He didn't know how Rosie could live there. She had gone back to buy the property, as soon as he had blessed her with her first bag. She was like an agent, taking fifteen percent off the top of all his licks, simply because she was his bloodline. He always took care of his bloodline. A real man did nothing less; so, when he got paid, she got paid...every time, on time. She was his sister and he had tried his best to do right by her. Out of obligation, not love, because he hadn't allowed himself to love anyone his entire life. It was why Morgan's love had snuck up on him. It had jumped him, delivering blows to his chin, kicks to his middle, folding him, like a little bitch with nothing more than a smile and the sound of his name on her lips. Morgan had beat him black and blue with her love. He felt the bruises even now. They throbbed unbearably. He loved her so terribly…even still…even knowing he couldn't stay…even if he wanted to, he couldn't stay with her. The possibility of that possibility wasn't even in his power anymore. He was leaving her, and the realization that the day had finally come made tears of anger burden his eyes. He would do anything to stay, but he couldn't. His head hung low, locs blocking out the bum straggling down the street. The sound of the bottles clanging inside the grocery cart he pushed serenaded the otherwise quiet street. Messiah was in a dreadful mood. He had to blow town. He should have been left town. If Ethic found out he was still in the city's limits, there would be no bullets spared. He had to do this one thing first. He didn't want to, but lately his choices weren't his own.

The headlights that shined on him pulled his attention. Rosie Williams was home. His little sister. He remembered the day his mother had brought her home. He didn't know how he remembered. He was only three years old, but he could vividly see her walking into his room, carrying a little, crying bundle.

"Meet your sister, Messiah. This is Rosie."

"Wozi?" he had asked. "Wozi is my sister?"

"Wozi is your sister and you're her big brother. You'll have to protect her. You'll have to be strong for her. Nobody comes before her. If you ever have to choose, you choose her."

"My Wozi."

Messiah had imprinted on her, instantly. That sense of responsibility had settled into him from day one. He had loved her back then, before trauma happened, before love made him feel weak, before he associated loving someone with pain. Before the love of Bookie had turned to something sadistic, something cruel, something unimaginable. After that, he had been afraid to let anyone love him…he had been terrified to love at all. He wanted no parts of it. Love felt like manipulation. Love was the pre-cursor to abuse. Love was the way Bookie had gotten Messiah to trust him, before robbing him of everything that made him a man. Fuck love. So, he couldn't love Wozi if he wanted to. Protect her? Yes. Love her? He couldn't. He just couldn't. Wozi exited the car and then reached into the backseat to retrieve her child.

"Messiah! He's gone! Daddy's gone!" she cried, hopping out the car. She snatched open the back door and pulled out her son. His nephew. Another attached un-attachment. He didn't move immediately. He sat there, brooding, contemplating, struggling, as she stormed over to him. "What the fuck you just sitting there for? Did you hear me? I got a call from the department of corrections, Messiah! He's gone! He was fine. He was in perfect health, and all of a sudden, he's dead?! I've been wondering why he hasn't called. Why he hasn't checked in. He's dead. He's been dead for days and they are just now calling! That nigga, Ethic, did this! I hope he kissed all his fucking kids goodnight last night, because every single one of them is fucking dead. Why are you just sitting there? Do you hear me? It's time to put this shit to rest."

Messiah stood. "Quit all that fucking yelling, Wo. You're being reckless right now. Open the door."

Wozi was so emotional that her hands shook, as she put the key in the lock and opened her door. Messiah followed her inside.

"I'm so glad you're done with that bitch. It's about time you came to your senses. I'm going to make that shit hurt. I want her in pieces, Messiah. She looks exactly like her sister. Exactly. I fucking hate her. I want her dea—"

The adrenaline that coursed through him, as he put the burner to her lower back and pulled the trigger, made his heart race. Wozi lost her legs, as the bullet ripped through her. No sound because Messiah knew better. Silence the shot. Two pulls of the trigger. One body, one head shot to make sure it was finished. Get in and out; but she was his sister. He couldn't just let her body hit the floor. He was having a hard time even curling his finger a second time for the kill shot. He caught her, as she stumbled backwards into him. She gripped her child and he gripped her, staggering to the wall, and then sliding down, as she gritted her teeth, gasping for air.

"Messiahhh," she groaned, crying.

He squeezed his eyes closed, pulling her head back to his shoulder, as his nephew screamed in the arms of his dying mother. "Shhhh," he whispered in her ear, stroking her hair as his heart bled.

"How could you?" she cried, coughing. "Mess—" Blood spurted from her mouth. "Why?!"

"For her," he whispered. He kissed the side of Wozi's head, as she kicked her feet, trying to push against him, trying to fight for her life. Her lungs were filling with blood. She was suffocating. She was drowning on dry land. Messiah, her brother, her flesh and blood, had shot her. "I told you not to make me choose, Wo. If you're alive, she's always in danger. She's never safe. I can't stay to keep her safe, but I can't leave her if you're alive. I can't, Wo. She's mine. I'll sacrifice anything for her. Even you, Wo. It was you or her. I'm so sorry."

"My son," she cried. "My baby. Messiah, my son."

"I got him, Wozi. Just sleep. Just close your eyes," he whispered. "Just like when we were little. Close 'em, Wo."

He gritted his teeth and put her head to his chest. His fucking eyes burned. He was at war with himself. He felt like a monster. Morgan had peeled back so many layers of his soul, he felt everything, every second of Wozi's life leaving her. He felt that shit and it was excruciating.

Her son wailed in her arms, as Messiah held her tightly. "Just like that, Wozi."

He lifted the gun to her temple and turned his head away. If he could have handled this any other way, he would have. If he could leave and be confident that Wozi would never seek revenge against Morgan, he would have let her live. He knew his sister, however. She was a menace; and once she had spoken the threat against Morgan, it was written that she would kill her. Wozi didn't make idle threats. She didn't speak without thinking. It would only be a matter of time before she touched Morgan, so Messiah touched her first. He couldn't do much for Mo, at this point, but he could take care of that. He could clear the danger out of her path. He was stuck between the blood that coursed in his veins, the DNA he couldn't help, and the blood that pumped his heart. Morgan made his heart race. She gave him purpose. He would never not choose her. No matter how difficult of a decision it may be. He would lay anybody to rest for her. Over her. Because of her. Morgan was justification enough to commit murder and condemn his soul to hell. He didn't give a fuck, as long as she was covered. He knew his mistakes made him less of a man. A lesser man than the one who was supposed to possess someone as pure as Morgan. He was figuring out life the hard way. Through trial and error. Making up logic that justified his wrongs, because in his mind, this was right. It was Morgan's law, Messiah's will.

"Just do it."

Messiah curled the trigger.

Wozi's body went limp in his arms and Messiah laid her down gently. He bent to pick up his nephew.

"I know, man, I know," he whispered. He grabbed the diaper bag from the floor and placed it over his arm. "Shhh, shhh. Fuck I'ma do with you, nephew? Hmm? What I'm supposed to do now?" he whispered, bouncing, as he stepped over Wozi's body. He didn't look back, as he made his exit.

CHAPTER 3

"Ethic…"

"Hmm?" He didn't even lift his head. He pressed it into his balled fists, as he leaned forward over Morgan's bed.

"You need sleep. You've been awake for days. I can have the nurses setup a cot for you."

"I can't," he said. "I can't sleep, baby. If she opens her eyes, she got to see me. It's important. I need her to know I'm here."

Alani placed a hand to his shoulder, then another, and then squeezed. He was so tense. His entire back was locked. The structure of him was so strong that it felt like she was trying to knead boulders. All the pressures of their world were balanced on his shoulders. He was balancing so much that it felt like he would fumble. He had fumbled. With Morgan. With his daughter. He hadn't seen this coming. She rubbed his neck, his shoulders. "She knows, Ethic. I promise you, she knows. Can you at least eat something for me?"

"I'm not hungry," he answered. "Where are the kids?"

"I sent them home with Nannie," she whispered. "I hope that's okay?"

He nodded. "Of course. You should go too. Doesn't make sense for all of us to stay. I can call if anything changes."

"No," she whispered.

"Just go home, Lenika!" he snapped.

"I'm not leaving," she whispered. She was so patient. His mood had been altered. His temperament short, and she didn't care one bit. "I'm staying as long as it takes. I'm staying. She needs you. You need someone too, though, and I'm not leaving."

He lifted his head from the bed and opened his arms to her, pulling her into his lap. "I can't even remember how I survived before you. Shit hurts so bad. I'm barely functioning. I don't mean to be short with you..."

"I know, baby," she whispered. "Don't worry about me. This isn't about me. I know."

She looked him in his eyes, soft fingers rubbing the sides of his face. "I'm so full of faith that I know she's going to wake up, Ezra. You don't know God like I know God. That's my nigga and He's got you. I promise."

Ethic gave up a reluctant smile, licking his lips, then licking hers, running his tongue over her bottom lip, like it was dry, and he was responsible for its lubrication. They showed love in the oddest ways. Like they had run out of ways to express how they felt, so they were forced to make up new shit. Alani kissed him.

The amount of guilt that pressed down on his soul was overwhelming because he had been through this with Morgan before...the depression...those days were so long ago that he almost forgot they had occurred. After Raven died.

The grief had been so heavy that it had drowned his entire house. The only thing that had warned him that Morgan's grief was greatest were the razor blades he had found under her bed one day. She had stolen three of his and hidden them there. When his maid had discovered them, Ethic had been devastated. Questioning Morgan had taken all his courage. He'd taken her for ice cream, just the two of them, and then placed them on the table. She'd been just twelve years old when she broke down in that shop. Tears of embarrassment and grief poured out of her that day. He was hurt behind Raven's death, but Morgan's pain was incomparable. They had tried to **manage** it for years, until that day.

"What are these for, baby girl?" he had asked.

Her lip had trembled so violently. He already knew the answer. She didn't even have to speak it. She was going to kill herself with them. Morgan had spent three years in therapy. Three, long, hard years of weekly sessions to get her through depression. He'd never thought those days would return. Her psychiatrist had cleared her. Her doctor had told him she was fine; but as he looked at her in this hospital bed, he realized she was anything but okay. Trauma after trauma had occurred in Mo's life. She had taken so many L's. She had said goodbye to so many people; now, she was trying to leave him. She was trying to follow them.

"If she dies, I'ma need you to take Eazy and Bella with you for a while," he said.

Alani pulled back, brow furrowed. "What?"

"I need to hear you say you will. That you'll take care of them like they're your own."

"They are my own, Ethic. I love them, but what are you saying?" Alani asked. Her eyes prickled. Fear erupted in her chest. Protesting. Screaming. She needed clarity.

"She can't go by herself. Mo won't make it. You say there's a God, she won't make it to Him, without someone to lead her there. If she doesn't open her eyes, I've got to close mine. I've got to make sure she gets to God."

Alani's chin quivered. "Ezra, no," she whispered. Her face was wet. Her tears fell without permission. "No! No!"

She was revolting against even the thought of his demise. One strong hand cupped her face. Four fingers wrapped around her neck and his thumb to her cheek. He pulled her forehead to his. He swallowed the lump in his throat, and she could see his despair. She was witnessing the undoing of a king. The weakening of a gangster. His child was dying, and Alani knew what it felt like to want to die too.

"If anything happens to you, I will not make it. You can't talk like this. I'll die, Ethic. I will. Mo dies, you die, I die, then what? Those babies grow up without anyone. They need you. I need you. So, Mo has to wake up. She just has to open her eyes and save us all. You can't lead Mo to God. You don't know Him. I know you're not all the way there yet because you wouldn't be giving up right now. You'd have faith. If you go, I go, because I've got to make sure *you* get there. No. She just has to wake up. She is going to wake up."

Ethic lifted his other hand to hold her entire face. His

somber filled the entire room. Alani was the sunshine he had been waiting on for years. The storm that had wrecked his life for as long as he could remember had finally cleared the day she had walked him into that church, but it didn't last long. As soon as they had gotten their stride, found their way, Morgan had lost hers and the happiness he had worked so hard for was snatched - once again. He pressed his forehead to Alani's. "Take care of my kids."

A sob destroyed her. There was finality in his statement, like his mind was already made up, and Alani was devastated.

The door opened, forcing the couple apart, as a doctor entered the room. Alani stood from Ethic's lap and turned away from the doctor, wiping her eyes. She could barely pull herself together.

"How's our girl?" the doctor asked.

"I'm waiting on you to tell me. She hasn't done anything yet. I'm holding her hand all day, talking to her every minute. No movement, no muttering. Nothing. I need you to tell me something, Doc," Ethic said. He was almost pleading.

"We found out why her heartbeat has been irregular," the doctor said. Ethic tapped Alani's bottom and she lifted.

"We ran a full blood panel on Morgan. She's pregnant, Mr. Okafor. About 18 weeks along."

Ethic's head turned to Morgan, then to the doctor, then back to Morgan.

He stood, swiping a hand down his head, as he turned away from the hospital bed.

"She's pregnant," he uttered. "A baby?" he whispered, in disbelief. "Mo is pregnant." That one came out in utter wonder, barely audible. "I'ma kill him. I'ma kill him. I'ma fucking kill him."

"Ezra," Alani spoke. He leaned against the wall, his fist acting as the barrier between his head and the plaster. He bit his knuckle and turned back towards Morgan. "Is the baby okay?"

"His heartbeat is so strong, we thought she had an arrhythmia," the doctor informed. "There could be some developmental issues because of the carbon monoxide ingestion, but we won't know that until birth, but he's strong. He's holding on tight in there. We're starting to see fluctuation in her brain activity as well, and that's a good sign. Right now, it's just a waiting game. We're waiting for her to wake up to determine what type of brain function she has."

Ethic leaned over Morgan and planted lips to her forehead. "Fight, Morgan."

BEEP!
BEEP!
BEEP!

Morgan's eyes felt heavy. It was like someone was pulling down her lids, trying to keep her in the darkness that she was fighting. She fluttered them open.

Bella.

They closed. Morgan's eyes lifted again, but they were so damn heavy.

Aria?

"Come on, baby girl. You can do it. Wake up. I'm right here waiting for you, Mo. Open those pretty eyes."

That was Ethic's voice, and she felt tension in her chest, like she wanted to cry. He sounded wounded, like he'd been crying, like there was something blocking his throat. Fear. Worry. Morgan heard them both, and as she fought against the invisible force pushing her eyelids close, she opened them...because her father was waiting for her to...because she heard it in his voice that he needed her to.

"I'll get a doctor."

That was Alani's voice.

Bitch, Mo thought, still hating the idea of her. Still loathing the fact that Ethic had been pulled out of the dark that they once shared; now, Morgan was standing alone in the grief of losing Raven.

She closed her eyes once more. Fluttering them again to see Eazy. Her eyes scanned the room before rolling closed again. Frustrations mounted in her because she couldn't keep them open long enough to set her sights on the one person she wanted to see. He wasn't there. Messiah. Where was he?

Gone. Messiah's gone.

The thought made her want to close her eyes forever. She remembered why she had done this to herself. He was gone from her life and she didn't want to live a life without him in it. She didn't want to raise a child alone, without a father, but there was no way that Messiah could be a part of her life, after what had been revealed. So, she wanted to see her daddy. She wanted to die so she could be with Benny Atkins, because he was the only one who could triage her broken heart. She needed him, but he was dead because of Mizan. Messiah was Mizan's brother. She wanted to be dead too, and it would all just go away.

"Mo, I'm right here. Come back for me, Mo. Morgan! Wake up! Baby girl, just wake up for me!"

Poor Ethic. I love you so much. I'm so sorry.

She felt cold fingers open her eyes and the face of a white man in a white lab coat hovered over her.

Get that fucking light out my face.

As if he could hear her thoughts, he released her eyelids and the darkness cloaked her, again.

"Give her some time. She should wake up soon. When she's ready, she'll come to and we can assess the damage then," the doctor said.

The damage is monumental. I'll never be the same.

Morgan laid there hearing, feeling, but not waking. She couldn't wake. The fog she was in was too dense. She couldn't quite see through it, but she could listen. She heard it all. It was an odd place to be. Stuck between breathing and not...wedged between life and death. In limbo. She could almost hear her other family, Raven, and her parents, calling her to them. She almost wanted to just let those eyes stay closed, but then there was Ethic. She heard him the loudest, calling her back. She'd had six years with Benny. Her time with Ethic doubled that and then some, and he was truly the most important man in her life. She had never loved anyone more, then Messiah had come into her world. She loved him that much…enough to consider going against her family to be with him, if it had ever come to that…and he hadn't been willing to do the same. He hadn't defied his family, he had been there to avenge *his* family. It could only mean one thing…he didn't love her at all.

"She's trying, Ethic, that's a good sign."

If this bitch don't get out my room, Morgan thought, annoyed by the sound of Alani's voice. *She's going to take him away from me. She's going to make him stop loving my sister. Get outtttt.*

"I know," he answered. "Shit just can't ever be right, you know? Like it's a constant juggling act. When I didn't have you, my kids were straight. Now, you're here and Mo's in this fucking hospital bed. It's just constant loss. I'm constantly dropping the ball. It makes me feel like I'm choking. She's laying here, fighting for her life, because of me. It feels like I can't breathe."

"I'll breathe for you," Alani answered. "I love you, Ezra. I'm in love with you and everything attached to you. I'll breathe for every single one of you. This isn't your fault. It isn't hers either. Sometimes, life just gets so hard."

Something about those words and the way they sounded made Morgan's heart lurch inside her chest. The monitors around her blared, going crazy, at Morgan's internal reaction. For so long, Morgan had to discern the world around her without the sense of hearing; now, she was discerning it with that sense alone, because her eyes just wouldn't cooperate. Morgan heard sincerity in Alani. Alani knew that feeling of losing so much that you wanted to check out and Morgan could hear it. Morgan heard commitment in Alani's voice, like no matter what Ethic did or how hard it got, Alani would never leave. Not again. They were past that point. Morgan wished she could have that with Messiah.

Dread filled the room for 48 more torturous hours before Morgan was able to muster the strength to open her eyes.

"Mo?"

Aria's face was the first face that blurred in front of her. Morgan's eyes were filled with emotion, but she wasn't crying. It was like she had been submerged underwater and was trying to see through the water that remained in her eyes.

"Girl, thank fucking God!" Aria exclaimed. "Now, I can kill you."

Morgan's lip trembled, and she felt Aria grip one of her hands.

She tried to speak but the endotracheal tube that ran down her throat stopped her. It was choking her, and Morgan panicked. Her eyes widened in terror and she gagged on the tube, as the machines around her went haywire.

"Somebody, help! We need help!" Aria screamed.

A nurse rushed in and Morgan cried, tears streaming from her eyes, as terror seized her.

"You're fine, Morgan," the nurse said. Her voice was calm, and she grabbed Morgan's face, staring her in the eyes. "You're fine. Don't fight it. This tube was breathing for you. This tube kept you alive. I'm going to remove it, okay?" Morgan squeezed her eyes shut and nodded. "Okay. It'll hurt just a bit. Your throat will feel raw, but you're fine, sweetheart. Your family is here. They're downstairs getting food. They'll be so happy you're awake. Just stay calm." The nurse turned to Aria. "Come hold her hand." Aria rushed to the bedside and laced her fingers with Mo's.

Morgan deadpanned on Aria. She had never seen fear in her before, but it lived in her stare. The nurse pulled the tube out of her mouth, and it seemed to go on forever, until finally Morgan felt relief.

"Just breathe, sweetheart," the nurse said. Morgan's breaths were shallow, and her entire chest burned, but she was breathing on her own and that was progress…it was a miracle.

"I'm going to have your family paged. They're right in the cafeteria. You take care of her until I get back," the nurse said. Aria nodded, clearing her own tears from her eyes.

"Bitch, I want to kill you, but I know I'd miss you, so I can't do shit but fucking cry," Aria chastised. Morgan laughed through a sob that escaped from her. "Everyone was so damn worried, Mo," Aria said, seriously.

Morgan opened her mouth to speak but the words jumbled in her throat. She wasn't strong enough yet, the tube had been down her throat for so long that scar tissue had begun to form around it. Morgan's eyes flooded.

"Aww, Mo. It's okay. Just breathe. You don't even have to talk. Just breathe, Mo," Aria urged. A mixture of embarrassment and gratitude filled Morgan. She had never had a friend like Aria. She represented a sisterhood. A level of loyalty that Mo was only used to receiving from family. If it were up to Morgan, she would have never divulged this to Aria. She would have kept it a secret, pretended like everything was fine, so that Aria couldn't harvest the information to use against her later. Looking at Aria in this moment, Morgan saw pure love...a genuine concern that reassured Morgan that there was no judgment taking place, there was only love. Aria had been terrified to lose Morgan, and the revelation that their friendship was indeed true made Morgan's heart so tender that it felt like pain.

Bella walked in, eyes glued to her phone.

Morgan parted her lips, eyes burning with tears, as she tried to call her name. It hurt too badly to get it out, but Bella's head snapped in her direction at just the attempt. The iPhone fell from her hands and she didn't even care. She rushed to Morgan's side. Her chin quivered, as she crashed into Morgan, clinging to her as she cried.

"You hurt me so bad, Mo," Bella sobbed. "Everything fell apart without youuu."

Morgan held onto Bella. Instant remorse filled her. She hadn't thought of Bella when she was sitting in that car. She hadn't thought of anyone except herself. The sight of them, these sisters, was so emotional that Aria rolled tear-filled eyes to the ceiling to stop them from cascading down her cheeks.

"Don't do that to me. You can't do that, Mo! Like ever!" Bella cried. Morgan caressed Bella's hair, soothingly, as they wept. Morgan pulled back.

"I'm so sorry, B," Morgan signed.

"I'm running down on Messiah. I'm beating his whole ass," Aria whispered, as she sniffled and dabbed her eyes.

Morgan's eyes widened, and she shook her head, panicking, frantic.

"No, please, Aria, please, don't say anything. You can't. Not to Isa either. I don't want anyone else to know," Morgan signed. "Please…"

"What is she saying?" Aria asked Bella.

"She doesn't want you to tell him or Isa. You have to keep it a secret, she says," Bella interpreted.

"You're in here because of him! This is his fault! What about the baby?" Aria protested.

Morgan sucked in air, freezing, fear-filled.

"The doctor told us, Mo," Aria revealed. "Ethic's been out of his mind worried about you. You've been out for a long time."

"How long?" Morgan signed, confused. It hadn't felt like that much time had passed. Bella's lip quivered, and she hesitated to answer. "How long, B?"

"Almost two weeks, Mo," Bella answered, sadly.

"And he hasn't come once?" she signed.

"What is she saying?" Aria asked.

"She's asking about Messiah," Bella whispered.

"I tried to call him. Ethic tried to call him. He's not taking our calls. Isa isn't even taking my calls. I'm not sure, but I think they're gone, Mo," Aria whispered.

Morgan broke. Her head collapsed against the pillow and her hands lifted to her face, as she sobbed. Gone? How could he be gone? How could he leave her? How could he really pick up and walk out of her life after promising that he would never desert her? She didn't give a fuck how mad she was...how deceitful he had been...how off track they had gotten. Messiah could cheat, rob, kill, steal and Morgan would be mad as hell...but she would never leave...they were supposed to hate each other until they loved one another again...fight until they felt like fucking...but never leave. He was never supposed to leave her. Morgan's soul was snatched from her body. Her love, her heart, her strength, the father of her child and the man she would have died for, the man she would have killed for, the man she had spoken first for...had left her. She wished she had never opened her eyes. If he was gone, there was no point in being here at all.

Ethic entered the room and both Aria and Bella moved out the way as he rushed over to her. He removed his jacket and climbed into bed with Morgan, wrapping his arms around her and kissing the top of her head as she sobbed. Witnessing such turmoil was enough to bring Alani to tears, as she lingered in the doorway with Eazy at her side. Such unbelievable grief filled the room that it choked her.

"Come on, guys. Let's give your dad a minute with Morgan," Alani said, voice weakened by the emotional sight. "Aria, Morgan needs a little time with her father, okay?"

Aria nodded. "Of course, yeah. I'll come back tomorrow, once things have settled. Oh, and Mo?"

Morgan looked up, wiping her eyes, as she tried to control her cries.

"I snuck into your courses and took finals for you. I knew you were waking up, and when you did, no way was I going to let my girl have to re-do freshman year. My ass probably flunked them bitches anyway, but you can't say I didn't try." Aria winked and elicited a much-needed laugh from Morgan. Amused through the sadness. She got a snicker out of Ethic as well, before waving, hugging Alani and Bella, and then giving Eazy a high five before exiting.

Mo watched everyone leave the room except Ethic. He just held her, rubbing her shoulder, and kissing the top of her head.

"It hurts so bad," she signed.

"I know," Ethic answered, signing his response. "It hurts because you're living, Mo. Life hurts sometimes. You have a lot of life ahead of you, baby girl, but you got to be here to get to the good part. You've got to be here…"

His voice broke and Morgan clung to him tighter.

"I'm so sorry," she tried to speak. It came out in a whisper, a pained whisper, and then a parade of sobs followed behind.

"Me too, Mo," Ethic replied.

"He's Mizan's brother. I didn't knowwwww. How could I not knowww?" she signed.

"We just learned that part. That part's no good. We've had a lot of hate for Mizan for a lot of years and I reacted off that hate, but he's this baby's father too," Ethic said. "He's shown us other parts, Mo."

"I can't have this baby," Morgan signed. Her hands shook so violently that she could barely express herself.

Ethic turned stern eyes to her. No way was he allowing Morgan to play that game. Alani had taken him through that game. It was a painful deceit, and nobody won in the end. "You don't keep a man from his kid, Morgan. And you don't make decisions about a man's kid without involving him. Ever. There's no undoing that. I know that hurt. That's not happening," Ethic said.

"But he's Mizan's brother," Morgan protested. "I can't..." Ethic reached for her hands, stopping her from signing, cupping her hands in his. He brought them to his lips and bowed his head. He was so fucking grateful. So indebted. She had opened her eyes and was functioning. They had problems to solve but she was alive to do it. That's all that mattered. He didn't want her worrying... didn't want her to give up again...Morgan reclaimed one of her hands, as he gripped the other, and she rubbed the top of his head. She knew he was crying because he trembled. Head bowed because he didn't want to show her this weakness he cried, and Morgan soothed him while tears flooded her. She had no idea he would be this hurt. She had never been more remorseful in her life. Hurting Ethic ruined her. He sniffed and released her, clearing his face with one hand, pinching the bridge of his nose, then swiping one hand down his entire face. He sucked in a deep breath.

"Before he was Mizan's brother...before we knew. Who was he to you? To this family?"

"He was my family," she signed, still crying. Ethic sat on the edge of her bed and cupped her face, clearing her tears with his thumbs. "We wanted this, Ethic…to start a family… together. We were going to have everything…be everything to each other, and now he's nothing," Morgan signed.

Ethic felt the turmoil in her soul because it filled his too. What was he to do? How could he reconcile this for her? What actions could they take as a family that didn't disrespect Raven's memory?

"I take it Messiah doesn't know," Ethic said. "I taught him everything he knows, and I find it hard to believe that even I could keep him away if he knew you were pregnant."

Morgan shook her head. "I was waiting to tell him and then everything went so wrong. I can't keep this baby."

"You can, Mo. If that's what you want. You're not obligated to make any decision on anyone else's behalf but your own. Not Messiah's, not mine, not Raven's. This is your body. If you decide to keep this baby, I'll be here for you through every single hard day. I'll come to every appointment, spoil you through every pain, because you're my daughter and I love you. I'ma hold you down even when a knucklehead-ass boy breaks your heart. You're not alone."

"I loved him so much, Ethic," Morgan whispered. Her insides burned with the words, but she didn't care. She needed to speak those words because they were fact. Nothing but truth. She had loved Messiah Williams.

Ethic nodded. "I know. I want to prepare you, baby girl. The doctors thinks there might be some damage…"

"Damage?" Morgan's voice was childlike, as she lifted sad eyes to his.

"The lack of oxygen. It might have hurt the baby. No one will know for sure until this baby is born, but I just want to prepare you."

"What did I do?" she cried, as her lip quivered.

"You tried to run from pain, but the only way to deal with pain is to feel it. Get through it, Mo, and I'm right here to help you find your way when you get lost. You hear me?" he asked.

She held him tighter and nodded. Ethic sat there with her, as she cried; and when she fell asleep, he lifted from the bed. Rage coursed through him, as he stepped into the hallway, pulling his cell phone from his pocket. Alani waited in the hallway, sitting in a chair against the wall, as she read to Bella and Eazy. When she saw him, she handed the book off to Bella.

"Keep going. I'll be right back," she said. She walked over to Ethic. He ended his phone call, in frustration.

"I've got to go...."

"After Messiah?" Alani asked.

Ethic pinched the bridge of his nose. His jaw flexed, and he gritted his teeth. Tension lived in his every expression.

"I'm trying real hard for you, but..." he paused, pointing a stern finger at Mo's door, and then swiping one hand over his mouth and finessing his beard. "He fucking...what he's done to her...he's fucking Mizan's..." Ethic was coursing with ill intent. His appetite for murder was restored.

Alani feared this side of him and her heart galloped as she saw it take over the loving man she knew. She reached for his face. "Hey," she whispered.

Ethic gave her his focus.

"I'm going to kill that nigga, baby. I got to. I got to. I fucking..."

"Ezra," she said, and the hurt he heard in her voice jarred him. Eye to eye, forehead to forehead, she whispered. "Forgiveness is for the strong. Be strong, Ethic. Like it or not, Messiah and Morgan have a baby on the way. He's your family now. If I can forgive you, you can forgive him."

"He was lurking, waiting..."

"And he clearly loves you," Alani said. "He clearly loves Mo. He had every opportunity to hurt you and he's resisted all these years. He's been around for years, Ethic, and he never struck. He fell in love with you. It's easy to do. So easy to do," she said, as she rubbed the side of his face and gazed at him in concern, while amazement...wonder... over the type of man he was, danced in her eyes. "You mean something to Messiah and he means something to you. That's why the betrayal hurts because it came from someone you love. We talked about this. You can't be judge, jury, and executioner. Morgan tried to kill herself over that boy. She loves him; and if you kill him, she'll never forgive that. So, you find him, and you fix it. That's how you protect your daughter in this circumstance. You go get her man and let him know it's okay for him to come back. Family is fucked up sometimes. It's not always perfect, but you make it fucking work. You're going to make this work for her."

"But Raven..."

"He's not his brother, Ethic," Alani interrupted. "He didn't kill Raven. Same way I didn't hurt Morgan. We can't help who we're related to."

That hit home. Alani heard the bat connect to the ball, as she hit the shit out the park. Recognition shone in his eyes and he entangled his fingers in her hair, as he gripped her head, kissing her…so deeply.

"I'm lucky to have you. You know that?" he asked, as he kissed her lips. A quick peck because he no longer had to pull her all out of her with every kiss, because she was readily available to him now.

"Eww, Daddy," Eazy said, as he covered his eyes from the chair he sat in. Alani chuckled.

"I'll be back, okay?" he said.

She nodded and pecked him back, unable to help herself.

"We'll be here," she whispered.

"I know you've got to meet your professor. I won't be long," he said.

"I know Morgan isn't fond of me, but I'm not going anywhere, Ethic. Fuck that book and my professor. Take as long as you need. I can reschedule."

This time, a deeper kiss, and Alani swooned, accepting his tongue into her mouth.

"Daddyyy! So embarrassing!" The protest belonged to Bella this time.

Alani turned from him, blushing. "Little girl, mind your business," she teased, as Ethic chased her face with his lips, kissing her, again. "Come here, baby, let me embarrass her some more." Alani kissed him again and again.

"Mmm," he moaned.

"Daddy!" Eazy shouted.

Alani laughed, as he bent her backwards, kissing her longer, just because his kids were protesting.

"I'm raising a bunch of fucking playa haters," he said, as he kissed her entire face, moving from her forehead to her cheeks, to her neck, then the tip of her nose. Alani hollered in laughter. This felt so good. It felt easy and she was so grateful for the love he gave. "Hurry back. We need you. I *need* you."

He bit the lobe of her ear, gently, and then he was gone. He had a score to settle with a youngin' he should hate, but somehow, mixed in the hate was a little bit of love that was keeping Messiah breathing…he just had to find him.

CHAPTER 4

"You ready, bro?" Isa asked.

Messiah looked around the master bedroom of his home and he tightened his face to stop the emotion from becoming evident. He could still hear Morgan's laughter bouncing off the walls in the room. He could still see her lying beneath him at night, refusing to utilize her side of the bed because Mo was clingy, and she didn't care that she made him hot as fuck at night. He tossed the last stack of cash from his safe in his Louis duffel and then zipped it. He wasn't taking anything but clothes and cash. Everything else could stay.

"Yeah, I'm ready," he confirmed.

"Yo, bro. You should go talk to her," Isa said. "Shit, a nigga need you to holler at her. I was this close to knocking Ali down. Now, you got a nigga dodging her calls."

Messiah snickered. "You wasn't hitting shit, nigga. Aria wasn't fucking with your ass," Messiah said, giving up a half smile at how hard his mans was chasing it.

"Nigga, I would have been knee-deep in that shit by summer, my G. The way she pop that shit on stage. Bruhhhh," Isa groaned.

Messiah shook his head, but he could relate. He headed for the door. Meek was in the living room waiting.

"Everything G, bro? You ready?" Meek asked.

"You know we can just pop Ethic and stay right here in town," Isa proposed. "We rocking with whatever you decide."

Messiah had considered all the possibilities, but killing Ethic would erase any chance he had to ever even speak to Morgan again. Odds were already slim, but taking that step would annihilate them. He wasn't ready to live a life that didn't have the possibility of her in it. He told himself he would come back one day, when things were calmer, when she had time to decompress...if he made it that long. Killing Ethic was not only dangerous but damaging. If Messiah was honest with himself, he would admit that he had love for Ethic. He was his OG, he had taught him too much to follow through with such a treacherous plan. Messiah would walk away with his soul clean on this one. He would take the L and love Mo from afar, because no one else was getting close to his heart.

"Nah. All this shit is dead. This town is dead. Let's shake," he said.

"And what about li'l homie? What we doing with him?" Isa asked, nodding to the sleeping toddler that rested on the couch.

"Bleu's going to take care of him for me," Messiah said. "Make sure he gets to a good family and shit. Somebody who won't fuck him up."

His heart was the heaviest it had ever been, as he walked out the door. It had been too long since he'd last seen her. Morgan was like air. She filled up his lungs every time he laid eyes on her. Without her, he was on E. He could barely breathe. It hurt. So. Fucking. Bad. If he could have one more day with her, versus a hundred years without her, he'd choose those glorious 24 hours and die happy. She had called so many times he had to block her, just to resist answering for her. He felt like a snake. Messiah had seen his share of grimy days and he knew he was a menace to most, but to her, he had been good. Living with her disappointment was crushing him. The voice messages she had left him didn't even sound like her. The begging tore him in half. Never ever was it okay to live in a world where Morgan Atkins had to plead for love. Sadness had transformed her. It was suffocating him, but his poker face was strong. He stepped out onto the porch and paused when he saw Bleu pull up in front of his house.

"Load up. I'll be there," Messiah called out to the crew.

"So, you're leaving?" Bleu asked, as she came up to him, standing directly in front of him, arms crossed, face bent in disbelief and anger, but the underlying emotion -the one that caused her eyes to glisten - was sadness. Messiah meant everything to her. She loved him, and watching him was an inevitable torture.

"I got to shake. Shit's hot," he said, as he swung his hands in front of his body, one hand catching the other balled fist as he looked down the block. His eyes stung, and he sniffed it away. If he had ever been capable of loving someone before Morgan, it would have been Bleu. From the very first time he'd laid eyes on her, he'd known she was a special girl. The friendship they had built over the years was valuable to him. It meant something, and he didn't realize it until this very moment when he was forced to let it go.

"Messiah," she whispered, sympathetically. "She loves you. I love you, boy. Saviour loves you. You have people here. You can't just run from this. Shit gets hard. You talk it out. You work through it. You don't run off. That girl is ruined. You chewed her up at my house. Don't do this. You can have an entire life here."

"We both know that's a lie, B," Messiah said. "A nigga lucky to have what I had with her. The time I had I wasn't owed. When you live foul, you fucking die foul. I never deserved her in the first fucking place." He had to frown, folding his emotion to stop himself from crying. He felt it. The sobs. The urge to fall into Bleu's arms and pour his pain all over her. He had been plugging that hole his entire life.

"She'll be by your side when it gets bad…because you know it's going to get bad, Messiah."

"I was going to put a bullet in his head, Bleu. Ethic ain't forgetting that shit. So, either I murk that nigga and she hate me forever, or I leave, and I miss her forever," Messiah said. "Or he kills me and none of the above is an option. Forever ain't that long. I'ma be good." He nodded like he was trying to convince himself.

"You're breaking my heart, Messiah," she whispered.

Bleu felt a tear fall down her cheek. She swiped it away.

"Yeah, apparently, that's all the fuck I'm good for," he said. The somberness of his tone told her he was ashamed of that. He didn't care about who he decimated in the past. His actions were his actions and he never apologized for them; but this time, he was filled with remorse…overwhelmed with a regret so strong that a tear slipped down the bridge of his nose.

"I'm fucked up, but never let nobody bend my name when it come to her, B. Never let niggas say I did what I did because I hated her. I never hated her. I love her. Don't let 'em run the stories back no different. I love her the only way I know how, B," he said, lip quivering. He had no control over his emotions. The vulnerability was painful to a man who was used to feeling nothing.

"My Messiah," Bleu whispered. She reached up to touch his face. "You're worth so much and don't even know it."

"The kid is in there. Make sure whoever gets him takes care of him, B. Make sure he's safe. Make sure nobody's doing no shit to him. Abusing him. Give him a chance," Messiah said. His voice was so weak, weaker than she'd ever heard him. He hoped Wozi's son had a better chance than he had ever been given.

"And the house? What am I supposed to do with it?" she asked.

Messiah looked back up at it. "Give it to Mo. She won't want it anytime soon. She'll hate me for a while, but one day, when she hate a nigga a little less, give it to her. Her name is already on the deed."

"Messiah, this isn't right," she whispered.

"I don't know how Ethic moving with it, so steer clear." He was ignoring her pleas to stay, diverting the conversation. "Last thing I want is for you to pay for being affiliated with me," Messiah said.

"Iman has me covered. You don't have to worry about me," she said. Bleu's lip quivered. "What if we don't get to see you again. . .before. . ."

Messiah reached down and wrapped his arms around Bleu, kissing her cheek. One peck, then burying his face in the groove of her neck, then another peck, before burying himself there again. She felt one sob, before he holstered his feelings. She broke down in his arms. "Stop, Shorty Doo-Wop. I'll see you one day."

She nodded, quickly regaining her composure.

"Nah, boy…there's only one Shorty Doo-Wop now and it ain't me," she said, with a smile. "I want to see you once a month. A lunch date, every single month, Messiah. You open my Christmas gift and you go there once a month. I'll meet you there. You've been my best friend since Noah..." She stopped speaking because it was so hard to reminisce about old times without breaking down…about the man she had loved and lost in the blink of an eye. "I need to know that no matter how far you go…" She paused, again, because it was so damn hard to tell her friend goodbye. She knew it might be goodbye for good and it was tearing her up inside. "I need a day to look forward to seeing you. Just open the gift and go there. Meet me there. Okay?"

Messiah instantly thought of Morgan, wishing he could somehow have the same arrangement with her…wishing this goodbye was being had with another…or better yet, that it didn't have to occur at all. He nodded. "You can bet on that," he promised. "Tell Saviour to be good. You be good too, Bleu. Stay clean." Besides Morgan, Bleu was the only other person he was worried about leaving. She had a dark history with addiction and he didn't want her falling off.

"Always," she said, with a nod and a tear-filled gaze. "She taught you how to love, Messiah. At least call her."

He nodded. "I will." They both knew he was lying, and as he got in the car, his entire chest felt split open. Bleu threw up a hand, as he watched her grow smaller and smaller in the side, passenger mirror. He tossed a hand out the window to bid her farewell, as he and the crew rode through Flint for the last time.

Ethic pulled up to Messiah's home, and as soon as he climbed from his Tesla, he knew Messiah was gone. The curtains were open. That was indication number one that Messiah had blown town. He didn't care who saw inside. Ethic gritted his teeth and gripped his steering wheel, in frustration, because he knew if Messiah went underground, he would never find him. Ethic had taught Messiah, mentored him, gamed him up from a young age. Messiah would move with precision now that he thought Ethic was a threat. Ethic wouldn't find Messiah until he wanted to be found, but they were on a timeline...a forty-week timeline, to be exact. Morgan needed him, and Ethic had a feeling that Messiah would miss the birth of his child. Burden filled him because he didn't want that type of heartbreak for Morgan. He had never wanted her to feel anything but love. If Messiah was going to take the job from Ethic, he needed to do it better. Familial ties and treachery lied between them, but bloodlines were now crossed. Morgan would bring Messiah's seed into the world. Mizan's nephew. What a sticky web love had weaved. Ethic didn't have a choice but to make it right, but it was too late.

"The one fucking time this mu'fucka want to follow directions…" he grumbled. Ethic pulled away from the block, knowing in his heart that he would have to equip Morgan with the strength she needed to raise her child without Messiah.

"Please, don't make me do this. Please, Ethic, pleaseee," Morgan cried. She bounced, as she begged him, stomping one foot desperately, hoping her tears were enough to get him to take her home. He always gave her the desires of her heart, when she threw a fit. He hated to see her cry and he was struggling with leaving her inside the four walls of this hospital.

"It's not up to me, Mo," he whispered.

"It is! It is up to you!" she shouted. "Ethic, please. I just want to go home. Don't leave me here. Messiah already left. You can't leave me toooo." She was hysterical. The terror that glistened in her tears tore the moxie right out of Ethic's spine. His stomach weakened, and he pulled a distraught Morgan into his arms.

"I'm never leaving you, Mo. You just got to get better, baby girl. You feel my heart beating?" he asked.

She nodded.

"As long as it's beating, you got me," he said.

"Then, just take me homeeee," she said, wrapping her arms around his neck. She locked her hands together, like a stubborn toddler who didn't want to be pulled away from her father. Two nurses approached the pair to break up the scene. The dependency Morgan possessed when it came to Ethic was showing. He was hers. Her protector and the love of her young life. She could depend on him. She always had, and she needed him to just save her. She didn't want anyone to fix her but him, because he was the only one who understood why she was the way she was. Soulmates of a different form, Ethic was the most important person in her life. Even Messiah didn't measure up when it came to prioritizing her love.

"You have to let go," one of them said. She pulled Morgan and Ethic wrapped a protective hand around Morgan's back, stiff-arming the hospital staff with his free hand.

"Don't touch her." The order came out with such force that it ricocheted through the room like a gunshot. Morgan clenched her eyes.

"Ethic, no, no, no. Don't let them take me," she cried.

"I don't know about this," he said, wavering. "I can hire the best therapist to come to the house."

"Mr. Okafor, she'll have to complete a 72-hour suicide hold. We recommend you commit her longer, but it's the law that we have to keep her for the 72 hours after regaining consciousness."

A male nurse approached this time, and Ethic slapped his

hand down, forcefully. "Don't fucking touch her. Who the fuck are you? You put your hands on her again and I'll put you in a box." Ethic pointed a finger at the man, sneering, as his temple throbbed, and his heart ached. This was the hardest thing he'd ever had to do and Morgan's fear, her absolute terror, was putting him in a position of defense. He felt inclined to protect her.

Alani stood off to the side, heart breaking, one hand placed over her mouth in disbelief. She now knew what she was up against with Morgan Atkins. This was no normal connection between father and child, this was a love affair with limits. Ethic and Morgan had created the purest form of love and wrapped rules around it that kept it appropriate, but she could see that he loved her differently than his other children. He loved her more than his other children. It wasn't romantic, but it wasn't platonic either. It was obsessive. Like Morgan didn't want to share Ethic with anyone, ever, and Ethic had unknowingly encouraged the bond over the years. She had lost everyone in her life, so she overindulged in loving Ethic, and he poured everything into her to make up for it. They had never healed from the trauma that connected them; instead, they bound their hearts together and let them bleed and scab over, leaving behind a gruesome scar. It was devastating to bear witness to this moment. Alani felt like she shouldn't be there. Like she was a fly on the wall, taking part in an interaction that she had no business being a part of. For the first time since meeting Ethic, she felt like she didn't belong.

"Ethic, they just want to help," Alani said, softly.

"She wants me in here. She just wants me out the way. Ethic, nooooo." Morgan's pleas ripped through him and he placed a hand on the back of her head.

Alani lowered her head and closed her eyes. The accusation stung and silenced her instantly. She didn't want that. She would never want that, but she knew it wasn't a time to discuss her wants and needs.

"Nobody wants you out the way, baby girl. We just need you to be okay. I need you to talk to somebody," he whispered. He kissed the side of her head. "This baby needs you. I need you. Eazy and Bella need you. Nobody's leaving you. Nobody's replacing you. We all want you home, Mo. Let's just try the three days. If you want to come home after three days, then we're out of here. They can't keep you after that, and if they try, I'll tear every wall down in this mu'fucka to bring you home. That's my word, but I really need you to try, Mo. I almost lost my favorite girl. I got to make sure you're getting the help you need. Make sure you're strong up here," he said, tapping her temple, as their foreheads met.

"I'm scared. This feels like I'm being punished. Like they're locking me up." Her lip trembled and spread wide in dismay.

"You know I would never let that happen, Mo," he said. "You're not in trouble. No one's upset with you, baby girl. I love you. You're mine. You think I'm going to let somebody take you from me?" he asked.

She drew in a shaky breath, as she calmed slightly. He would never. She believed that much.

"You can do this, Morgan," he said.

He held both her hands and she wrapped her fingers around his so tightly that it hurt. He brought her balled fists up to his lips and kissed them.

"Three days?" she asked.

"Just three days," he answered.

"Okay," she gave in.

A black woman with silver hair and a white doctor's coat stood next to Morgan, placing one, gentle hand on her shoulder. "My name is Dr. Gates. I'm the head of psychiatry here. I'll personally be handling Morgan's evaluation, and hopefully her treatment plan, if you decide to pursue it after the three-day hold. I promise you I will take the utmost care of her. This is the hard part, admitting that a loved one needs help…that prayer can't fix it…Morgan didn't cut a wrist for attention. She created a death chamber inside your home. She's a danger to herself, and I know leaving her feels like torture, but taking her would show that you don't care, Mr. Okafor. It would be the biggest form of neglect because your love can't fix the depression rotting in her mind. Let me help her," the woman said.

Ethic pulled Morgan to his chest and gritted his teeth, locking his jaw, as he looked the doctor in the eyes.

"I need you to understand what's at stake with her," Ethic said.

"I understand. She's your child…"

"She's my soul," he stated. "One person mishandle her in here, and…"

"Ezra," Alani interrupted.

She was his owner. She stopped his bark. She wouldn't even allow him to get his bite off.

Morgan squeezed his waist tighter.

Ethic looked at Alani and then to the doctor.

"Take care of her," he said, clearing his throat. He grabbed Morgan's arms and had to physically pry her from his waist. Her tears were endless. "I'll be here every day," he said.

"She won't be allowed visitors during evaluation," the doctor said.

Ethic swiped a hand down his face. "Three days, Mo."

She nodded, and he kissed the top of her head, before walking out the room. Alani hesitated, wishing she could say something to Morgan, but she opted for silence, before following.

Ethic stood directly outside the door, palms to the wall, doubled over in agony. This was causing him physical pain. His stomach was in knots of torture, because more than anything, he wanted to carry Morgan out of this hospital.

He was like a ticking bomb and Alani didn't know what would set him off. Her hand shook, as she placed it on his back, easing closer to him.

He felt her shaking and he stood upright, peering at her. He knew she was afraid, and he pulled her into him. "Life is never easy with me, Lenika. I'm sorry it's so hard. I'm sorry I can't give you simple. You deserve simple."

"I just want you," she whispered. "We've been through the worst. We can get through this. You can't ask for miracles and then not want to put in the work to make sure they last. We prayed that she'd wake up. She did. God blessed her. I felt her heart die beneath my hands when I was giving her CPR. She's not supposed to be here but she's here. Doing the work to make sure she never hurts herself again is not optional. She doesn't want to, you don't want to, but she has to. It's not an option. You're her parent. That comes with tough decisions. You have a phenomenal heart and you want to see them happy. But being a parent is about more than just giving them everything and saying yes to everything. You have to make the hard decisions that may not feel so good right now but will build her up in the long run. She needs this. You are not hurting her by keeping her here. You're helping her. You're doing the right thing, Ethic."

He pressed his forehead to hers, eyes closed.

"I don't even know why you fuck with me," he admitted.

"Because my love for you has no limits," she whispered. Their normal dynamic had always been him wrapping her, securing her in his hold. This time, she placed hands to his chest and ran them north and then around his neck, securing him in the safety of her. Their embrace created alternate universes, where nothing could penetrate, nothing could harm them, as long as they were trapped there. A hug. So simple. Their connection. So complicated. E & A. So fucking tragic they were beautiful. Like a sad poem that was read so many times it became a masterpiece. Ethic and Alani's love was art. Witnesses may grow confused. They may wonder how it was considered great. Looking at them inside a frame required one to squint really hard and turn their head to the side, just to attempt to understand such a piece. The artist was the greatest of them all. God. God held the paintbrush and He had perfected His stroke on the two of them.

She pulled back and took his hand, lacing their fingers, as they headed for the exit. They both knew that they were leaving behind an intricate piece of their puzzle, because the picture of their family could not be complete without Morgan Atkins.

CHAPTER 5

Shoelaces," the intake nurse said.

"What?" Morgan frowned. Morgan was relieved that her voice had returned, but she wished it hadn't, because now she was expected to speak. She was required to communicate, and she didn't want to talk about it. If it wasn't Ethic or Messiah, she didn't want to say one word. They were the only two people in the world who understood her. Not these doctors, with their fake sympathy and their note pads. She would never trust them, could never trust them to interpret the woe in her heart. What she felt was like a foreign language. Not many people understood the way she loved. Her love was like a tattoo. Permanent, almost impossible to remove. To even attempt it was painful. One had to think twice before committing to it in the first place. She couldn't talk to these doctors. They didn't know her pain. They didn't even speak her love language. They could never understand.

"We need your laces. It's a safety concern. You can hurt yourself with them."

Morgan wanted to protest, but she didn't. Humiliation stained her, as she lifted one foot and removed the laces, and then did the same with the opposite foot.

"Your father dropped off some personal items. I need to go through it and remove all the items on our prohibited list, okay?"

Morgan nodded. Surviving suicide might have been worse than dying. Now, she had to face people; now, she had to stare into judgmental eyes. She knew they thought she was crazy. Perhaps, she was. Perhaps the desperation she felt to escape this anguish was too great. Immeasurable. The pain was overwhelming, and Morgan just wanted it to ease some. It was the opposite of love. Whatever that was. Couldn't be hate because Mo didn't hate Messiah. She kept waiting for him to realize she needed him. Kept anticipating his rescue because he had to feel that she was in trouble. Why couldn't she feel him? Why hadn't he come? His words kept ringing in her ears. Over and over.

"I don't give a fuck anymore."

A permanent echo because he had left her chest vacant. He had snatched her heart right out of it and now his words just bounced off the chambers, forcing her to hear it again and again.

He had sealed her fate in that moment. She cared too much, and he cared too little. The unbalance was killing her. It was like the last year of her life had been a dream. Like she had made it up in her head. It couldn't have been real because Messiah would never have been able to stand this space between them if it was. He would feel the anxiety she felt, just from the separation alone. She spun the hospital bracelet that decorated her wrist.

"I need any hair pins you have in your hair," the nurse said. Her tone froze Morgan. She was cold, sterile even.

"My hair pins? It's all that's keeping my hair in place. Why do I have to take them out?" Morgan asked.

"They're sharp. You can't have them."

She lifted shaky hands and removed all her bobby pins, placing them in the biohazard bag.

The nurse rifled through her things, removing her Fenty blush because the mirror could be broken and used to slit her wrists. She removed her rat tail comb because of the pointed end. Morgan's Louis Vuitton planner was opened and shook out.

"What are you doing?" she asked.

"I don't think you understand the magnitude of what you've done. You are not allowed to keep anything that you can potentially use to hurt yourself or others," the woman snapped.

The woman took the pen Morgan used to write with and tossed it in the bag. Even her cell phone was confiscated. The Hermes belt that Ethic had packed was rolled up and put inside the plastic bag. Morgan shivered and pulled the blanket over her shoulders like a cape.

"You need to keep your hands in plain sight. You can use the blanket, but please don't pull it higher than your waist," the nurse said.

Morgan, reluctantly, let the blanket slip.

The security guard at the door stood, hands clasped in front of him, and looking straight ahead. Morgan wasn't sure who he was there to protect but his presence made her feel threatened. It made her stomach feel empty and her heart pound. Ethic had told her this wouldn't be like punishment, but as she stared at the gun on the man's hip, she felt like she was trapped. She just wanted to go home. No one made her feel safer than Ethic. She just wanted to get out of there. The nurse removed the strap from her duffel bag and then placed it on the table. "You'll change into these," she said, placing folded, tan, scrub-like clothing next to the bag. Morgan's eyes burned. This felt permanent. It felt like more than a three-day evaluation. Why did she need a uniform if she wasn't staying? Had Ethic committed her without her knowledge?

"Can I call home?" she asked, her voice trembling in terror.

"Not right now, Morgan. There is a schedule you must adhere to here," the nurse informed.

"If you want to climb in the wheelchair, I'll take you up to the psych floor. Get you settled."

"I don't want to get settled. I won't be here long. Three days... and I feel fine. I can walk," Morgan answered.

"It's protocol. You must be escorted in the wheelchair onto the psych floor."

The psych floor? They thought she was crazy. She was being handled like she was crazy. *Messiah took my heart and my mind. It's with him. Wherever he is, it's there, next to him. Ssiah, I need you. Where are you? You promised me. I need you and you're not here.*

I know I made promises, shorty. I know I said shit to hurt you. I know. I'm fucked up. I told you I was fucked up. Why I got to be so fucked up? I should have never touched you. Never loved you. I can't fucking take hurt like this, shorty. Fuck did you do to me?

The thoughts ran through his head. They had been running through his head for weeks. Almost like he could hear Morgan's thoughts. Like he was responding. Sending a response through midair and planting them right into her mind, without speaking one word. Two lovers, so connected that they were having one-sided conversations that made sense. Two, young souls, so attached that the pain they had caused one another was shared; they could feel it, they had manifested it, and it was killing them. Two hearts fused so tightly together that ripping them apart had proved deadly.

Messiah sat in the waiting room of the hospital, head bowed, as he gripped the manila envelope in his hand. The huge cross that hung above him caused his lip to tremble.

"God, please. I know I put in a lot of work for the other side. I know, Man. I know I'm fucked up. I know this prayer fucked up too, but You gave me something that was fucking beautiful, Man. I just need a little more time with her to be able to let her know I'm sorry. To show her why I'm fucking insane in the head over her. She don't even know how good she is, Man." Messiah scoffed, shaking his head, as he curved the envelop in his hand, turning it into a cylinder that he gripped tightly. "You put an angel down here just for me and she has no idea she even belongs to You. Just give me time with her. Please, Man. I ain't even fuck with You like that until You gave me her. She's the only thing You've ever gave me that made shit down here easier. Don't take her away. Just give me more time. I need her."

Messiah had never been this weak. He didn't even recognize the feeling. He had thought the hardest times of his life had passed him by, but they paled in comparison to this.

"Mr. Williams?"

Messiah turned to the door to find a nurse staring at him. "We're ready for you now." Messiah felt his stomach sink. This was it. This was what he had avoided for months.

He stood and followed the woman into the back.

"Stand on the scale," the woman said.

Messiah stepped up onto the metal plate.

"When's the last time you've seen your doctor?" the nurse asked, frowning.

Messiah thought back, his mind floating back in time to the day he'd taken Mo to Stepping Stone Falls to let her high come down. That morning. He'd found out that morning. He had been diagnosed with cancer. It was the biggest reason he had warned Morgan that he would never be able to stay. That he would hurt her. That they would never be. There was no future with him. No wedding. No growing old together. He knew that it would hurt her to only have him for a little while, but that small moment of time that they had carved out was the best days of his life. Those days outweighed every ounce of pain he had ever felt. He looked at his illness as a blessing, because he would have never crossed the line with Morgan if he hadn't been diagnosed that day. Hearing that he was sick made him want to risk what little time he had left on her. Messiah couldn't allow himself to die without indulging in an angel. Morgan had been his biggest blessing and he had been her biggest curse. She would never know how sorry he was. He would never be able to tell her.

"It's been awhile. About a year or so," he said.

"You're 180 pounds. According to your records from your doctors in Michigan, you were 225 at your last visit. You know what that means, right? They should have told you what to look for. The signs. You should have…"

"I know," he said. "I was busy living. I didn't want to take the time out to die. I found a girl to love me for a little while. It was worth it."

Messiah stepped down and the woman looked at him in stun.

"Let's get you in a room," the woman whispered, clearly affected, barely audible. She cleared her throat and led the way down a hallway, and then into a private room.

He opted for the chair in the corner. He didn't want to see the little, leather bed that was for patients. He wanted no parts of any of this, but he had promised. He had promised Bleu to meet her there.

On my fucking nerves, man, he thought, shaking his head. As soon as the thought manifested in his mind, there was a knock at the door. It opened, and he saw her peek through.

"Messiah," she whispered, a bit of relief in her tone, as she pushed the door open all the way and stepped inside.

She laughed a little, scoffing, in disbelief.

"Stop being dramatic, man. I said I would show up," he said. Bleu laughed a little more, swiping her tears away.

"I'll give you two a minute. The doctor will be in soon."

As soon as the door was pulled closed, he stood, and she ran into his arms. She couldn't help but sob.

"I didn't think you would come," Bleu said.

Messiah pulled back. "I'm here, man."

"That's the first step," she answered. "You could beat it, you know? There's a reason I borrowed all that money from Iman to pay for this."

"Some fucking Christmas gift," Messiah stated, shaking his head, as he sat down in the chair. His head hung in turmoil and Bleu reached for his locs, pulling until Messiah looked up at her.

"Why are you here, Bleu? You know who I am. You know I ain't shit. I fuck up everybody around me. You stay long enough, I'ma hurt you too," he said.

"So, I'm supposed to run from you, Messiah?" she asked. "I'm supposed to abandon you?"

"Yeah. That's exactly what you're supposed to do, B," Messiah said. "Self-preservation. A nigga ain't shit."

"You're everything, Messiah," she whispered. "You saw so much good in me when I was at my worst. I'll never forget that. I'll never not see the good in you. I don't care how much bad you try to cover it with."

"Don't ever bring nobody here," he said, stubbornly, chin quivering, as he reached for her, pulling her close and burying his head in her stomach. "Nobody, B. Not Isa, not Ahmeek, and especially not Morgan. Don't ever bring her. I don't ever want her to see me sick."

Bleu was hesitant to touch him because she was afraid that it would remind him that he was exposing himself. If he remembered that he was showing vulnerability, he would stop.

"This shit is gon' hurt, B. I can already feel it. I've been feeling it," he admitted. "Been dying. The shit is killing me and it's like every day I breathe a little different, a little bit less every day."

Bleu placed a delicate and shaking hand to his head. Her fingers explored his locs, massaging his scalp, as he placed both hands to her hips, burying his face into her body. She felt him shudder, but she didn't hear the sob that accompanied it. She knew he was holding it in with all the strength he had left. Messiah Williams hated to be weak. He hated this...showing her this...but he couldn't help it because she was all he had left. The only person capable of coming with him. The last man standing on his team was a woman. "I'm so sorry, Messiah," she whispered, as a tear trailed down her cheek and fell through midair, landing in his hair. Her tears watered him. She was raining emotion and she hoped her flood would nourish him enough to grow. The thought of Messiah dying tore Bleu up inside. She had been through this before...the loss of a great man. She dreaded the grief that was to come. The only thing that had kept her from giving into addiction when she had felt it before had been Messiah. His friendship.

His insistence on showing up for her. But if he became the one she mourned over, who would keep her together? Bleu could already feel herself falling apart.

A polite knock on the door forced Bleu to take a step back, and Messiah pinched the bridge of his nose, clearing his throat. A black woman with blonde locs entered the room. She had too much hope in her eyes to be an oncologist.

"I'm Dr. Autumn Nash," she said.

"Messiah," he stated.

"And you're his…"

"His friend," Bleu finished for her. "Bleu Montclair."

"She's the unlucky mu'fucka who gets to watch me die," Messiah said.

"Well, she seems to love you very much," Dr. Nash answered.

"Yeah, she likes torturing herself," Messiah snapped.

"Messiah, stop," Bleu whispered.

"It's okay," Dr. Nash spoke. "I'm sure it's been a hard thing to wrap your mind around. There are stages of acceptance that patients must go through. Anger is one of them. Resentment too."

"I ain't none of those. I don't even want to be here," Messiah stated. "I'm just trying to speed this shit up. Get it over with. Everybody got to die one day."

"Well, Messiah, I'd like to do all I can to try to slow this down. If you're willing to let me try," Dr. Nash said. Dr. Nash clicked the lights and pulled out a scan, before turning on a monitor that illuminated the images she hung on a monitor.

"These are the scans from the last time you were seen by your doctors in Michigan," the woman stated. She switched the images. "This is you now."

"Oh, Messiah," Bleu gasped. She felt the squeeze on her hand and it surprised her. She didn't hesitate to lace her fingers through his and hold on tightly. They would need to hold on, because the ride was about to get bumpy and he had no one else to hold him down.

"As you can see, the cancerous cells have spread drastically," Dr. Nash said. "I'd like to cut it out." She turned on the light.

"Nah, man. They already told me. You cut and I'm dead. They said it's a 3% chance that I come off the table alive. Look at that shit, man. How do you cut all that out?" Messiah asked.

"With skill. With patience. It will be a very long surgery. I have a team in Baltimore, at Hopkins, that I trust to assist. We could airlift you there and have you in surgery in days," Dr. Nash answered, as she sat on the rolling stool in front of Messiah.

"The chances are very dismal, Messiah, I won't lie to you; but I am the very best. There is a reason why people come to me from all over the world. With me, your chances go from three percent to twenty," the woman answered.

"A twenty percent rate of survival. He would have surgery and the cancer could be gone? You could get it all?" Bleu asked.

"I could. Then, I'd run him through intense chemotherapy treatments. It'll be miserable. I won't lie to you. Then, for good measure, radiation as well; but you'd be alive. It'll be the toughest time of your life, but it's a shot."

"So, I either die fast and use the time how I want to, or die slow and let you carve me apart," Messiah said. "I don't want to die on an operating table. Twenty percent isn't enough. No. I'm not having the surgery."

"Messiah, let's think about this…"

"Ain't shit to think about," Messiah stated. "It's my body. My life, B. If I'ma take a L, I'ma do it my way."

The doctor nodded. "Okay, let's get you through intake and checked in. We'll begin normal rounds of chemotherapy. We'll try to attack as many of these cells as we can, give you all the time we can, Messiah, without surgery."

"How long?" Bleu's voice barely worked, but she had to know.

"Three months. Four, if we're lucky," Dr. Nash said.

It felt like the clock began ticking at that very moment…a countdown to Doomsday. Bleu's eyes prickled in distress.

"I know it's a lot. I'll give you some time to process things. A nurse will be in to escort you to your room."

"I've got to stay here?" he asked.

"At this stage, it's wise to continue fighting the disease in hospice. It's time you make some preparations, Messiah. I'm sorry."

Messiah broke. His head collapsed between his knees, but he quickly recovered, lifting his head high as he stood. His face convulsed, betraying him, exposing him.

Bleu stepped in front of him, grabbing both hands. She brought his hands to her heart. It was racing. She was wrecked. Her entire body trembled, she was so devastated, but he didn't need weakness…he needed strength. He was terrified. She could see it, so she couldn't show that she was too.

"Look at me, Messiah," she whispered.

"I ain't did shit right, B, and I ain't got time to fix it," he said. "If I've ever hurt you, Bleu..."

"You haven't, Messiah."

"I have, B. I saw you down bad. I saw you on the block, strung out, and I served you. I poisoned you more, Bleu. I don't even know why you're here...how you put up with me all these years. You should be gone too."

"You know why I've stayed clean all these years, Messiah?" she asked.

He shook his head, unable to even form words.

"Because I knew you were coming by. For breakfast, for dinner, because your ass don't cook, and you can't live off fast food," she said, snickering through tears that blinded her. "Sometimes, for nothing. Sometimes, just to feed Saviour when he was first born. Sometimes, just to look me in my eyes. I knew you were coming by, so I couldn't get high. I couldn't backslide. I couldn't let my emotions drown me because you were always on your way over. You would call at six in the morning, sometimes, and not show up until dinner. So, I couldn't. I couldn't get high all day because you were on your way. Always there. Even when I didn't want you there, you came anyway. We are connected through someone we both lost. Your best friend was my best friend and we lost him, and we've been stuck together ever since. You've done his job ever since, Messiah, and I love you for that. Not the shooter, not the goon, not the crazy nigga with the temper and a street resume a mile long, but my friend. I know you think you're heartless, Messiah, but you have shown me love in ways that prove you aren't. I don't know anyone better than you. Just because you've done bad things doesn't mean you haven't given out good too. I'm not going to let you believe that lie. You have been the very best friend to me, Messiah. It's my turn to be that to you."

Messiah opened one hand over her heart and ran it up to her neck. Bleu was at his mercy. He could squeeze the life out of her, if he wanted, and she knew he wanted to. Messiah handled pain by inflicting pain. He was frustrated, and he had a taste for murder. He wrapped one large hand around her neck, while staring at her. Bleu stepped into him and wrapped her arms around his waist, laying her head on his chest, as he rested his chin on top of her head.

"Fucking annoying, B," he complained. Bleu burst out into laughter, as he held her tightly.

They had such a hard road ahead of them, but Messiah was grateful for her presence. He was already dying without Mo, but Bleu made it a little better. She made it a little less lonely; and as he stood there, holding her in his arms, he realized that Morgan Atkins may have been the love of his life, but he hadn't loved her first. Bleu had cracked through his shell long before. He just hadn't realized how valuable her friendship had been to him until now.

CHAPTER 6

Alani rolled over and the vacancy beside her caused her eyes to pop open. Ethic was gone. Missing from the spot beside her. She knew because she was unsettled. They slept so intertwined with one another that too much space felt foreign, and she was roused from her dreams because his hot skin wasn't overheating her. She complained about how hot his body always seemed to be, but she secretly loved it, silently adored the warmth he covered her with at night. It was cold in this empty room. A chill had settled over the entire house, in fact. It had only been twenty-four hours and the mood in the Okafor home was dismal. From Ethic to his children, everyone was cloaked in angst. Alani placed nude-painted toes to the floor and reached for the robe hanging off the back of the bathroom door. The matching version was on the hook beside it, and even that subtle detail made her smile. His and hers bathrobes. He had purchased her one to stop her from hogging his. She covered herself and eased out of the room. Alani took the top floor of the house by memory. It was like she had designed it herself, the way she maneuvered around the plant in the hallway and the hutch that sat against the wall to get to Eazy's room. She pushed open the door and found Eazy pointing a laser pen at the glow-in-the-dark stars that were stuck to his ceiling.

"Hey, Big Man," she whispered, as she stepped inside. "What are you doing awake?"

"I can't sleep. I keep dreaming about Mo and my mom," Eazy said.

"Well, that doesn't sound like such a bad dream," Alani answered.

"It's a nightmare. If Mo is with my mom, then that means she's dead too. It means she's never coming home," Eazy answered.

It was like he had put a dart through her heart.

"Oh, Eazy," Alani sighed. She walked over to his bed. "Scoot over."

Eazy made room for Alani and she laid down next to him, staying on top of the cover, while he was nestled underneath.

"Mo is coming home. She's going to be back here, safe and sound, before you know it," Alani said. "And you know dreams don't really work like that. You can dream about people who are no longer with us and people who are, Eazy. It doesn't mean Mo is going anywhere. Your mom is probably with Mo right now, watching out for her, to make sure she's alright. You don't have to be afraid to dream about them together."

"Are you sure?" Eazy asked.

"I'm sure," she said.

"Can you sleep in here with me?" he asked. "If you're next to me, maybe you'll show up in my dream too. I really want my mom to meet you."

Alani nodded, and she was grateful for the darkness because he couldn't see the tears that accumulated in her eyes. Alani knew that Ethic was the man for her, but he wasn't her favorite; he never could be, because the little people in his life held those spots in her heart and they weren't letting up. Eazy was the love of her life. The unknowing way he loved on her was unlike anything she had ever experienced. That mother-and-son bond he gave her was flawless.

"I'd really like to meet her too. I'll stay right here until you fall asleep," she whispered. She turned her face to kiss the top of his head. She began to hum.

"I release alllll disappointment. From my mental, physical, spiritual, and emotionallll bodyyyyy. Cuz I know that spirit guides me, and lovvveee lives insidddeee meeee. That's why, todayyy, Iiii take life as it comesss..."

It was her favorite mantra. An India.Arie song that always reminded her to let go of what she couldn't control and live for today, to accept what the present brings and let go of the rest. This day brought her motherhood, not for the one she thought she'd spend the rest of her life nurturing, but to a little boy and girl that she had never expected to receive. Alani laid patiently, with Eazy tucked beneath her. She didn't rush his sleep or try to sneak out early. Her need to check on Ethic had transformed into her need to make sure Eazy slept without fear. Eazy trumped Ethic every time. His children always would. If she ever had to choose, she would always rescue them first. It was what made Ethic love her. "God, please let me be useful to him," she whispered. She didn't climb out of his bed until two hours later, when she was sure he wouldn't stir. Bella was next. She opened the door to find Bella sleeping soundly and she didn't disturb her. The master bedroom was still empty, and she knew exactly where to find Ethic. She walked down the stairs and into the basement. She would never get used to seeing him like this. Black, Nike, athletic tights, bare feet, big and ugly, because he was a whole man, and shirtless. The evidence that he was king rested between his legs and Alani's body reacted. Everything about him called a response from her. Her head spun, her nipples peaked, and her clit ached. Alani had to close her eyes and shake her head, he was so damn fine. He was so lean, so strong, and those fucking tattoos just did something to her. The whole reformed gangster thing he had going made her river flood. She knew that no matter how well he hid it, there was nothing reformed about his G. It was always present. Like the holy ghost. His authority was omnipresent. There was no retiring that, but she appreciated his effort. He was doing all he could to be better for her. He was who he was, and Alani had never met anyone like him. The eight-angle pose he held effortlessly was amazing. The ways he controlled his body was incredible, but the ways he controlled his mind was a gift. One she felt privileged to unwrap every day, exploring his depths, soaking up his knowledge. God, she loved him.

"Ethic," she interrupted.

He didn't answer but she knew he heard her.

"It's late, baby," she said. "Or early, depends on who you ask. Have you slept at all?"

He took his time coming out of the difficult pose, and every muscle in his body worked until he stood on his feet. Sweat wet him. Alani wanted to drench him.

He snatched the towel from the couch and took it to his forehead, and then his neck, before lifting worried eyes to her.

"Mo's awake," he said. "She's been awake all night."

Alani was speechless. "How do you know that?"

"I can feel it," he answered.

Taken aback by the connection they shared, Alani held her breath. She knew he wasn't lying because she felt him that way. She felt his energy for miles and miles. Distance didn't matter.

She closed the space between them. "She'll be home in less than 48 hours."

"Might as well be weeks," he said, closing his eyes and pressing his forehead to hers.

"I know," she whispered, stroking his cheek gently with the back of her hand. Ethic was so heavy, so brooding. She massaged his ear, and then moved to the back of his head, as he nudged her with his face, baiting her. Alani knew that sometimes Ethic liked her challenge, but today, after all he had endured, he needed her submission. He nudged her, again, and she fought her instinct to lead, choosing to follow, as she dipped her head back, submitting to his tongue, as it invaded her mouth.

"Come on," she whispered, pulling back and grabbing his hand, forcing him to follow her upstairs.

She pulled him all the way into the master bedroom and then to the adjoining bathroom. She reached for the oversized tub and turned on the water, adding lavender bubbles. Alani could see the wear that life was putting on him.

He came out of his workout attire and stepped into the tub.

"Come here, where you going?" he asked.

"I'll be right back," she said, with a smile.

She returned with a handful of candles and a stick of sage.

"She lit each candle and placed them around the bathtub and then lit the sage.

"There's way too much bad energy in this house. It's choking you," she said. "I burn sage when I feel like I need to clear my house of bullshit."

"So, you're burning it here?" he asked.

"This is my house, ain't it?" she asked.

He bit his bottom lip, his eyes slanting in amusement. "This your castle, queen. Burn away," he said, throwing his strong arms over the side of the tub and leaning his head back.

Alani placed it in an abalone shell and put it on the counter.

"Come over here, baby. I'm trying to see something."

She smiled and grabbed a sponge, before walking over to him, sitting on the side of the tub.

"I'm a patient man, but I want that, Lenika," he said, reaching for the belt on the robe. Alani snickered and gripped his chin, forcing him to look at her. She pecked his lips.

"This isn't that," she said.

"It should be that," he countered.

She dipped the sponge in the water and poured liquid soap all over it, before taking it to his back. She washed his skin with one hand and massaged his tense shoulders with the other.

"Mmm," he groaned.

"You have to sleep, Ezra," she said. "You can't take care of Mo, or anyone else, if you don't take care of you. Nobody has ever taken care of you. I won't let you be neglected." She washed his body like she was washing a child; and to her surprise, he complied. He had done this for her. Cleansed her. Now, she was cleansing him. Mind. Body. Soul. Home. Heart. It would all remain spotless under her care. His head hung low, as she let water drain from the sponge over his head. He took one hand and cleared the water from his eyes, before wrapping both arms around her. Alani's heart was old and raggedy, it was bruised and bullied, but damn if it didn't beat for this man. He had made sure of it. He had resuscitated her, when everyone else had given up.

She dropped the sponge into the water and cupped his face, as he stared up at her. "I'm gonna be so good to you," she promised. "While you handle everything else in our world, I'm going to handle you... love you, as long as you'll let me." He pulled her into the water, robe and all. He slipped the shoulder of the robe down and sunk teeth into her shoulder, and then palmed her breast, lifting her nipple to his mouth. Alani's head fell back, and she gripped his thighs, as he feasted there before moving to the other one. She felt his dick beneath her and she shuddered, as he peeled back the robe, tossing the soggy mess of fabric onto the floor.

"Come," he said. The order she always followed. "Ride my face, baby."

Alani's eyes widened slightly. *Nasty-ass.* She stood, hovering over him, as he looked up into her womanhood, exploring, fingering. His strength was remarkable, as he picked her up, gripping her hips, as she let her thighs plié over him. When his lips touched her, Alani's hands lifted to the wall. He was arresting the pussy, she might as well assume the position. He smacked her ass so hard it stung, and she knew what it meant. He was putting her to work. Alani worked her hips because she knew he wanted her all over his face. *Feed this nigga.*

"Mmm," he groaned, sucking on her clit like she used to do Kool-Aid baggies back in the day. Ethic wasn't the man to make a mess while eating. He made sure everything she served went in his mouth. His tongue was just wet enough; not sloppy, not disgusting, but juicy and warm, and the texture of his taste buds against her sensitive clit put a frenzy in her soul. She couldn't ride him hard enough, couldn't quite fuck his face deep enough. Her mind was gone, as she chased ecstasy.

"Aghhh!" she cried, between clenched teeth, as she pressed her pussy down so hard on his face she was sure he couldn't breathe. Alani didn't care where the orgasm came from. His lips, his tongue, his nose. She covered all three bases, as she went for that home run.

His hands gripped her thighs so tightly, she was sure his fingers would leave bruises behind.

He lifted her and ran his tongue from her clit to the parts where his tongue shouldn't touch, and he ate her there too. *This. Nigga. Here.*

"Oh my god," she moaned. "Ethic, baby, why do you do this to me?"

The way he manipulated her clit made Alani go crazy. She came hard, gripping his head, as he sucked her soul from her body.

She let one leg fall to the bottom of the tub, for balance, as he stood. She placed both hands to the wall, as she felt him hanging behind her. Hot dick on her wet ass, he grunted, as he lowered a bit and then split her in half.

One stroke straightened her spine, as he reached around her body and gripped one breast, while devouring her neck. It was sensory overload. It felt too good. Sinful. Alani lifted one leg onto the side of the tub, as he folded her in half. His hand spread wide over her lower back, fingers lifting, as he pulled her back, forcing every inch of him into her. "Ethic, I can't take it," she whispered.

"Take it, Lenika. Take care of me, baby," he said, hitting her deeper. "Damn."

He hit it harder. Faster. Alani threw it back, biting down hard to stop her moans because she was going to wake up the entire house. The entire floor was wet, and the water had gone lukewarm, as Ethic hit the bottom of her depths, daring deeper with every stroke. It was so good that she felt herself running all over him.

"Mmmm… shit."

Ethic gripped her ass so tightly, going so hard that Alani's legs began to shake. He wrapped an arm around her waist and sat back inside the water, pulling her onto him, reversing their roles, giving her the power because he felt her getting weak while he was in control.

A fist to her hair, he pulled her backwards until she leaned her back against his chest. His dick was rooted in her, so long and wide that she felt him everywhere, stretching her limits, breaking her in like a new pair of shoes. Ethic did all the work, still stroking upward, as he leaned against the back of the tub while reaching around her body to roll her clit between his coarse fingertips.

"Ezraaa," she whined.

"Nut for me," he groaned, in her ear.

"I ammmm," she cried. "God, I am." She could barely breathe. Bitches had to train for dick like this. Stretch, warm-up, and then do a few laps, before hopping on, because it took endurance to finish this marathon. She felt him pulsing. Felt his dick throbbing, as he had his way with her. She lifted and turned, not hesitating to put her mouth on him. Sucking dick was personal for a woman, and Alani had hated it before Ezra. You just couldn't eat everybody's food, without inspecting the kitchen. Same for dick. Couldn't wrap your lips around something if you didn't know where it had been, but Alani knew. He was for her. She was the only chef in his kitchen and she waxed that wood until it was shiny and wet.

Ethic buckled, stomach caving, abs tensing, as he gripped the sides of her head and watched as she sucked the orgasm right out of him.

Alani kept going until she tamed him, and then she kissed the tip of him, before climbing up his body.

"Now, we sleep," she whispered. She kissed his lips and climbed out of the tub. She placed extra towels on the floor to soak up the water. "I'll clean this up when we wake up."

Ethic followed her to their room, and as Alani went to pull the curtains close, she paused. Hints of orange, purple, and yellow blazed against the horizon, as the sun ended night's reign.

She relaxed into him, as he came up behind her, wrapping tattooed arms around her waist.

"The light always comes after the dark, Ethic. You just have to be patient," she whispered. "Morgan's going to get out of there and you're going to make sure she's strong… strong, without a man making her strong. We're all going to be okay."

He gruffly replied. She knew he was lost in thought, and she placed her hands over his, as they stood there, staring out the window, watching the sunrise. "I love you."

He kissed the back of her head and it was enough. It was all the reciprocation she needed. She was enveloped in his love, every second he was in her space - and even when he wasn't. She had never felt anything greater. She just hoped they could get to a place of peace, because he deserved it… they had earned it. They just had to get through the dark and the light would eventually come; just like the sun, they would rise.

CHAPTER 7

Morgan stepped into her old room. Her timid steps and curious eyes took in the luxurious space. It was exactly as she had left it. She had been a girl when she occupied this space. It seemed like so long ago. The months she had spent with Messiah had felt like an eternity. She was a woman now, grown and burdened with the ills of love, like every other woman of the world before her. Men had a way of disgracing a woman, of marking up the walls of her heart, destroying it and then expecting them to function afterward. Morgan was barely putting one foot in front of the other. She really just wanted to go back to her apartment, but Ethic wasn't having it. He wanted her under his watchful eye. She could see the fear in him. He thought she would try to finish the job if she had enough space and opportunity. There was no convincing him otherwise.

"You good?" Ethic asked, as he stood in the doorway, watching her, eyes filled with angst, forehead riddled with lines. Morgan felt bad because she knew he was terrified to lose her. Ethic was terrified to lose everyone he loved. He had lost so much over his lifetime that he tended to hold on too tight, but Morgan needed that right now. She appreciated that he didn't want to let her go. Messiah had let go without thinking twice. She needed someone who wanted to tie a knot of loyalty around her. Her father. She needed him. Ethic was that and more. She nodded.

"I'm fine. I promise," she whispered.

Ethic opened the pharmacy bag he held in his hands and removed two, orange bottles. His big hands twisted the tops off and he placed two pills on the desk. His eyes prickled, as he screwed the tops back on. Morgan could see that he was struggling, and she felt so much remorse that she couldn't bear the sight of him. "I'll keep the pills with me." Ethic could barely get the words out. Xanax and sleeping pills. His beautiful Morgan was burdened with pain so great that she had to numb it. Pain so great that he couldn't trust her to keep an entire bottle in her possession. He wasn't pleased with the fact that she was taking them while pregnant, but her sanity was at stake, and the doctors had assured him that the low dosage wouldn't affect her baby. Still, the fact that she needed them at all tore him apart inside.

"Mo, I'm..." Ethic started and then stopped, unable to find the right words. "I'm sorry, baby girl."

Morgan shrugged, her lips so heavy with sadness that they poked out in an effortless pout. It was the face she had made when her heart was broken, ever since he had known her. Every other time he had been able to fix it. He couldn't fix this, and it made him feel helpless; because, if he wanted nothing else at all...if he could have one wish, it would be to heal Morgan Atkins.

"Messiah..." Ethic started.

"I know. He's dangerous..." she interrupted.

"He is..." Ethic nodded. "But he's also tied to you now, so keeping him out of the loop isn't an option, Mo. I don't know where he is, but if he contacts you, you let me know. I don't want you around him until I've talked to him. He and I need to come to an understanding about some things."

"You're going to kill him," Morgan said. She wasn't like Bella. She didn't scare at the notion of Ethic's gangster. She had never been naïve to the fact that it existed. Benny Atkins had been a gangster and she had loved him anyway. Morgan knew exactly who Ethic was and she loved him more because of it. The notion that girls found boys like their fathers proved true, because Messiah reminded her so much of Ethic.

"For fucking knocking you up, I could wring his fucking neck," Ethic said. "But the rest we're forced to work out. There's a kid on the way. I can put ghosts aside for that, but I need to tie loose ends. He was here on behalf of Mizan. On behalf of his family. He needs to know that this is the last pass I'm extending. Until I talk to him, until he knows, you aren't to see him, Mo. Just let me make sure his intentions with you are what he says they are."

"They aren't," Morgan said, shaking her head. "If they were, he would be here. I know him. I know him like no one else knows him. Everything he ever said to me was a lie." Morgan's face melted into destruction, as she tried her hardest to keep the tears at bay. "I loved him and he lieddd," she cried. Ethic crossed the room and she buried her woes in his chest. He could feel her body quaking and Ethic saw red. Oh, the ways he wanted to peel Messiah's top back. Not for targeting him. Ethic had been sent for before. He had faced opposition in the game many times…he could handle that part. The pieces of Morgan that Messiah had broken, that was all the motivation Ethic needed to cover Messiah in six feet of dirt.

"I know, baby girl. Feel that shit and then learn from it, Mo. Use it to become a stronger woman, a stronger mother," Ethic said. "I want to talk to you about maybe going back to the hospital for counseling. A couple times a week. I know we've tried in the past, and you didn't like it, but…"

Morgan pulled back, shaking her head. "I don't need that, Ethic. I'm fine. Please, don't make me do that." Her eyes watered, and her lip trembled. Pure fear seized her. She didn't trust many. She didn't trust any, in fact. Just Ethic. Just family. No way could she bare her soul to a stranger. She hadn't said one word over those three days. She just sat there, staring at the doctors, as they tried to get her to open up. She just bided her time, counting every hour until Ethic came to get her.

"You tied a pipe to the back of a car, Morgan. That's not fine. Do you know what that would have done to me, if you had killed yourself? What it would have done to Bella? Eazy? We need you, Mo. Every fucking sip of air that I've taken since you walked into my home has been for you. You may not love you, Mo. You have some things in your past that have jaded your perception of yourself, but I know you love me. I know that. You love me more than you love you. Do you want to kill me, Mo?"

"Never," Morgan cried.

"You will, Mo. You almost did. If you die, I'm out of here, Morgan. Morgan fucking Atkins, you're my whole damn world. I love Eazy and I love Bella, but you…" he choked up, as his face lost control. He had to grit his teeth to continue. "You are the love of my life, Mo. Not Raven, not Alani. You. It's you, Mo. You're a gift. You're a piece of a woman that I'll never have. She trusted me with you and you have been light in my darkness. You have given me purpose, Morgan. You love me. I need you to love me enough to never hurt yourself again; because if you do, you're hurting me. If you die, I'm dying, Mo. These insecurities you have, they kill me, Morgan. You're my all. There is no family here, no life in this house, without you, baby girl," Ethic whispered.

Morgan was crying. Her entire face was wet, as she looked at Ethic. He poured out his heart to her. A love letter she had always wanted. A devotion she had known she had, but somehow didn't believe. She felt it in this moment and she was guilt-stricken for taking him through hell. It was like Ethic had aged in days. Worrying over her had aged him, it had taken time off his life, and she was so sorry.

"It just doesn't feel that way sometimes," Morgan said. "I know you love me. I know you do, but I'm not your blood."

"What does blood mean, Mo? You ain't got to be my blood, cuz you're the fucking heart that circulates it," Ethic said, beating his chest, softly. "Blood can leave you just as quick. Blood don't make people stick around." He thought about his father, abandoning him without a second thought, and the pain of the memory struck through him like lightning. "That don't mean shit, Mo. It's the people who love you back. Who stick with you when you're fucking up, when you're being unlovable. Those are the people that count. Men leave every day. Women too. I'm a father to you because you're mine. You're mine because I said you were mine, and I take that commitment seriously. You aren't disposable in my life, Morgan."

Morgan was crying so hard that her lip trembled violently, and her nose ran, as she twiddled her fingers.

Ethic sighed, running his hand down his face in exasperation. He sat on the bed and patted the space beside him.

"What am I not doing, Mo? What else can I do to show you that I love you?" Ethic asked.

"I don't like her," Mo whispered, unable to look Ethic in the eyes. He didn't have to question the *her* Morgan was referring to. He knew. He didn't know how to respond to it because he liked *her*, a whole fucking lot. Morgan shuffled hesitant feet over to him and sat beside him.

"Her being here, it feels like you're forgetting Rae, and she reminds me of her brother. Every time I look at her, I see him. She almost had your baby. That baby would have been related to everyone here except me. If she gives you a family, I'm no longer family. I'm just alone. She's taking my place. She's erasing Raven."

"No one will ever erase Raven," Ethic said. "Or you." He bent over, elbows to knees, as he pinched the bridge of his nose. It was always something keeping him from *her*, but of all the reasons he had ever had to not pursue Alani, Morgan was the best one. "Nobody matters to me more than you, Bella, and Eazy. You're my children. We may not share blood, but you're mine, Mo. I've had more time with you than Benny and Justine were given. Do you know how lucky I feel because of that? I chose you, Mo. Nobody popped up on my doorstep pregnant, forcing me to stick around. I stuck around for you because you're my heart, kid. That smile you hit me with at six years old melted me. You mean everything to me. I know you better than anyone, Mo. You belong to me. You're a part of me. You're my daughter. No one can sever that. I do love her, though, Morgan. I won't lie to you about that; but she doesn't replace you, and she's not her brother. I don't even know how the same people who made him, made her, because she's nothing like him. Her heart, her intentions are..." Ethic paused because he couldn't put into words how far from malice Alani was. All Mo knew was that Alani was related to her rapist and that Alani had shot him. She didn't know the parts that Ethic cherished. The love. The rarity of her spirit. The ways she made him feel whole. He didn't want to seem like he was defending Alani. He just wanted to be clear. "Me loving her doesn't decrease my love for you. My concern right now is you...getting you through this. I won't have her around here, if she hinders your healing. I just want to get you right. I need you to be stronger. I need you to live, Mo. Live the life that Raven was supposed to. You're so much like her, but so different. You're supposed to turn out different."

A knock at the door caused him to look up. Alani stood with a plate of food in her hands. Her show of love.

The way she expressed it when she didn't know what to say. She fed people…their souls, their stomachs… she was filling...she was nourishment. Alani cleared her throat and the tenderness in her eyes told him she had overheard. Her feelings were hurt, and she was holding it in, trying to be strong.

"I have food. If you're hungry," she said. Her voice was small, as she held up the plate. It held injury in it. Her feelings were hurt, and Ethic knew she had overheard Morgan's distrust. Morgan shook her head. Alani had been there for her after the fight at Messiah's, but Morgan was a stubborn girl. No way would she betray her sister, no way would she let Ethic love Alani more than he loved Raven. She couldn't. She just couldn't.

"No thanks."

Ethic felt like he was suffocating. He was stuck between the love of his child and the love of a once-in-a-lifetime woman. It felt like they both held onto one of his arms, pulling in opposite directions. God, how he just wanted to walk in the same direction with them. Together…his girls…his loves…on one path. That would be too much like right. He sniffed away the burning in his eyes and rubbed his hands on his sturdy thighs, and then stood, kissing the top of her head on the way up. He grabbed the plate from Alani's hands and took it to Morgan. "Eat, and then get some rest, Mo." Morgan reluctantly reached for the plate. Ethic paused in the doorway, looking at Mo skeptically.

"They told me to strip your room, Mo. Belts, scissors, razors, pens…" Ethic said. "I don't want to treat you like that, Mo, but I will if I can't trust you. Can I trust you?"

"Yeah," she mumbled. She was mortified. She wondered if this would be what the rest of her life would be like. Would everyone always expect the worst from her? Would they look at her through skeptical eyes forever?

"Can I trust you, Morgan?" Ethic asked, again.

"I'm not going to try to kill myself," she stated, louder this time. "You don't have to watch me every second. I just want to be alone."

"Just give her a little room to breathe," Alani whispered. "Everybody just needs to take a breath. If she needs you, she'll tell you. Right, Morgan?"

"Yeah," Morgan said, unenthusiastically. "Right."

Alani tugged at Ethic's hand, pulling him out the room.

He pulled Morgan's room door closed, on the way out.

"I'll head home," Alani whispered. He placed a hand on her face, four fingers wrapping behind her neck, as he caressed her cheek with his thumb. He could hear her disappointment, but sympathy reflected in her eyes. She understood. It was the reason why she had his heart. She was a mother. First and foremost, even without any children walking the Earth in the physical sense, she still mothered shit. His kids, even him; she had a way about her that illuminated the fact that she had experienced the miracle of having two heartbeats at once.

"I just need time to get Mo together. Everything around her is changing. Maybe now might not be the best time for you to move in." The words on his tongue tasted like shit. The impossible choice that Morgan wanted him to make only had one option…his child. Morgan came first. It obliterated his soul. The words, the taking a step forward to be pushed two steps back, tore him apart. He had worked for this, he had hurt for this. Shit, he had bled for this…to get Alani to a place of comfort where she would merge her life with his, despite the odds. It was a bitter pill to swallow. Their interruption… possibly, their disruption, but Mo needed him. Mo needed him more than he needed Alani and it was his duty to provide. He could feel Alani holding her breath. She did that, when she was in anguish, when an emotion so strong was consuming her…when it was tearing through her like a storm, she held her breath, forgetting that she needed the next sip of it to stay alive. "Breathe," he whispered, and she exhaled, while nodding with tear-filled eyes.

"We just can't get it right, can we?" she whispered.

"I still want this, Lenika," he said. "I just have to get a handle on Mo first. I have to figure out how to do both."

A tear fell out the corner of her eye and he kissed it away. His lips to her face felt amazing. Goddamn, this woman touched him in ways she couldn't even comprehend.

"Okay?" he asked.

She nodded. "Of course," she whispered, passionately. "Of course, Ezra. She's your daughter." Her understanding made it hurt that much more. He indulged in her lips and Alani lost strength in her legs. Every, single, fucking time he touched her, she weakened a bit. One hand wrapped around her waist and went to the cuff of her ass, grabbing, pulling her into him. Time stood still. Time, which waited for no man, somehow slowed a bit for Mr. Okafor. It always did, whenever he was with her, allowing him to savor the moment that would inevitably pass. Her senses heightened for the ten, glorious seconds he helped himself to her tongue. Alani could never fathom how women would just fall victim to the hypnosis of men. She had seen friends switch up and become completely wrapped up in a man, losing all sense of self, and she could never understand it - until now. Now, Alani got it. Now that she had a man capable of making her change up, she felt like a hater for ever being upset about another woman having it. Because this nigga here. Babbbbyyyyyy. Alani would lane switch so quick on a bitch…there was nothing that she wouldn't do or give or sacrifice or tolerate to make sure this worked. He released her, and another tear slipped from her eye. She was so damn grateful for him… to have survived all they had endured so that she could have him. It was hard, but it was worth it. She was going to feel the loss anyway, might as well let him love her through it…let him love her back to health…love her for the rest of her life, if he chose to put up with her that long, because Alani had her ways, ways that no one else deemed worthy to stick by her through. Then, here came Ezra Okafor, sticking and shit. Sticking with her through the worst, through it all, sticking like duct tape, like lash glue, like two, thick thighs on a sweaty day. Ethic was stuck on her and it felt glorious, even with the pain that came with their bond. She would rather love him with all the heartache that came along with it, than be carefree with someone else.

"Back to dating," she said. There was something in her tone, something he couldn't identify. Sadness. Disappointment, like he had gotten her hopes up only to pull out. He felt it, because it filled him as well. The letdown of it all.

"I'm not test-driving you, Lenika," Ethic said. He kissed her once more, just a peck, to the tip of her nose. "Although, I wouldn't mind test-driving you, baby." She giggled. She didn't even know where it came from. The bubbly snicker that fell off her lips. It was flirty and light and cute...it was everything she would normally roll her eyes at, but he had her floating. Everything he said made her feel like she could fly.

"I'll take your Tesla," she said. "It's probably not a good idea for you to leave her alone to drop me off. I'll be careful with it."

Ethic smirked. She was naturally bossy. Assertive. He would enjoy breaking her in, dominating her, earning the right to lead her. It took a lot more than good sex to get a woman like Alani to submit. He was up for the challenge. He looked forward to it, in fact. It would take some patience to find their natural roles and then adjust them to each other's comfort level. They had so much to work out.

"Your Tesla," he corrected, as he pulled the key fob from his pocket and held them up in front of her.

"What?" She frowned.

"It's yours now. It's a little small for me anyway," he said. "I'll call you later."

She smiled, then nodded, before she took the stairs. She paused halfway. When she turned to him, his eyes were on her; his gaze never left her until distance forced him to look away. He was a man who gave his woman his full attention - every time. No staring at a phone screen while she spoke, no half-listening with unenthused responses. He focused on her, not just absorbing her words, but responding to the language her body spoke as well. "Should I cancel with Nyair tomorrow?"

"No, I'll be there," he answered.

Alani continued down the stairs, but his voice halted her once more.

"I got priorities here, but you're a priority too. One isn't more important than the other. I just have to figure out how to balance it all. This is new for me, juggling a woman and my kids. Nobody's been in your seat before. You loving me back is brand fucking new, Lenika," he said. "So, believe me when I tell you, you're at the top of the list, right next to each one of them. I won't miss our session with Ny."

"I believe you," she assured.

He shook his head. "Nah, there was a time when you didn't believe in me. I don't want that to happen again. If you can't believe in your man, that ain't your man."

"You've been mine since the day you rescued me from my job. I believed in you even when I said I didn't. Even when you thought I couldn't. I can be stubborn sometimes. There's a lot that comes with me. I know you love the parts I've shown you, but there are others you haven't seen yet. I'm not easy to love," she said.

He descended the steps, her words drawing him near. His legs lifting in a confident swagger, causing her eyes to zero in on the dick print enunciated by his

Nike sweatpants. She told herself she would burn every single pair he owned when she finally moved in. When she looked up, they were face to face. He trapped her against the wall, his arms making a jail around her, as his eyes bore into hers. She wanted to serve a life sentence in this cell.

Why the fuck can't I stop tasting her?

He bullied his way into her mouth, kissing her so deeply that she moaned in satisfaction.

"I." His thick tongue filled her mouth and she sucked on it, feeling a pulse in her clit.

"Don't." He pulled her bottom lip into his mouth, pursing his full lips around hers.

"Want." He pinned both of her hands against the wall above her head, as he focused on her top lip, licked the valley above it…the oddest place, but somehow, he made it pleasure-filled.

"Easy." He pulled back and pecked her chin, and then wrapped his lips around her chin, licking her, tasting her in the oddest place. Another quick kiss to her lips before he nudged her head to the side with his face and trailed kisses down her neck, still arresting those hands above her.

"I could never live without this. I don't even know why I ever tried," she moaned. "My god, Ethic, you're going to make me…" Her mouth fell open in bliss. How he had assigned a new recipe to her orgasms, she didn't know. She had needed the same ingredients to get there her whole life, and dick was the main one, but Ethic finessed her in ways that just made that oven heat instantly…no waiting, no penetration needed. With him, she came on sight. He wasn't even using his hands and Alani was climbing the walls. He kissed her like he was afraid to lose her, like her tongue was his favorite candy and he had a sweet tooth. Hardness pressed against her belly and he scooped her, hands under her ass, leaning into the wall, his chest against hers. The friction against her clit had her delirious. The audacity of him to be this bold in the stairway, with his children spread throughout the home. She wanted to protest, but she was held hostage by euphoria. He had her mind gone. In one way or another, she was never truly sane with him. She had been crazy in love, lust, or hate with him since the day they had said hello. She couldn't quite seem to find sanity, and the way he made her feel, she didn't want to. They had so much fucking to make up for that their every interaction was erotic. A kiss couldn't just be a kiss. It ended up with him inside her, every time, and she found it mind-blowing that he kissed her clit the same way he did her lips. He didn't play with it. He didn't approach it like he was afraid of it, he kissed that kitty with aggression, with wanting, and Alani was desperate to have him between her thighs. They lost time, as they hid there like two, lovesick teenagers, groping one another. She couldn't ever recall kissing anyone like this...or even enjoying it enough to allow it to last so long. Her panties were destroyed, like they were made of paper towel and she had tried to absorb a huge mess. Nobody had ever aroused her like this man. She dripped for him.

"Daddy!"

He groaned, and she snickered, as their lips separated. They had been kissing for so long that hers throbbed a little. He gripped her face, using his thumb to trace her lips. She opened her mouth, licking his thumb, and Ethic grunted in awakening.

"The shit I want to do to you," Ethic whispered, as if it pained him to stop.

"Daddy!" Eazy was persistent. "Never mind, Dad!" Ethic went back in for a kiss, but just before their lips touched… "Alani!"

Alani slid out of Ethic's entrapment.

"Yo, I swear that boy need an ass whooping," Ethic stated.

Alani lifted a brow in amusement. "You leave him alone," she snickered. "I'll check on him on my way out. I've got to go meet my professor; and thanks to you and your little, half hour make out session, I'm late," she said. She pointed at the erection he was instinctively gripping with one hand. "You go handle that."

"You already late, might as well be late as fuck. It's only one way to handle this," he insinuated. She took one step and was pulled back into him, only this time, he didn't kiss her. He fisted her hair and pulled. Her neck snaked backwards, their eyes met. So much passion. Lovers, unable to depart without it hurting just a bit.

"I love you."

Alani blushed, and her heart went tender. Her smile was uncontainable, as she returned, "I love you." No too on the end of her sentiments. No saying it just to say it because he had said it first. She loved him. She had loved him before he had ever known she loved him, and she meant those three words with every fiber of her being.

"Come back to me," he said. Her brows pinched, as the words penetrated. *He's afraid that I'll run. Every time I walk out the door, he's going to wonder if I'll return.*

Her heart cracked, right down the middle. She could see the apprehension behind those soulful eyes.

"I will," she promised. "Ezra, I always will."

Every step she took made her feel sick, because she didn't want him to have the insecurity of her leaving. She knew what that felt like. She had lived with that her entire life. From her mother to her father. They always left. No one ever stayed. No one… but him. He was the only one who loved her enough to do so. As she beelined for the living room, she found Eazy on his video game.

"What's up, Big Man? What's with the yelling?" she asked.

"I'm starvinggg!" Eazy said.

"There's food right in the kitchen, Eazy," she said.

"But I don't want that," Eazy protested.

Alani's eyebrows lifted. Coming up with Nannie, options hadn't been an option. You ate what she cooked. Alani was cut from an old-school rearing, so these protests were new to her.

She looked to Bella who sat in a chair with her earbuds in. "Did you eat?"

Bella nodded. "Yes, but Eazy's super picky," she explained.

"Does he have food allergies or something?" Alani asked, confused. Bella pulled out one earbud.

"No. He just hates anything that isn't pizza or nuggets. Lily usually makes him a separate meal," Bella explained.

Ethic has lost his mind, Alani thought.

"Come on, Big Man," Alani said, as she made her way into the kitchen with Eazy in tow. She pointed to the island. She was really going to be late now, but this was her new normal. Eazy, Bella, Ethic, and even Morgan. If she was going to be a part of it, they had to do some adjusting too.

"Have a seat," she said. She fixed him a plate of the meal she'd made. Baked chicken, Caesar salad, mashed sweet potatoes, and macaroni and cheese. She placed it in front of him. "I spent a lot of time and put a lot of love into making that for you. You don't have to eat everything if you don't like it, but you should try everything at least once. Does that sound fair?"

Eazy picked at his plate, as Ethic strolled into the kitchen.

"Dad, can I just have a peanut butter and jelly sandwich?" Eazy asked, frowning, as he eyeballed the plate.

Ethic went to answer, more than likely to oblige, but Alani interrupted, "No, you may not, Eazy. I cook every, single day, and I'm going to be here sometimes, which means I'll be cooking for you." Ethic knew this would not go well. He had been accommodating Eazy's palette since he was a baby. Lily knew his favorites and made them every day like clockwork.

"But I don't like this stuff," Eazy complained.

"I think we have chicken nuggets or something, E…"

The look Alani gave him stopped Ethic in his tracks and he held up hands of surrender, as he leaned against the countertop. He would be a spectator in this bout. Alani versus Eazy. He was curious as to how it would end.

"You can't dislike what you haven't tried, baby boy," Alani said. "We can come up with a menu together, and you can choose one dish every meal that you want me to make, but I'm only cooking one meal for everyone in this house. We'll eat together, all at the same time, and we'll all enjoy the same meal. Today, this is all that I prepared; so, if you're hungry, you'll have to try new things. After you eat, you can ride with me to run my errands, and then we'll go to the grocery store to put together the dinner menu for the rest of the week." Alani held out her hand. "Okay?"

Eazy squared off with the plate, frowning, and then he nodded. "K," he agreed. They shook on it and she motioned for the plate, holding up crossed fingers.

"Go ahead and try it out."

Eazy took a small bite and chewed, skeptically. "Hmmm… I guess it's edible," he said, as he dug in for a second and larger bite.

Alani laughed. "I'll take edible."

Ethic crossed his arms and looked on in wonder. "Yo, you've got some shit with you. Some voodoo dolls stashed somewhere or something. I don't know how you do what you do, but…" He shook his head. "He's eaten the same, five foods his entire life, and one conversation with you and he cooperates."

"I don't play those type of games with my kids. I speak, they listen," she said.

Her kids.

He noticed the pride that she expressed when she said it. She was staking claim, not forcefully, not trying too hard to insert herself into his life. She moved naturally around his home, correcting and adjusting things that she felt were awry. He had seen Dolce try to attempt the same with Eazy and Bella before. Her tone was always too sugary to be real. She tried too hard, sucked up a bit too much, and it never resonated with him as real. His children had resisted her every step of the way, to the point where Ethic had to ask her not to attempt to parent them. Alani was simply mothering. She was making a home out of his house, making admirers out of his children, and making a better man out of him.

"Apparently," he said, impressed.

"And I'm taking him with me. That way, you know, I have to return," she whispered. "We'll stay the night at my place. I'll meet you, Bella, and Mo at church tomorrow. Maybe Nyair can do a group session with everyone?"

"Family counseling?" The question was rhetorical, and she could see him retreating inside his head to consider the notion. They weren't technically a family, but she loved him, and he loved her. She loved his kids and they loved her. Morgan hated her, but Alani hoped to work on that.

"Is that okay?" Alani asked.

"Yeah, I think that's okay," he answered, his eyes taking her in with such intensity that she looked away.

Ethic kissed her lips and Alani headed back toward the front of his home. "I'll be in the car when you're done, Eazy, and rinse your plate and put it away before you come out!"

Ethic's eyes followed that ass all the way to the door.

"Hey, Daddy?"

Ethic turned his attention to Eazy.

"Are you going to marry her?" Eazy asked.

Ethic blew out a breath of unease. "I don't know if she would agree to that, homie. Right now, we're just feeling things out."

"You should ask her. I'll bet you one hundred dollars that she says yes," Eazy said.

"You're that confident, huh?" Ethic snickered.

"Yep, you should just man up and ask her already," Eazy said.

Ethic's brows rose in amusement. "Man up, huh?"

Eazy nodded, stuffed a few forkfuls of food in his mouth, and then hopped up from the table.

He was halfway out the kitchen, running full speed, before he slid to a stop, ran back to the table and grabbed his plate. He stunned Ethic, once more, by clearing the dish from the table, putting it in the dishwasher and then rushing out. "Bye, Dad!"

Man up.

CHAPTER 8

"Yo, B, if I don't wake up from this…"

"Messiah, the doctor said it's a simple surgery. This isn't anything major. They're just putting your port in," Bleu said. He laid in the hospital bed, hands behind his head, elbows pointing East and West, as he bit his lip. His eyes were on the ceiling.

"I'm just saying. When I die…"

"Make sure she knows that you loved her. I will," Bleu whispered.

Messiah was so insistent, always double and triple checking that Bleu knew to tell Morgan Atkins that his love was real. She wouldn't forget. She would carry out all his last wishes. Anything he asked, she would do; because if the shoe was on the other foot, she knew he would do the same.

The doctor walked into the room and pumped hand sanitizer into her hands, rubbing them, as she smiled. "You ready, Messiah? You and I have a date."

"This a fucked-up date, Doc," Messiah shot back.

The woman smiled, shaking her head, and then turned to Bleu. "I'll send an intern out to keep you updated along the way. It won't take long."

Bleu nodded. The nurses broke down Messiah's bed, lifting the rails and unlocking the brakes, as the bed began to move.

"Yo, B!" Messiah called. He held out one tattooed arm and the nurses stopped, as Bleu went to him, grabbing his extended hand.

"If I don't wake up..."

"Messiah! Stop talking like that," she complained, with tears in her eyes. "I'm going to tell her. If you weren't so damn stubborn, she would be here."

"Tell yourself too, B. You're my best friend. A nigga love you too."

She laughed through her tears, as he lifted one hand to her cheek, swiping the tears away with his thumb.

"I'll see you when you wake up," she said.

Bleu stood in the empty room, as they wheeled him out. Her heart broke; because although he would wake up this time, she didn't know how many more times Messiah would be blessed to open his eyes, and it tore her apart that his time was coming to an end.

CHAPTER 9

Alani pulled down the visor above the driver's seat and flipped open the mirror, as she applied a coat of gloss over her nude-painted lips.

"Do I look like an author?" Alani asked, as she turned to Eazy who sat in the passenger seat, eyes glued to his handheld game, thumbs moving a mile a minute.

"No, you look like a teacher," Eazy said, without looking at her. Alani frowned and flipped the visor back down, inspecting herself. Did that mean she looked blah? Boring? Old? Suddenly, she agreed with Ethic. Eazy definitely needed an ass whooping.

"A teacher?" she exclaimed!

She reached over and closed his game.

"Hey!" he protested.

"I need you in the real world when you roll with me, Big Man," Alani said, with a chuckle. "Now, tell me…how does one look like a teacher?"

He shrugged. "You just look like you're always going to say something smart. Like learny…"

"Learny, huh?" Alani laughed. "I guess I could look like worse things."

"Plus, you like my dad and all teachers like my daddy. There was this one, Ms. Greenwood. She used to always send letters home to Daddy and smile really big when my daddy came to pick me up. She even baked him a whole pan of lasagna one time, and Daddy sent flowers to her as a thank you."

Alani's neck snaked backward, and her eyebrows lifted. "Ms. Greenwood, huh?"

"Yep, you look teachery, like her," Eazy confirmed. "Teachers are simple pretty, not pretty, pretty like Dolce. You don't have to paint your face..."

"Paint my face?"

"Yeah, Dolce's face always had paint on it and it never matched her neck. It was just always a lot of gold paint on her face. You don't do any of that and you're still pretty. Teacher pretty, like Ms. Greenwood."

"How about I take you to school tomorrow?" Alani proposed, as she got out of the car. Eazy followed along, oblivious to the ways he had ruffled her feathers.

"Really?" Eazy asked, his short legs moving double time to catch up with her long strides.

"You would like that?" Alani asked, laughing, amused at his enthusiasm.

"Yeah! That would be great!" Eazy said. "All the other kids get dropped off. Their moms walk them in and kiss them goodbye in the mornings. It's always just me. They get good luck from their moms and I don't, so I always get clipped down because I don't start off with the mama magic like the other kids."

Alani held open the building's door and motioned for Eazy to go inside first.

"Well, I guess we'll have to make sure you get a little bit of mama magic in the mornings, so you can have better days," Alani said. "I'll take you every day."

"Really?!" Eazy's excitement over something so small made Alani's heart explode. This little boy had never had a mother's affection and it was obvious that he craved it.

"Really. I won't miss one day for the rest of the year," she said.

"What if you get sick?" Eazy asked.

"Mamas have this thing we do when we're sick; even when we feel the worst, we pull out our last bit of strength from our secret hiding place to make sure we are there for the people we love," Alani said.

"And that's me? I'm a person you love?" Eazy asked. "I mean, I know you love my daddy, and Bella, because you're always with her, but me too?"

Alani stepped into the elevator and Eazy followed her. She bent down so that she was eye level with him. "Especially you."

The smile he rewarded that answer with warmed her and she pressed the button for the second floor. She made a mental note to spend more time with Eazy and then stepped out of the elevator, headed to her professor's office.

She entered the space, knocking, but peeking her head into the opened door.

"Alani, please come in. Have a seat," the man said. He was tall and dark, with a bald head and goatee. His kind eyes thinned, as he smiled, then bit his bottom lip. "It's been too long. Who do we have here?" he asked, nodding to Eazy.

"This is Eazy. Eazy, this is Professor Gates," Alani introduced.

"Only I'm no longer your teacher. This is a friendly visit. We're friends," he said. "Call me Alex."

Alani sat and pulled out Eazy's chair for him to relax beside her. "Okay, Alex, soooo…my book?" she frowned and put both hands over her mouth, before biting on her thumb nail. "Did your editor friend hate it?"

"My editor friend loved it. She said she hasn't read something this gripping since she discovered Ashley Antoinette," the teacher said.

"No shit?" Alani asked, a chuckle of disbelief leaving her lips.

"No shit," Alex repeated, finding her amusing. His eyes sparkled with interest, as he sat on the edge of the desk and leaned forward. He placed a hand on her knee. Her eyes followed that hand to her skin and Alani looked up at him, slightly uncomfortable. She knew when a man was flirting with her. Didn't she? She crossed her legs; a movement to get him to remove his hand without having to ask. He was smooth, sharply dressed in an expensive suit, and distinguished. She could only imagine the number of undergrads who fell for him at first sight. Alani had eyes for one man, however.

"They want to get a deal on the table right away. They want to print up unedited copies for reviews, get them out to New York Times, Ebony Magazine, Essence…I can represent you in the deal, if you like. I've negotiated a few publishing deals in my day."

"Wow, really?" she asked.

"Really," Alex confirmed. "The entire book was gripping, Alani."

"Lenika," she corrected. She could tell he was getting used to calling her by her first name and she didn't like it.

"Excuse me?" he asked.

"Please, call me Lenika. No one really calls me Alani," she said, giving him a muted smile.

"Lenika it is," he complied. "Well, Lenika. We must celebrate. Our new, agent-author, relationship, must be toasted over a glass of wine and an expensive meal."

Alani's mouth fell open, but she couldn't find a reply. His body language told her this was not a professional invite.

"She'll celebrate with my dad," Eazy said.

Alani rolled eyes of shock to her side and the look on Eazy's face was one of pure possessiveness. He looked her professor in the eyes, unsmiling, and unflinching, not at all intimidated like most children would be.

He was staking a claim. Alani had a man to take her to celebrate things like this, and it was his father.

"I guess I have plans," she said, with a smile, as she reached over and rubbed the back of Eazy's head.

This little boy here. Protective like a son. Jealous like a young man. No nonsense like his father.

"Yeah, I guess so," Alex said, standing. He held out his hand and extended it to Eazy. Eazy looked at it, letting it linger in midair for an awkward beat, before shaking it.

"Thank you for everything," Alani said.

"I'll be in touch about the contract and I'm sure right after you sign, a reading will follow to generate press," Alex said.

She nodded and then grabbed Eazy's hand as they left. Her life was changing rapidly. She had found her footing. She had found purpose, after losing it all, and feeling like she would never be able to breathe again. Here she was, full on living, succeeding, climbing out of that darkness with a man by her side, a book getting ready to hit the shelves, and an entire city block with her name on the deeds. Who was this woman? How the hell did this woman survive all she had endured? She was walking, hand in hand, with the most beautiful little boy with a smile on her face, as the sun shone down over her. How had this happened? It had just been so dark, so lonely, and now she was living. *God, how?*

CHAPTER 10

Fuck all this pretty Shawn Carter shit, nigga... HOV

Ethic pulled onto Nannie's old block, subwoofers knocking, as Bella rode shotgun, nodding her head.

"Shawn was on that gospel shit, I was on the total opposite."

Ethic's head whipped right, surprised at her for knowing the lyrics. Surprised even more that she had the moxie to recite them in front of him.

"You think you're growing up on my watch, huh?" he asked.

Bella poked out her lips and nodded her head more, turning up the energy in her bop, as she frowned at her father.

"Lace front to the back, don't front," she rapped. Her soft voice didn't even sound right saying the callous words.

Ethic didn't know when it had happened, or even how it had happened, but Bella was blooming right before his eyes. Baby girl wasn't a baby anymore.

"Watch the language, B," Ethic said, feeling tender on the inside. Her growth hurt like a motherfucker.

"Sorry, Daddy," she said, smiling. She leaned over to kiss his cheek, as he threw the car in park, and then popped open her door.

"Yo! Where you going? You ain't gon' help your old man clean out the garage?" he asked.

Bella shook her head and laughed mockingly. "She called *you* over here to clean it out. *I'm* going next door to Lyric's."

Ethic shook his head, as he climbed out the car. The block was alive. A group of teenage boys had a hoop game going on right in the middle of the street. An everyday event in the hood.

Ethic saw a black Audi pull up and park behind him. The dark tint hid the driver and the loud sounds of Childish Gambino oozed out the car.

This is America
Gunz in my Area
I got the strap
I got to carry 'em

Hand lingering near the hip where his pistol was tucked, he stood, waiting to see who emerged from the vehicle. Everything about Ezra Okafor was territorial. If anyone was pulling up to Nannie's house, then they better do so with respect. Niggas needed to know that this entire block was under his watchful eye. Especially, if Bella was determined to spread her wings here. Nyair stepped out of the car and Ethic relaxed as he approached. He was the most thugged-out pastor Ethic had ever encountered, but somehow the realest. Tattoos covered his forearms that were exposed by his sleeves that were pushed up to the elbows. A rosary, a cross, Jesus wearing a thorn crown, black ink covering black skin of a minister. Nyair was a walking puzzle, as he swaggered over to Ethic, while he scanned the block. Ethic couldn't quite figure the good pastor all the way out, but he trusted the energy that surrounded Nyair. It felt familiar. A gangster's shake and a brief embrace served as their greeting.

"That ain't preacher music," Ethic stated.

"It's genius, though. That's art, my G. Certain things I ain't giving up. Me and God will settle that score when it's time," Nyair snickered. "Nannie called you over here too for this garage?"

"Yeah, man," Ethic said, scoffing, as he put his keys in the pocket of his Nike sweats. "Glad it ain't a one-man job."

"Nannie got stuff from when we were kids in that garage, G. Two men ain't even enough."

Ethic chuckled and followed Nyair up the driveway.

"Hey, Ethic!" Connie called from next door. There seemed to always be a crowd at her house. The billow of smoke that rose from the barbecue grill emitted a mouthwatering smell into the air

He threw up a hand, in greeting. Not rude. Not friendly. The way Connie beamed, you would have thought he had blown her a kiss. The Ethic Effect had permeated the block, wetting panties instantly.

"I got a plate over here for y'all! I got ribs on the grill, chicken, polish sausages and some sides in the house!" She shouted.

"You whipping it up, huh?" Nyair called back.

"Every day, handsome," Connie called back. "I know how to get and keep a man."

Nannie stepped out onto the porch, a cigarette fired up in her hands.

"You ain't kept a man since '95, Connie, hush up," Nannie fussed. "Leave my boys alone."

Ethic chuckled and then ascended the steps, pulling the cigarette from Nannie's fingertips, before wrapping her in a loving embrace.

"I know Lenika don't know you back smoking these," Ethic stated, as he put it out against the metal railing on the porch.

"You run Alani. You don't run me, baby. Nannie would run circles around you, young man." She patted his cheek and pulled out another cigarette, as she moved by Ethic and hugged Nyair. "Thank you for coming over for an old girl. I know you're dealing with a lot over there right now. How's Morgan?"

"She's doing the best she can," Ethic stated. "Her friend is at the house with her right now."

"That first heartbreak feels like it has the power to ruin the rest of your life. When she realizes another man can come along and make her feel the same, she'll be fine. You only mourn the loss of a good man. Losing a nigga that ain't shit is a win. She's young. She'll learn," Nannie preached. She turned to head back into the house. "The garage is unlocked. Mr. Larry ordered the dumpster for y'all."

Ethic and Nyair made their way to the back and the overwhelming amount of junk piled in the garage made Ethic pause. He looked to the overgrown grass in the backyard.

"Yo, we might as well clean all this up while we're here. I'll put someone on a weekly rotation for the grass. This is crazy,"

Ethic stated, scratching the back of his head and grimacing. It would take most of the day to take care of this, but he wouldn't leave it undone. They dug into the boxes. Within an hour, the heat from the early summer sun beat down on them. Ethic came out of his shirt and spun his hat backwards, as he draped the white fabric around his sweaty neck. Connie and her friends had come to the backyard just for the visual.

"Lord knows, He did a motherfucking job, do you hear me?!" Connie shouted, as her girlfriends laughed and high-fived. Their cackling and commentary as Ethic and Nyair emptied the garage only made Ethic shake his head.

"This is sexual harassment like a mu'fucka," Ethic snickered.

"Indeed," Nyair answered, laughing. "I'll bust that down though, G. She can cook, and she got that little pouch in the front a nigga like to hold onto while he in that. Guarantee it's amazing."

Ethic laughed deep and hard because he knew Nyair's assessment was likely truth. The same way women assessed men at first glance, men sized up women. Alani had that little pouch, the evidence that she had carried life inside her before, and he loved that shit. In this moment, he craved it... craved her. He just wanted to finish the job, so he could get back to his woman. He didn't want any issues with Lenika. There would be no accepting of compliments or food from next door, no matter how good it smelled. Alani would murder him dead, and then beat the case.

"I know Nika got you locked down, but what about you handsome?" Connie asked, as she switched over to the chain-link fence.

Ethic chuckled and patted Nyair on the back, before moving back into the garage for more boxes. Connie wasn't an ugly woman. Pretty face, big hips, a little gut on her from having kids, and Ethic would bet his bottom dollar she had pussy that had put a few niggas names on a notice down at the friend of the court. He shook his head, again, and went back into the garage to retrieve the next box.

Nyair smirked, a half smile creeping at the corners of his lips, as his dimples settled into his cheeks.

"I'm not looking. Just tryna get my walk right before I try to lead a woman, you feel me?" he asked. He swept one hand over his head and trapped his bottom lip between white teeth. "I will take that plate, though, if the offer still stands."

"Nah, I got a new offer," she said. "Whenever you feel the need, you can slide through anytime and I'll feed you. Whatever you want. Whenever you're hungry."

Nyair's entire face heated, glowing in a red undertone, as his eyes sparkled in amusement.

"Just a couple ribs and some greens would be more than enough," he said, eyes smiling, as he chuckled a bit. The dimples in his cheeks were enough to make women swoon, but put it on his flawless face, accompany it with the chiseled jawline and athletic physique, and women fell in love at first sight. Connie was no different.

"I'll send baby girl, Bella, back over here with a plate for you," Connie said.

Ethic emerged, frowning, as he lifted a box over his head and tossed it into the dumpster.

"Yo, let me talk to you for a minute," he said to Connie. Connie shifted her gaze to Ethic, looking him down and up; yes, down and up, because she started at the print in those damn sweatpants and then lifted her eyes until they met his.

"My daughter don't deliver no plates to grown men. I know she's spending a lot of time here lately, and she's with your daughter a lot, but I don't play no games about mine. As a matter of fact, if there's ever a nigga over here while she's here, you send her back to this side of the fence, you understand?"

Connie placed a hand to her chest, taken aback and a bit speechless. She shook her head. "I know you fucking Nika real good. Motherfucking perfection," she muttered. "Her mean-ass done hit the fucking jackpot. They don't even make 'em like you no more, babyyyyy. I understand. I'ma follow every damn order with a smile on my face."

She walked away, shaking her head.

Nyair chuckled.

"La gon' beat yo' ass, bruh," Nyair said. "That's trouble."

Ethic snickered and bent down to grab another box. He saw a picture frame lying on top. He placed the box down and opened it. The face had aged but that smile was the same. He wasn't staring at a picture of Lenika. His Alani was all that was present in the photo.

"These her parents?" Ethic asked, passing the picture to Ny.

"Yeah, that's them. Cecil and Joi. Nannie had to take all the pictures out the house a long time ago. They used to make La cry so hard she'd make herself sick."

Before Ethic could respond, a sound that was too familiar, too close, too fucking deadly, erupted on the block.

BANG! BANG! BANG! BANG!

Ethic's entire body reacted. His stomach hollowed. His mouth dried, and his heart stalled, but Ethic didn't freeze. Gunshots meant go, to a man of his pedigree. His daughter was on this block and bullets were flying. He drew his burner, without thinking twice. It was as automatic as his next breath.

"Bella!"

Nyair was right behind him; and to his surprise, brandished a gun of his own. Ethic raced to the front yard, and to his horror, Bella laid in the middle of the front yard. Her hands covered her ears and her eyes were squeezed tightly.

"Daddddyyyy!" Her shrill screams cut through the air, as a boy he'd never seen covered her with his entire body.

Ethic advanced on the car that had brazenly stopped in the middle of the block. Three gunmen hung out the windows. Even the driver sat on the windowsill, busting shots across the top of the car's roof.

Ethic fired, hitting the back tires first, to stop the car from being able to peel away. Nyair banged alongside him, busting cover shots, like he didn't have a God to answer to. Like he repped sets and brandished colors instead of crosses.

Ethic ran around the back of the car, snatching the driver out with so much aggression, he pulled him through the window, causing his shoes to fall off his feet.

He slammed the shooter to the ground and stuck his gun in the middle of his forehead. He was grateful for Nyair because he had the other two shooters handled. Young niggas underestimated the reload. They emptied their clips all at the same time, so there was no cover fire to stop a nigga from running up on them when their clips ran out. It was amateur hour. Ethic knew because they didn't alternate their shots; and as he stared into the eyes of the kid under the barrel of his gun, he realized how young the kid was. He couldn't have been a day over sixteen.

He grabbed him off the ground, relieved him of his pistol and pushed him to the curb. "Sit down," he said. "On your fucking hands."

Nyair pulled the other two from the car and walked them to the curb. The entire block was silent. Nobody knew what would happen next. They knew what could happen, and no one dared breathe, let alone move.

"Move and I'ma send you back to your mama zipped up," Ethic said.

Ethic put a foot to the chest of the driver, pushing him back into the dirt.

"Aye, man!" the kid shouted.

This was why Ethic kept his family out of the city. Whenever he stepped foot inside the city limits, he became a gangster. That's what it took to stay alive in Flint. He bent down, patting the pockets of the kid until he pulled out a wad of money, with a school ID, wrapped by a rubber band.

"He a fucking kid, man," Ethic said, flicking the ID and the money back at the boy. "Turn around. Get on your fucking stomach. All y'all. You want to be a shooter? Shooters ain't afraid to get shot."

"Please, man!" one of the other boys said, trying his hardest to stop the quiver in his tone.

"You turn around too, homeboy," Ny said, gun still trained on the other two.

"You see that girl over there?" Ethic asked.

The driver lifted his chin to look up at Bella.

"That's my daughter, nigga. She be around here. That house. This entire motherfucking block, and the one behind it - on both sides - is off fucking limits," Ethic sneered, pressing the gun in the back of the kid's head.

"Okay, man! Okay! I ain't know! I ain't know! Ethic, man, please!"

The fact that they knew who he was spoke of his legend on these streets.

The three, teenaged boys were trying not to bitch up, but they trembled like leaves in the wind.

Stupid, little mu'fuckas. Ethic was livid. So many young, black boys walked around brandishing guns, letting bullets fly, to mask an inadequacy that wasn't being filled at home. Trying to be men before their time. Wasn't shit fun about manhood, yet they rushed to it, fucking up because they were nothing more than adolescents with aggression.

Ethic wondered what circumstances had brought them to this block, what ghosts had put chrome pistols in their hands, instead of books, instead of basketballs. At this age, these little niggas should have been getting their first taste of pussy and jumping out of windows, so that they didn't get caught, not wetting blocks. Kids didn't even go through the stages of maturity anymore. They bypassed all those parts. They went straight from their mama's laps to prison, behind dumbass shit just like this. He had once walked their path and turmoil filled him because he knew these boys were living by a creed that was meant to destroy black boys. He stood, forcing himself to stifle his anger. This was a factory. This was a system that produced this. Black on black crime. US versus US. Guns in the hands of black boys aimed at other black boys. It both hurt and angered him. His son could be one of these boys. He used to be one of these boys.

He swept one hand over his head, frustrated, as his jaw locked, and his nostrils flared.

"Yo, hear me fucking clear!" Ethic shouted. "I got five hundred dollars and a job for anybody who bring they burners and they package to me today. This house and this block is off limits. As long as my daughter is around this bitch, nothing's moving on this block! Nothing! I don't want a dime bag of weed sold on this bitch! You want to make some money, I'll show you little, stupid niggas how to get some money; but this street shit is done over here. Take that shit to the other side of town. I don't give a fuck who got beef. I find out it's heat on this block, and I'm coming straight to your mama house. I'll be around here for the next few hours. You bring me the guns and I'll give you the cash. Get up." Ethic put both, his gun and the driver's gun, in his back waistline. "I see you back over here again and I'ma kill you," Ethic said, sneering at the boys on the curb, before stepping over them. Bella rushed into his arms, trembling, and it made Ethic want to kill the three teenagers all over again.

"Shhh," he whispered. He kissed the top of her head. His blood was boiling. "It's okay. Go in the house, B. Go with Ms. Pat."

Nannie pushed through the screen door and Bella rushed up the steps and into her arms.

"Go inside, lock the doors and stay away from the windows, just in case there's smoke," Ethic said.

"Ain't gon' be no smoke, O.G."

Ethic turned around and saw three, different, young men come off the hip. Ethic reached for his gun. Nyair reached too.

"No, big homie, nah. NO SMOKE! We ain't know this was your block, man. It's all respect. We know who you are. We heard you loud and clear. This block and the ones that circle it...all off limits from here out. I don't even want the money, O.G." The young man said, bending down to place his gun on the grass at Ethic's feet. "I'll take the game, though. If you give me the game, I'll make sure these blocks stay dry. I'm trying to move like you, big homie. Get out this shit with my life and my name. I don't want them to put numbers on my back."

Ethic knew he was referring to a prison number.

Ethic looked over at Nyair.

"That's powerful, G," Nyair said. Ethic bent down to pick up the guns and then he gripped the handle, feeling the weight of it in his hand. It was better than having the weight of another life lost on his soul.

"All y'all feel that way?" he asked.

"Hell yeah, man, my daddy and my brother died out this bitch. I'm just tryna eat. If you can show me how to eat, and I ain't got to do this shit, I'm with it," another spoke up.

Ethic sighed. "Come grab a box," he said, leading the way, with reluctance, back to the garage. Somehow, a two-man job had turned into a five-man task. As the afternoon sun burned out, turning light to night, Ethic had collected over 30 guns. His pockets were $15,000 lighter. He didn't even carry that much cash on him at once. He had to make a bank run, just to keep his word.

By the time he was done, he and Nyair were sitting on the front porch with Nannie, as the young men and teenagers from the block finished the garage and tended to her bushes. Nannie added the basement to the list of things to do, while they were at it.

Nyair looked at the box of guns at Ethic's feet.

"Yo, G, you could do some real good work in the city. They respect you on these blocks. The police hold the same type of drives and nobody shows. You raise your voice a little bit and every shooter on this street gave up their burner."

"You can get rid of them? Turn 'em in without no blowback?" Ethic inquired.

"That's not a problem," Nyair said. "You probably saved a lot of lives, G. When you ready to do it on the regular, hit my line." Nyair stood and slapped hands with Ethic, and then leaned down to kiss Nannie's cheek.

"Alani get with you about that counseling thing?" Ethic asked.

"Yeah, Sunday after church. I'll pull up on you around four o'clock," he said.

Then, he was gone, and the night was still. He rested his head against the back of the chair.

"Bella, baby, come out here for a minute!" Ethic shouted through the screen door. Fireflies floated through the yard and the street was unusually quiet. It had been tamed by Ezra Okafor that day. Enough action had occurred on these cracked sidewalks and pothole-filled streets to keep the grapevine ringing all summer. Bella appeared in the doorway moments later, pushing open the door. Ethic deadpanned on her.

"Who's the boy?" he asked. "The one who covered you when the shots rang out?"

Bella's eyes widened slightly, but she kept her poker face strong. He had taught her that poker face, that way of concealing her hand, so no one could outplay her. She had mastered that face. Months of lying to her father when Alani had been pregnant had given her plenty of practice.

"I don't know his name, Daddy. Just some boy from around here, I guess," Bella answered.

"He's just a neighborhood kid, Ezra," Nannie added.

Ethic stared at Bella long and hard, before standing and pulling her into his arms. He kissed the top of her head, lovingly. "Go get in the car. You're driving," he said, tossing her the keys.

"Say you swear?!" Bella shouted, in excitement, as she caught them.

Ethic chuckled and then leaned down to kiss Nannie's check. He stood and scanned the block one more time.

"Don't you think it's time to leave the city? I can buy you a nice house in the suburbs," Ethic started. "I wouldn't mind if you moved in with us either. When Alani and I figure things out, you're always welcome, Ms. Pat. In fact, you're needed."

"I'ma stay right here. The neighborhood will never change, if all the good people move out and leave the bad behind. We just got to love on our own streets. Love on our own boys until they're good too. You did a good thing today, baby. Should have blown them little rascals to kingdom come; but the fact that you didn't, means you're seeing the God in you in the reflection in Alani's eyes. You're a good man. A real good man, Ezra. Don't you let nobody tell you different."

CHAPTER 11

Alani rushed around the family room, placing flowers in vases and fluffing the couch pillows. She even put lavender oil in a diffuser. Ethic stood in the threshold, hands tucked away in the pockets of his black Ferragamo slacks. He leaned against the frame, as he watched her add life to the room. Fuck the room... She added life to the entire house. Her visits were less frequent than he would like because he was trying to accommodate Morgan's needs; but today, watching her move freely in his space, it made him crave her essence. She just added an aura to his life that was irreplaceable. He missed her terribly, whenever they were apart.

"It's just Ny, baby. I don't think you have to do all this," Ethic said, jarring her attention and forcing her to turn his way.

She pulled one of Eazy's gaming controllers from the couch's cushions.

"This boy," she said. "I bet he's been looking for this for days."

She sounded like a mama. She sounded like Eazy's mama, like she was ready to march upstairs and demand that he come clean up his mess. Ethic scoffed and shook his head.

Fucking incredible.

Alani wasn't all sugar all the time, pretending to drip her sweetness everywhere. She was sour too. She was stern and maternal and correcting. It's what told him she was genuine. She didn't care if his children liked her all the time. She parented them all the time and they loved her for it. Something as simple as her fussing about Eazy's mess made Ethic want to fuck her. Something as simple as sex between a man and woman was not so simple between Ethic and Alani. His need to be inside her, to bathe in her water, was a spiritual cleansing. She purified his dark soul. She was his soul mate. Yep, Ethic wanted to fuck her good.

"I'm not doing this for Nyair," she said. "I just want Morgan to be comfortable. You said she's been holed up in her room for days. The flowers should lift her spirits. All girls like flowers. The lavender is calming. I just want her to give this a chance. To give me a chance," Alani said. "I brought over food, in case anyone's hungry. Let me go take it out the oven and…"

Ethic grabbed her hand, as she attempted to walk by him, pulling her into his body. She was flustered, anxious, moody…Lenika was present today and he would bet his last dollar that she was on her period. Didn't stop shit. He still wanted to fuck her. Only her in that state. Another woman, he would never. With her, it was a blood pact, something to tie him closer to her, make them blood, make her his life source. His love for her was other worldly, living in a place rooted so deeply that nothing could ever destroy it.

"I missed you, baby," he whispered. His hand on her neck, then gracing the side of her face, as she bent to his will, face melting into his palm. She closed her eyes and rested there. A sigh left her lips and the same breath filled his lungs. She breathed life into him and didn't even know it. She supplied. He received. He was so grateful. He pulled her closer and looked down the bridge of his nose at her.

"Breathe," he whispered. Her entire soul stirred. His baritone commanded her, like he had trained her to obey. She felt her chest rise and then fall, pulling in air, following, obeying. Her king. *God, this man was a king.*

"Kiss me," she whispered. His queen. The only person on Earth that could lay out her own orders...ones he followed without hesitation. He kissed her and felt her go weak, but he was strong, strong enough for them both, as he held her up.

"I love you," she whispered, while cupping his face. "I've never known love like this, Ethic. I love you too much."

The *too much* bothered him. He craned his neck back. "What if you leave one day? I'll be destroyed," she whispered.

"It's never happening," Ethic returned.

"Promise me?" she returned.

He deadpanned on her, and then gripped her chin with two fingers, tilting it up. "On Love."

She wrapped her arms around his neck and he held her flesh to his body.

"Never happening, baby," he repeated.

The clearing of a throat pulled them apart and Morgan stood there, staring at them. Her face was pale and ashen, her lips dried, her hair pulled back into a ponytail. Her swollen eyes held a story of woe. The hoodie and leggings were a far cry from her usual, pulled-together attire.

Alani lowered her head and took a step back from Ethic, finessing her tingling lips.

"Hi, Morgan," Alani greeted.

Morgan gave her a tight-lipped smile. It was polite but short. She slipped between them and headed toward the couch.

Alani blew out a breath in exasperation. "She hates me," Alani whispered.

Ethic ran a hand down the side of his face, massaging his beard. "She hates everybody right now. Messiah isn't here for her to take this out on. There has been a lot of morning sickness, a lot of crying...we're all targets, not just you," Ethic informed.

Alani shook her head. "No, I think this is about my brother. It's like she hates me for what he did," she whispered. "I hope she knows how sorry I am. I've tried to tell her, but..."

"You're not him. You're nothing like him. You can't make up for what you didn't do. We'll take it slow with Mo. I hope one day she gets to know you the way I do. She can't help but love you, once she knows you. I need you to be patient with her...patient with me, while I help her through this."

She nodded. It didn't even need to be said. Alani wasn't going anywhere, and she wasn't rushing Mo's healing. She prayed for true healing, because after the video she had seen of Mo's rape, the fight she had witnessed with Messiah, then Messiah's admission, she knew Morgan had to be losing it. Alani knew what it felt like to lose it a little behind a man you thought loved you.

DING DONG

"I'll get the door. Grab B and Eazy," Ethic instructed.

Ethic went to the door and pulled it open.

"My G," Nyair greeted, as they slapped hands and embraced.

"Come in," Ethic said, as he held open the door and extended an arm.

Eazy and Bella came down the stairs, followed by Alani.

"Hey, Ny," Alani greeted, as she delivered a kiss on his cheek. "We're right in here."

The group traveled to the family room where Morgan sat. She had moved to the bay window and sat on the sill with her knees pulled to her chest. She stared outside, like she was being held captive, like there were chains on her that kept her from leaving.

"Mo, why don't you join us, baby girl?" Ethic stated, going to her and extending his hand. Morgan looked at his hand, glanced to the seating area in the room, and then looked back out the window.

"I said I'd come. I don't want to sit in a circle and hold hands. I'm here. I can hear just fine from over here," she said. It was the Messiah in her that made her resist so hard... that gave her a little bark behind that pretty face.

Ethic took a seat at one end of the couch, beside Bella, as Eazy sat in Alani's lap. Ethic warmed at the sight of Eazy. He was so comfortable. He was as big as Alani, but he knew that the physical discomfort of having his son in her arms was outweighed by the emotional bliss Eazy gave her. They were mother and son, not by blood but by bond, and Ethic found it hard to look away.

"First thing we got to correct is this," Nyair said, as he looked toward Morgan. He motioned to the picture of the foursome on the couch. "The four of you are beautiful together. I can see the instant need that Alani is fulfilling and it's amazing. It's what she's here for and that's godly. Babies transition well. They are resilient. The older we get, the more set in our ways we become, which is why baby girl is not on the couch. She's so far away from the couch that she's not in the unit. She feels like an entity of her own. So deserted that maybe it begins to make more sense to just get out of everyone's way altogether. Makes her feel like she could not be here, and it might be better. This picture on this couch could really exist, if she were gone...like she's in the way... like she could die..."

Ethic looked toward Morgan, who refused to look his way, and his chest hollowed.

"Mo..." he called.

Her chin quivered.

"Morgan," he said, his voice filled with emotion. He stood and crossed the room.

"Go get your cub, G. She crawled out on a limb and she's stuck. It's not that she doesn't want to come to you. She just doesn't know how to get back to you," Nyair said.

Ethic stood and walked over to Morgan. She still couldn't look at him, but tears were streaming down her face.

"Mo..." Ethic paused to clear his throat, because he was so

damn affected by her distress. "I just want you to be okay... I'm right here, baby girl. I'm never going anywhere."

"They all go. Daddy. Raven. Messiah," she whispered, still unable to face Ethic. "Now you, because of her...now you have her."

"And I'm still going to be right here," Ethic said. "I'm here, Mo."

Ethic stood directly in front of her and Morgan's head collapsed against his stomach. She sobbed into him, as he wrapped his arms around her head.

"He's Mizan's brother..." she whispered.

"I know," Ethic said. "I know."

"Why do I still love him when I know that? Why do you still love her when you know what her brother did?" Morgan cried.

"Because we can't help who we love, Mo, and because she isn't him. Messiah isn't Mizan. If he was, I wouldn't be here to hold you right now. I would be gone because he had opportunity. He had ample opportunity to kill me and he didn't. They aren't their brothers," Ethic said. "And no matter who comes, who goes, I'm never leaving you. I'm never excluding you. You're mine, Mo. You know how selfish I am with what belongs to me? You know what I'll do to a nigga over what's mine? You'll never not be mine."

He pulled her to her feet and she buried herself in his embrace, crying. Ethic practically picked her up off her feet, he held her so tightly, fisting her hair while she clung to him like a little girl because she was desperate for this love. Messiah had left her so empty and Ethic was filling her up.

"Mo, is it?"

Morgan placed eyes on Nyair and nodded, still looking over Ethic's shoulders because she didn't want to let go and neither did he.

"Will you join us? It's not a family session if you're over there," Nyair said.

Ethic finally released her, and Morgan walked over to the couch.

"Mo Money, are you okay?" Eazy asked.

Morgan swiped at her tears and shook her head. "Not this time, Eazy. I'm not okay," she admitted.

"Maybe I should go," Alani said, lifting Eazy from her lap and standing.

"No," Nyair said. "Too much desertion in this family. Mo's desperate for an exit, so she pulls the stunt in the garage. You leaving him after Kenzie, him leaving you after Love... no. The five of you need to stay...you stay, and you fight for family. You fight for unity. You work it out; because like it or not, all three of these babies are yours now, even the rebellious one you can't handle."

Alani looked to Morgan who looked away. Ethic swiped a hand down his face. He was struggling with this...with loving a woman that Morgan hated.

He looked to Nyair. "I need help with this. I don't know what I'm supposed to do here."

"You're supposed to sit with your family, man. Family don't always like each other. They don't always agree. They fight. They fucking tear each other apart...

"Ny!" Alani protested.

"My flesh, my bad," he said, lifting hands in surrender, as he licked his full lips.

"What kind of preacher are you?" Morgan asked, finding laughter and living in it for a moment, as her chest lightened some. She took in his casual attire and the tattoos on his forearms.

"A dope one," Nyair said, with a wink, licking his lips, again, apparently a habit, as he ran one hand over his head. "But I'll keep it clean. My fault, G. No disrespect," he said, looking at Ethic. Ethic nodded.

"The point is... Family has the power to destroy family. Families go to war with each other, and that's what this is…a battle between members of this family, but I'll bet if somebody walked in here and tried to hurt any one of you on this couch, there would be a problem. Alani would fight for you; and I'd bet if you saw someone trying to hurt Alani, it would be a problem for you."

Morgan rolled her eyes. She didn't respond, but she felt a pulling at her heart. She wouldn't go super hard for Alani, but she maybe, kinda, sorta, would be offended if someone came at her. If you caught Morgan on a good day when she was feeling good, she might pull some hair if Alani was getting jumped. Morgan crossed her arms across her chest and Nyair gave a half smile.

"The kid who needs love but is too grown to ask for it and too proud to receive it. Bruh, she gon' keep you busy," Nyair said.

Ethic shook his head. "Tell me about it."

"That's what we not gon' do," Morgan said.

"Morgan just has to be the center of attention or she isn't happy," Bella whispered.

Everyone turned to her, in stun. She sat, thumbing through her iPhone and slouching against the couch cushions.

"Bella..." Alani whispered.

"No, I want to hear this," Morgan said, voice trembling. "Is that what you think, B?"

"You've always been that way," Bella said. "If Daddy wasn't always paying attention to you, you'd have a fit. So, he took some of mine and gave it to you. He took some of Eazy's and gave it to you. He loved us half the time, so he could extra love you. Now, he loves Alani, and you want to take what he's giving her too. You're selfish with him, Mo, but he isn't just yours. He's all of ours! The whole family needs him, not just you."

Morgan recoiled, as she turned on the couch, hanging halfway off, so that she could stare Bella down.

"B..."

Nyair held up a hand to stop Ethic from interrupting.

"So, that's how you feel?" Morgan asked.

Bella's eyes were glued to her screen. She didn't even look up at Mo, as she continued to scroll. Morgan reached for the phone, snatching it from Bella's hands.

"Give me my phone, Mo!" Bella shouted, as she lunged across the couch. Morgan held it out of Bella's reach, while blocking Bella with one arm.

"No! Tell me! That's how you really feel?" Morgan asked.

"You're selfish! We love you anyway, but you want everything to be about you. You always have, but you're not here all the time. You're off loving Messiah, but you don't want Daddy to love Alani. He's so happy with her. He smiles, Mo. He can't even stop kissing her for five seconds, he loves her so much. Things were normal, and it felt good, but as soon as you saw that he was focused on someone else besides you, you tried to kill yourself. Now, he's back on you, and when you're hurting he'll give you anything. He'll even send Alani away just because you asked, but how is that fair? When you're off at school, we're here and we need her. You didn't even make time for my pageant, and I'm not mad because I know you have your life, but she did. She did what a mother would do. She was here. I need her, but because of you, she'll be gone."

"Bella..." That was Alani's objection this time, but Nyair raised a hand.

"How long have you wanted to tell Morgan that?" Nyair asked.

Bella shrugged. "Since the day her and Raven came to live with us. Morgan's always been his favorite. He'll do anything for her."

"I'll do anything for every person sitting on that couch," Ethic interrupted. "There are no favorites, Bella. It's equal. Between all of you. Alani too," he said, making eye contact with her. "I love all of you. Will die for all of you. If I ever made it seem like there was a pecking order, I'm sorry. B?" he beckoned her, and Bella lifted glossy eyes to her father.

"I'm sorry. There's no order, no favorites. Just love."

"I don't try to take his attention from you, B. I love you. I would never not want him to be there for you, or Eazy..."

"But not Alani, right?" Bella asked.

Morgan lifted disdain-filled eyes to Alani. They had such a complicated history. They had moments that were less tense than others, but Morgan was still struggling with acceptance. They both held their breaths because this was a standoff. This was the moment where they aired their grievances out. In front of the man they both loved.

"I don't know," Morgan whispered. She looked at Ethic. "I want you happy, but what about Rae?"

"Daddy said he will always love my mom," Eazy interjected. "That he's just making room for Alani. You should make room, Mo. We have all this space and no Alani. All we have to do is make a little room." The brilliance of childhood…the simplicity of seeing the world through Eazy's eyes. He made it sound so easy.

Alani's lip quivered, and she placed four fingers over her mouth. She closed her eyes because she knew that Morgan's answer was important. She braced herself for the worst. She felt it coming…the blow that would end her and Ethic…and she would have to suck it up, because Morgan needed him more. She was a young woman who had lost her way, and she needed her father. Alani knew in her bones that this love she had fought herself to finally have was about to be flushed down the drain. A sickness swept over her and wetness teased her lashes.

"Take your time, Morgan. You don't have to know how you feel right now. It's been a trying time for you. Just think about the people in this room. They are your family. They love you. You fight with these people, but no one will help you breathe like these very people. Even the one you think you need the least. You may have more in common than you know," Nyair said.

Morgan stood, and Ethic did too, pulling her into his body, hugging her tightly, as he kissed the top of her head. Morgan hid her face from the others. "I'm going to make it better, Mo. I'ma fix it for you, baby girl, like I always do."

She nodded, but never let him go. She just needed to be held...she just needed to be protected...she just needed attention...from Ethic. No one else would do. Well, one other would do, but he was gone, and now Ethic was all that was left.

Maybe I am selfish, but I don't care.

Alani sat on the couch, sipping the red wine from her glass. It was midday, but it was happy hour somewhere. This drink was needed. She had earned it. Morgan Atkins had pushed her to indulge. Morgan Atkins. The girl who would never accept her. The girl who was going to ruin her relationship with the man she wanted more than anything. Perhaps, Morgan was the sign she had asked God to send her regarding Ethic. She had pleaded for it so many nights...any indication to direct her steps...to tell her if she should love him or leave him behind. Ethic descended the steps and blew out a breath of exasperation. Anxiety filled his frame.

"I'm not sure if that hurt or helped," he said, placing a hand on her knee, as he took a seat next to her. He groaned, as he melted into the expensive cushions. He was exhausted... emotionally spent.

"Me either," she said. He laid his head in her lap and she rubbed his waves so gently that he closed his eyes...such a tender touch...the touch of a woman...his woman...but for how long? How long could he keep her? The days seemed numbered.

"I don't want to lose her. I'm so fucking scared I'm going to lose her," he whispered.

"Ethic, we don't have to do this. I love you, and I know you love me, but we both knew we would have so many obstacles between us. We knew it was a big chance that this might not work. Morgan tried to kill herself. That attention thing...this time, she needs it," Alani said. "Then, Bella feels neglected and Eazy needs you. Your plate is so full."

"And it's too much for you." Ethic's deep voice cut through the air, carrying so much solemn with it that her belly hollowed. His forehead wrinkled but his eyes remained closed. Ethic was the man who gave love but could never get it. He was the strong one...the one expected to carry the burdens of others, but no one thought of the ones he possessed...the weight of his own.

"No. I'm not saying that, but she doesn't want me here. She hates me," Alani said.

"So, I've got to choose," Ethic said.

"No, I've got to walk away," Alani whispered. It had taken so much just to get here...to a point where she wanted to stay…where she could commit, now she had to leave…it didn't seem fair. "I only have myself to consider. You have three other souls who depend on you. What might be right for us, might be wrong for them."

"I really do love you," he said, as he rubbed his palms together and leaned onto his knees. His hands went to his head and he rubbed the back of it, and then slid down to his neck to rub there too. The tension, the anxiety, the pain…all the things she provided relief for was returning because she couldn't stay. He had to sacrifice her for Morgan and it killed him, but there was no other choice. Morgan's life was at stake. Morgan was his child. "She's my baby. She's been my baby since she was six years old. From the very first time she smiled at me, she just dug a spot right in my heart. I know Bella's right. I've spoiled her, but she deserved it. She needed so much. I just wanted her to know that she had somebody. After her parents and then Raven…I wanted her to know that she always had me. How does she not know…what didn't I do right?"

"You did everything right…"

Ethic and Alani looked up to find Morgan in the doorway. "You've loved me perfectly, every day for almost my entire life. I don't want to be selfish. I want you to be happy," she said. "Even if I'm not happy about the person that makes you happy. I don't want to be selfish and keep you from someone you need. I know what that feels like. I felt like that…with Messiah. You don't have to choose. I don't like it, but I can try…I can give her a chance," Morgan said. "And I think I need the therapy thing. I don't want to do it at the hospital. I'll do it with Nyair. If that's okay…I'd like to keep going."

She swiped tears from her cheeks and walked away, as quickly as she had come. Morgan hadn't realized she had pulled so much from the people she loved…that she had taken some of the love from Bella and Eazy because she was trying to get her fill. She didn't want to do that to them. She didn't want to do that to him. They were her family, and she promised herself, going forward, that she would consider their feelings from now on; even if she had to hurt a little bit in order to do so. Selfless. Morgan wanted to be selfless for the people she loved. Letting Ethic love Alani was the first step.

CHAPTER 12

The scent of the Palo Santo stick filled the air, as Messiah sat in the leather chair watching Bleu, as she clipped the dead leaves from the sage plant she was insistent on growing in his room.

"You and all this energy bullshit is funking up my mu'fucking room," Messiah said.

"Your grumpy-ass needs some good energy, shut it," she countered. A nurse entered the room and Bleu took a seat across from Messiah.

"Will it hurt?" she asked, as she watched the nurse pull out the items necessary to administer his medication.

"Just a little pinch when I insert the IV into the port," she said. "Nothing Mr. Williams can't take."

Messiah flexed his muscle and winked at her. "A nigga built Ford tough," he said.

The blonde, young nurse turned beet red. "I can see that," she flirted.

Bleu rolled her eyes and shook her head, smirking, as the nurse hooked Messiah up to the drips.

The infusion room was empty. Bleu had paid extra to make sure his treatment was private. If he had to be weak, she knew he wouldn't want anyone witnessing it, even if it were only other patients.

"We'll start with an agent to relax you and take the edge off," the nurse said. "Then, I'll add chlorambucil. That medication will attack the cancerous cells in your body that are trying to divide. The more we can stop the division of those cells, the more time we give you. The port acts as a vein that will carry the medicine throughout the rest of your body."

Messiah's chest locked. It was his first chemo treatment and he didn't know what to expect. He felt like a shell. Like his life had already abandoned him and he was a hollow representation of the man he used to be. He remembered this feeling. He hadn't had it in a long time because it was accompanied by fear, and he hadn't feared anything in a long time; but damn, he was terrified of this.

"My hair will fall out?" he asked.

"It's a side effect of the chemo. We could cold pack you. Put packs of dried ice around your head for hours during the treatment. It could help stop the hair loss," the nurse said.

"How cold?" he asked.

"Negative temperatures. Extreme cold is necessary if we take that route," the nurse informed.

He shook his head. "No, let's just get it over with."

He closed his eyes and leaned his head back. He felt the nurse pull down the hospital gown to access the device they had implanted underneath his skin. He gritted his teeth and disappeared in his mind… to Morgan Land.

"Messiah, I love you."

Those zz's. He felt the tear slide out of the side of his eye and then felt Bleu's dainty hand as she reached for him. He gripped it tightly, as the pain from the port being hooked up seized him. It was over in seconds, but then a tingling filled him.

"It'll feel like something burns, or like your chest is going numb, as the medicine moves through your system," the nurse said.

"Hmm, hmm," Messiah grunted.

"You just hit your call button if you need anything. I have ice and clean buckets in case you need them."

"Thank you," Bleu whispered.

"So, I think Saviour has a girlfriend," Bleu said, trying to distract him.

"Say worddd?" Messiah said, popping his eyes open. "My little nigga," he snickered.

"Yup," Bleu answered. "I found a picture some little, fast-ass girl drew him. He's a baby and he's getting hearts drawn for him already. I think I want to go up to his school swinging."

Messiah laughed. "I bet you do. You treat him like he's your boyfriend. Yo' ass gon' be sick when he get older and he get the real thing, cuz you for damn sure ain't giving Iman no play," he stated.

"Who says I ain't giving Iman no play?" Bleu said, cocking her neck back.

"You ain't coming off that, Bleu. With your celibate-ass," Messiah snickered. Messiah's entire face turned green, as he sucked in a deep breath.

"Messiah?"

"The bucket, B," he gasped.

Bleu reached for the bucket and held it up, as vomit

spewed from him. She turned her head, as he heaved up so much clear fluid that it came out his nose.

"It's okay," she whispered. She hurried to the bathroom to empty the vomit and then emerged with a wet towel. She lifted his chin, wiping what remained. When he looked in her eyes, Bleu felt her eyes prickle.

She snapped them closed and shook her head to gather herself, before opening them again.

"It's okay," she said, again. "We don't have to talk. Let's just watch TV, okay? Let's relax."

She reached for the bottled water in her bag and handed it to him. He drank it all only for it to come right back up.

Bleu grabbed a new bucket and clenched her eyes closed, as she held it up for him. She hadn't been fast enough. He was covered in vomit.

"Bleu, get the nurse," he heaved. "This shit got me fucked up. They got to take it out, B. Take this shit out."

"No, Messiah. If you stop these treatments you die, Messiah. You die, and I can't live with that," Bleu stated. "Just, wait…"

She carried the bucket to the bathroom, repeating the process and emerging with fresh towels and a fresh hospital gown.

She cleaned him up and helped him into a new gown, before sitting in her seat.

"This ain't your job, B. I'm sorry I'm putting this on you," Messiah said, tone low…discouraged.

"And it wasn't your job to keep me clean all these years. To watch over me after Noah died. To come cut my grass when Iman is in California. To teach Saviour how to shoot a jump shot or come cover my windows in plastic before the first snow fall," Bleu whispered. "But you did it. You do it and you never complain, and you never not show up for me. I'm always going to show up, Messiah. Other people seem to come and go, but we all we got," she answered, tears falling. She held out her hand and Messiah snickered, clasping four fingers in a gangster's shake and then extending their pointer fingers before interlacing all five fingers into a joint fist. Their handshake. Some old-school, gangster shit Messiah had forced her to learn that they did effortlessly now.

"You so G, Bleu, it ain't even funny," he said, snickering weakly. "Make sure you give my nigga some pussy when you get home."

Bleu burst into laughter and Messiah gave up a weak chuckle as well.

Bleu grabbed the remote and turned on the TV, as Messiah lifted his feet onto her chair.

Bleu pushed his feet off her. "Get your dogs off me. You know I hate feet. Them crusty thangs," she said, frowning. He smiled and lifted them back into her lap anyway. Bleu didn't fuss. She turned up the volume of the old, black and white movie and they sat in silence. Messiah was in for quite a road and it was almost impossible to stay optimistic; but as he sat watching the delight on Bleu's face, as she watched old episodes of *I Love Lucy*, he felt a calm he had never experienced before. Despite the circumstances, despite the pain, despite it all, when he zeroed in on the amusement that played in her eyes, everything inside Messiah stilled…he felt no anger, no pain, no shame, because if he hadn't done anything else right in his life…his friendship with Bleu…he had done that well, and her being there, fighting death with him, was proof of that.

CHAPTER 13

How did you get here?
Nobody's supposed to be here
Myyyy heart says no, no
Nobody's supposed to be hereee
But you came along and changed my minnnddd

Alani's neck bobbed with every soulful note that floated through the living room, as she sat, folding the pile of clothes that rested in the basket at her feet. The glass of Moscato that sat next to her toes lifted her spirits. There was no crying today, so a bitter red wasn't necessary. Her wine choices matched her mood. Today, she was feeling light and sweet, so Moscato it was. She swore she was fancy, so she had cut up a block of cheese and some salami and pepperoni to pair it with. She was being fake bourgeoise and she smiled, laughing at herself a bit, because Ethic's massive estate had her forgetting that she was just a regular ol' girl. She was so comfortable in his home. The longer she stayed, the more it felt like she belonged. It was Saturday and she had taken her normal routine of R&B and weekend cleaning to his house. Ethic was still sleeping. A long night of lovemaking was holding him hostage. Alani quivered, thinking of the ways he had handled her mere hours ago. He deserved every, single second of rest he was getting. He had put in work and she still felt the effects of the orgasms he had delivered. Nannie and Mr. Larry had come by to get Bella and Eazy, so the normal noise that filled the walls was nonexistent and Morgan was barricaded in her room. She hadn't been very vocal, since the therapy session, opting to stay in her room for most of the day. Alani heard the tears, though. In the midnight hours, she heard music coming from behind closed doors. Love songs and crying. Alani's heart ached for Morgan because she knew what that felt like. She took a pile of the finished clothes upstairs and knocked on Morgan's door.

"I'm fine!"

It was Morgan's answer every time they checked on her. An emotional confirmation that was barely audible through the wooden door. She didn't want to talk, didn't want to participate in activities with the rest of them. She just stayed secluded in her room, wallowing, and everyone was so worried that they knocked all day long. Sometimes Eazy, most times Ethic, a few times Bella, never Alani. This was her first time knocking and she was disguising her presence with a clean clothes delivery.

Alani pushed open the door.

"Morgan?" she called. The room was so dark. The blackout curtains blocked out all light.

"Get out my room," Morgan whispered, voice cracking because the tears hadn't stopped. They would never stop.

"I have clean clothes, sweetheart," Alani said.

Morgan didn't answer, so Alani set them on the dresser. Morgan was barely a shadow in the distance. All she could see was that Morgan was balled up in the fetal position and she was facing the wall. Morgan may have been breathing but she was far from living. Alani stood there for a few seconds, trying to will herself to say something, anything, but she didn't want to give Morgan any reason to push her away. Alani's heart pulled inside her chest. She could hear Morgan's heart break. It was just festering, rotting the poor girl from the inside out. Alani turned to leave, but she paused at the door frame, and then walked over to the windows, pulling the curtains open some.

"What are you doing?" Morgan asked, as she popped up, in irritation.

"Maybe just leave the curtains open?" Alani suggested. "Even a little light might make you feel better."

Morgan hopped up and stormed to the window, snatching the curtains closed. "This isn't your room. This isn't even your house! Just get out! You can pretend like you belong here. You can try to replace your dead daughter with Eazy and Bella, but leave me the fuck alone," Morgan snapped.

"Mo!"

Ethic's baritone startled them both and Alani turned pained eyes to him.

Alani felt like Morgan had hit her and she felt anger bubbling on the tip of her tongue. This was the second time Morgan had disrespected her daughter's memory. Alani scoffed and pointed a warning finger at Morgan. It took everything in Alani to control her emotions.

She curled that finger into a balled fist and closed her eyes, as she sucked in a deep breath.

"The curtains stay open, Mo. I've been where you are. I know it's killing you. I know it hurts so bad you can't even breathe. You're mad as hell and your little-ass is mean as fuck, and the baby in your stomach isn't making it any better because you're sick all the time. I know, Morgan! I was you. Only I did all the wrong things and my baby ended up dead. If you want that. If you want to kill what you and Messiah made, you certainly are doing just that. If you want it to all be worth something, then leave the goddamn curtain open. At least let the sun hit your ashy-ass face. That's a start, and eat the food I send up here." Alani picked up the plates of food that Morgan hadn't touched, as she headed to the door with tears in her eyes. She turned to Morgan before exiting. "And I can take all the cheap shots you got. I've survived worse. So, you want to talk about my dead daughter? Go ahead. I'll eat that, because I know you're hurting so bad that you want everybody else to hurt too. I've been there. I know; and when you want to talk to someone who knows how to climb out of it, I'm here."

Alani stormed by Ethic and he reached for her elbow, but Alani pulled out of his hold.

"Don't," she said. "I'm going to finish sipping my wine, cleaning this house, and singing old-school love songs because I'm fucking in love, damn it."

Alani left Ethic upstairs with Morgan and she took the stairs back to the main floor.

"Don't let Morgan Atkins make you cry," she whispered. "Just breathe. You can do this."

Alani needed fresh air. She slipped into a pair of house shoes that sat by the front door and hurried outside. She gulped in air, like she had been deprived, before heading to the mailbox. She needed something good to come to her today. Her contracts were on the way. She prayed for the distraction because the mention of Kenzie had shaken her. Morgan was trying to pull her back into the dark and she felt the anxiety building. Alani walked the distance of the long driveway until she got to the gate. She entered the code and stepped outside its safety to pull open the mailbox. Only one letter rested inside. She pulled it out and her stomach plummeted when she saw the name on the return address.

Disaya Okafor

Alani's eyes lifted to the house and then drifted back to the fancy writing. It burned Alani that even YaYa's script was pretty.

Is he married to this girl?

She was no fool. She knew YaYa had to be short for Disaya. She recalled Eazy's birthday party. The chemistry she'd felt between YaYa and Ethic, the familiarity, the smiles they shared, the laughs he extended to her. Alani felt jealousy burn through her veins like someone had doused her in gasoline. She tore open the letter, not caring that she was invading his privacy.

Ethic,

I can't even tell you the ways I miss you. I'm so grateful for the connection we have. I know you have someone now, but I just need you to know that you always have me. Always. Nobody. Not Indie. Certainly, not that girl you're trying to make things work with. Not any other person between us is actually between us, because you and me will just always be you and me. Nobody else has ever really mattered. What we have is for us. I love you so much. I can't wait to see you. Same time. Same place. Same room. I'm still cumming for you. Thank you for the money. You don't have to. I always say no, and you always send it anyway. Every month. I'm so grateful for you. You will forever be the love of a lifetime. The greatest one I've ever known. Next lifetime, we'll live it up. Until then, we have our day, once a year. It's coming up. I'll see you soon.

Forever,

YaYa

The picture that accompanied the letter was the final nail in the coffin. YaYa's green eyes stared back at her, as she held the baby boy Alani had seen at the birthday party. Alani's heart was no longer functioning. She could barely see, as she made her way back to the house. Tears blinded her. This man. Her man. Was a motherfucking liar. He waited for her, sitting on the staircase that faced the door, as Alani entered crying.

"I'm sorry. I talked to Mo. She's going to apolo-"

Bop!

Alani swung on him.

Slap!

She followed up with a slap so hard that it jerked his neck to the left. Ethic stood, wrapping her in his arms, restricting her from moving.

"Yo! What the fuck is wrong with you? Calm down! Lenika!"

"Get the fuck off me!" she cried. She pushed him away. "What is this?" she asked, tossing the now crinkled letter at his head. Before he could even read it, Alani pointed an accusing finger at him. "You're a liar. You are the world's best fucking liar!" She couldn't breathe. She was hyperventilating, she was so upset.

Ethic didn't even have to read the letter. He saw the name and knew her reaction was justified. He knew that he had fucked up.

"You gon' let me explain or you want to keep assuming?" Ethic asked.

"The bitch is using your last name!" Alani screamed. "You're sending her money! You're supposed to meet up with her! That's not assuming. That's facts."

Alani was devastated.

"Lenika," he said, taking a step in her direction.

"I SWEAR TO FUCKING GOD, IF YOU TOUCH ME, I WILL TAKE YOUR HEAD OFF, EZRA."

He rubbed the back of his head, in angst, and took a seat on the staircase, giving her space. "I told you that's done."

"My nigga ain't my nigga if he's sending the next bitch a monthly check," Alani scoffed. "I'm done."

Alani didn't even bother to dress. She marched to the living room, snatched up her purse, and then headed for the door. He hadn't moved from the step. He just sat there, brows hiked in concern, legs open wide, elbows resting on top of his knees. Alani reached for the door and pulled it open so hard that the door handle put a dent in his plaster.

"Lenika!"

He came off those steps, barking her name like she was the one in the wrong. Alani kept walking, tears burning her eyes so badly that she had to close them to ease the pain. She was sobbing. Chest quaking, as she pulled open the door to his Tesla. She climbed inside, and when she looked up, Ethic was standing in front of the car. She wanted to run his ass over. She opened her purse and rifled through the contents, in frustration.

He knocked on the hood of the car and then opened his balled fist to expose the keys that hung from his middle finger. He turned and walked back into the house. The confident swagger in his step normally made her swoon; today, it set her soul on fire. He was so damn arrogant.

Alani sat outside for three hours, stubbornly, refusing to go inside for the keys. The first hour was fine. Her phone kept her entertained; but when it died, she was miserable.

Fuck him and that bitch.

Her lip quivered. She was only so angry because it hurt, and Alani hated to let another motherfucker be the cause of her pain. She had told herself that he wouldn't hurt her again, that he had already hurt her so drastically, so he would be more careful next time, but he hadn't. He had still fucked up. He was still mishandling her. The fact that YaYa had mentioned her in the letter made it worse. It made it seem like he had spoken to YaYa about her, and that even still considering her as a factor, he hadn't decided to end the affair. If he didn't live so damn far away from the city, she would walk her ass home; but instead, she stayed outside, crying, and cursing him out in her head. Alani wasn't new to heartbreak. She had been hurt before. Men had cheated before, but that disloyalty cut differently when you didn't see it coming. It burned more when you put a man on a pedestal and he hopped off that bitch with disregard. She had chipped away ever piece of bitterness that had weighed down her heart, just to make sure she loved him right, and now she remembered why she had it up in the first place. Men were no good for her. No matter how much they pretended to be, somehow, Alani always ended up hurt.

Niggas ain't shit.

She looked up at the house and saw Morgan staring at her from the upstairs window. Alani wanted to swing on her little-ass too.

Alani sat in that car until she couldn't sit anymore. She had to pee so badly, she didn't have a choice but to go back inside.

She sighed and grabbed her purse, before climbing out.

Her chest tightened, as she pushed open the front door. He was sitting on the steps. The expression on his face told her the angst that was choking her was suffocating him too.

"Why the fuck you just sitting there looking stupid?" she asked.

He shook his head and pinched the bridge of his nose. Alani was nowhere to be found. He was facing off with the guarded version of this woman, the mean-ass version of her. That mouth was so reckless, he wanted to put something in it, but her heart was so damn enraged, he feared her little-ass would bite it off.

"You're sitting outside looking equally stupid, no?" He didn't even look at her. He just sat there, rubbing his hands together, slowly, contemplating how he could explain away what she had read. He knew an explanation was owed, but he also knew her emotions would block her from hearing him.

Alani hated that he had a point.

She saw Morgan appear at the top of the staircase.

"Can you not bring all that crazy back in here?" Morgan asked.

"Oh, Morgan Atkins, you have enough crazy up in here for all of us," Alani snapped. Ethic's head jerked up and he watched Alani point her finger at Morgan.

"This is not your business. Go find you some, Mo," Alani stated.

"You don't pay bills in here," Morgan countered. Ethic's head turned in shock to look up at Mo. This had to be the Twilight Zone. No way were they arguing like this in front of him.

"Let me give you some grown woman game, Morgan. When you fucking the nigga who pays the bills the right way, it makes you the boss; and I'm fucking Ethic real goddamn good, so take your spoiled-ass to your room, now, so I can figure out if I'm going to keep fucking him or if I'm going to let that little, fake-contact-wearing bitch have him back," Alani said, with bass.

Morgan smirked and rolled her eyes, but she walked away mumbling, "Y'all crazy as fuck." Morgan made it all the way to her room before she yelled, "And that's why her eyes are real!"

Morgan slammed the door and Alani was so pissed at that revelation that she punched Ethic's ass, again. Ethic had endured enough of the laying of hands. Her blows did little to hurt him physically, but inside, they bruised him. He hemmed her up against the wall, pinching her chin in the U of his hand. "Keep them hands to yourself, Lenika. I ain't with the fighting. I don't want to fight with you at all. Right now, I just want to fuck you, cuz that mouth real slick and that shit drive me real crazy, baby."

"Fuck. You." She sneered, moving her face out of his grasp.

Ethic cleared his throat. "You came in here to argue or to talk?" he asked.

"Don't flatter yourself," Alani spat. "I came in here to pee."

She walked right by him and into the first-floor half-bathroom. Ethic pushed the shit open, as she lingered on the toilet.

"Ethic, close the door!"

"I've turned that pussy inside out, Lenika. I'm not closing shit," he countered.

She knew he was angry because his mouth was crass. Mannish Ethic only emerged when he was feeling a type of way. He leaned against the frame, arms folded against his broad chest, dark eyes penetrating hers. Tears fell down her cheeks.

"You know I hate this shit. I'm not giving out bullshit, Lenika. I'm not fucking with Ya..."

"I'll slap the shit out of you, if you say her name," she said.

She wiped and flushed, and then adjusted her clothes, before washing her hands. She didn't even dry them. She flicked the water in his face, before trying to push him aside. He didn't budge.

"Why is she sending you pictures of that ugly-ass baby?!" she screamed. She knew she was being childish, but she didn't care. Her feelings were crushed. The possibilities of what this letter meant and what value YaYa had in Ethic's life was burdening her. "A baby and your name? You gave her both? Is that baby yours? Did you marry her, Ethic?" Alani placed a hand to her stomach and damn near folded, as she slammed down the toilet seat and sat down. She couldn't even sit upright. The palms of her hands caught her tears, as she bawled. She was trying. She was attempting to be rational, struggling to calm herself so logic could return, but she was so damn emotional that she couldn't think straight. Ethic got on his knees in front of her, gripping her wrists to force her to let him into her sorrow.

"Lenika. I'm not married," he said. So earnest. How could someone so good hurt her so badly? "I'm not fucking with that girl. I did for a while. It was something serious, until you. I thought I wanted her, until you, baby."

"Oh, and regular ol' me came along and made you change your mind, huh?" Alani cried. "You put me against her and I came out the winner? Nah, Ethic, you're a liar. You have me here, and then once a fucking year you planned to have her too. Right? That's what her letter said. Nobody else matters but y'all, right? You're sending her money. Once a month. Have you sent her money since I've been under this roof?"

Ethic's jaw locked, in frustration, and his silence was an admission of truth.

"How much?" she asked.

"Five thousand dollars," he answered, truthfully.

"Nigga, per month?" Alani shrieked.

"It's nothing, Lenika. It's minimal," Ethic responded. "The shit means nothing."

"So, let me get this straight. You're sending her sixty thousand dollars a year? It's for that baby, isn't it? Your baby?" she grilled, staring him in the eyes, silently hoping he said no, praying that there was another explanation for such a hefty sum of money.

"For whatever she needs," he said.

"I want out of this," Alani whispered, devastated. Her chin trembled so violently. She couldn't even look at him. "I want out. I want out. I don't want to do this, Ethic."

"I don't care what you want, Lenika. You not deciding shit. I'm deciding. You're here and you're staying, baby. You mad cuz her eyes green? Fuck it, fuck me up. I fucked with a few bad bitches before you came along, Lenika. We can get all the fighting out the way over them right now. They're in my past. I can't change what I did before you. You're right here in front of me right now. She's sending letters asking for love I'm giving you, setting appointments for dick you get every fucking day, baby. We had a thing. A once-a-year thing, in case we ever lost touch along the way. That shit is over. I forgot the shit was even coming up. I wouldn't fucking do that to you. It's not how I choose to move when I'm serious about a woman. I'm serious about you. Nobody else."

Alani saw his lips moving, but just like a woman, she heard what he didn't say. What he refused to acknowledge was louder than anything he had said.

"Look at me and tell me that baby isn't yours," she said.

Ethic blew out a sharp breath. "She says it isn't."

"What the fuck do you mean, *she* says it isn't? Did you get a test, Ethic?" she asked.

He lowered his head, scratching the back of it.

She scoffed. "You didn't, did you?" she accused. "You know it's yours."

"Leave it alone, Lenika," he said.

"Nah, I'ma leave *you* alone," she said.

"That's never happening," he stated, pulling her hips off the toilet. "We're past that stage. I'm never fucking allowing that to happen. So, tell me what you want me to do." His tongue was on her, before she could stop him.

"No!" she shouted, attempting to stand. He stayed right there on his knees, pulling her pants down, placing one hand under her thigh and lifting it, as he sucked her clit into his mouth. "Ethic, nooooo," she cried.

"Yeah, baby. I'ma keep you cumming," he groaned. "You don't run from me." He stood, pulling down his sweatpants and filling her.

"I hate this," she whispered, as she planted teeth in his shoulder. She bit him. Hard, and he, in return, showed no mercy, inflicting pain, as he hit the bottom of her.

"This isn't fair," she whined, as he lifted her onto the sink. "You're not fighting fair."

The back of her head hit the mirror and she felt the knobs to the faucet dig into her lower back, as he put a beating on her. She had thrown too many blows for him not to hit back. He jabbed that pussy until it was black and blue, while Alani cried out in ecstasy.

Her body was betraying her, enjoying him, while her heart was in turmoil.

"I hate you," she whispered.

That one went right through the center of him because he knew there was a part of her that could mean it. He gripped her chin, pushing her cheeks in with stern fingers, as he paused. He looked at her through clouded eyes and then finessed her tears between his fingertips, rubbing them in, like he was pinching salt. Alani could see how her words hand injured him and she wished she could "un-speak" them. Even after the letter, she still didn't want to hurt him. He pressed his forehead to hers. He pulled out and turned her around, kicking her legs open, before sliding in from the back.

"Don't hate me, baby," he whispered, before devouring her neck. His lips on her body, his dick in her, so far in her that he was her.

"PUT. SOME. FUCKING. ACT. RIGHT. IN. YOU." Ethic beat it up, with every, single word. This fuck wasn't for nothing. It was chastisement. It was scolding. They weren't making love this time. He was teaching a lesson and Alani was a motherfucking A-plus student.

"Baby, slow down," she groaned. She tried to run, but Ethic pulled her hair with one hand and her hip with another.

"Bring that ass back. Talk tall, walk tall, baby. Damn, take that shit," Ethic groaned. "I'ma hit this pussy just as hard as your crazy-ass hit me. Knock your little-ass right out."

"Goddd, Ethic," she moaned.

"Say you sorry," he whispered in her ear, as he stroked forward. Alani gritted her teeth.

"Nigga, fuck you. I'm not saying shit."

She didn't even realize she had said it aloud until she felt him go still.

Alani's eyes popped open, when she heard the snicker leave his lips. "Stubborn-ass," he said.

SLAP.

It stung so fucking good. She felt him open her ass so wide it felt like he would rip her in half, as he pushed himself so deep inside her it felt like he was pushing that apology to the tip of her tongue. She bit her bottom lip.

"Agh!" Alani cried out, passionately. She lost the fight, as she creamed him. She came so hard that she reached behind her to hold onto his neck and put bloody scratches in his skin.

She felt him release inside her and he leaned over onto her, bracing one hand against the mirror as he caught his breath.

"You leave this house and I'm lighting up your whole block. There are plenty rooms in this house. Choose one, and go be mad in there," he said. His tone held no play, and he put a kiss to the back of her head, before pulling out of her wetness.

He adjusted himself and Alani stared daggers at him through the reflection in the mirror.

"So, you're holding me hostage?" she asked.

Ethic ignored her question. "When you're ready to talk without all the yelling, come find me." He left her standing there, fuming, as he walked out. She hated that, even with the anger she felt, he was right. She wasn't going anywhere.

The amount of space that had accumulated between Ethic and Alani had never been so great. Even when they had been apart, the yearning they had felt for one another kept them connected somehow. This fight was the first time since meeting him that she had completely shut him out. It had been two days of silence between them. He had told her to pick a room. She had chosen the master and had put him out, forcing him to sleep in Eazy's bed because his guest rooms were being renovated. Eazy slept next to her each night.

Ethic had given her space. He had expected her to come to him sooner to talk but he had underestimated her stubbornness. Once Alani had her mind made up about something, she didn't budge, and he was learning that the hard way. He climbed out of Eazy's bed. His big body on the full-size frame just wouldn't do. He groaned, as he stood, shrugging tense shoulders, as he made his way down the hallway. He smelled the sage coming from the room, before he even opened the door. Alani had been burning it non-stop. A box full of Emergy sage had shown up on his doorstep overnight and she hadn't hesitated to put a stick in almost every room of his house. Her energy was off balance. The PH to her mood had been disturbed and the infection was spreading. She was unhappy with him and her silence was loud. Alani was the only person he knew who could pull guilt out of him without saying one word. He walked over to her side of the bed and got on his knees. Eazy was curled up in her arms and Ethic was jealous as shit. He wanted to disturb them, but they both were so peaceful…too peaceful to bother. He leaned in and kissed Eazy on the forehead and then kissed hers as well, before standing. He ached on the inside. Every inch of him felt her disposition. They had such a perfect love, when it was on track, but when it derailed, it was catastrophic. It was the most painful thing he'd ever endured…her disappointment was his kryptonite. Yes, he had sent YaYa her usual payment, but it wasn't his intention to disrespect. The shit was a monthly expense. Like the lights, like the cable, YaYa was a bill, one he paid on time, every time. Five thousand dollars to a man like Ethic was equivalent to a hundred bucks. It was a utility. Ethic was a man of his word. Anyone he had ever loved, he felt obligated to take care of, because it was rare that he gave a fuck at all. He didn't think it was necessary to stop the payments. YaYa wasn't a threat to Alani. YaYa was used to getting her way. She was used to him coming when she needed him to make her cum. He had no intentions of continuing that. He had no plans to attempt to balance both. He was just keeping his word; and if he was honest with himself, he wasn't sure if YaYa was being honest about her child, so he was covering his bases, making sure that she was always good…that the baby boy that had sent sparks through his heart when he'd held him was always good. YaYa said the baby wasn't his, but he hadn't seen proof, he hadn't even requested proof. Ethic wanted to trust YaYa. He felt like he could trust YaYa, but now that Alani had brought it up, a nagging in his gut told him that he didn't trust her at all. Now that he had Alani and he trusted her wholeheartedly, he realized he couldn't trust YaYa at all. YaYa didn't want to blowup her marriage. She was holding onto it for dear life, so why would she tell the truth, if the baby did belong to him? He didn't want to think about what it would mean if that child was his. He knew Alani's limitations. He had exhausted her forgiveness. She wouldn't be able to accept more heartbreak from him. He would never want her to. The jealousy that sprouted in her whenever YaYa was around was indication enough that she would never accept her as a staple in their lives. If he was the father of YaYa's child, it would end them.

There was so much discord in his home. Alani was miserable, Morgan was miserable, even Bella had been walking around with something different in her tone. She spent as much time out of the house, visiting Nannie, just to get away from the tension that had taken over his house. The three women in his life were stressing the hell out of him. He was so grateful for Eazy. His big man was the only sane one under the whole damn roof. Alani had his back hurting from sleeping in Eazy's bed, dick hurting because she wasn't coming off no pussy, and heart hurting because she was mean as hell when angry.

He traveled back down the hall and sat on Eazy's bed, rubbing all over his wavy head, in distress.

"I'm ready to talk now."

Her voice was like a snake charmer, pulling his heart right out of his chest and in her direction.

She stood in the hallway, in one of his shirts and leggings. Her arms were folded, a scarf was tied in a unicorn knot on her head, and one foot was propped up on top of the other.

"Come."

She hated to hear that word because her body responded on instinct alone. She crossed the room and sat on Eazy's bed, beside him, tucking her hands between her thighs.

"I think I should go back to my place for a few days, Ethic," she whispered.

"Lenika, on Love, I'm not fucking with her or anybody else. I was never going to meet her. I sent the money because I'm a man who likes to keep his commitments. I loved her once, I can't lie about that, but the way I love you doesn't even compare. It makes what I had with her look trivial; but the same way I bought a block for you when you weren't mine at all, is the same thing that made me send her that money. I just wanted to ensure that the people I loved was taken care of, whether our time has passed or not. I didn't think about how it would be disrespectful to you. I didn't think about it at all. It just goes out automatically. It won't happen again. I'll take care of it. Anything and anyone that's stopping me from progressing with you is expendable."

He finessed her chin and Alani pulled away. "A baby isn't expendable, Ethic. Morgan isn't expendable. She doesn't want me here. She barely comes out of her room because I'm all over the house. I just think I should have followed my first mind and never moved in here. We aren't married. I have no right to tell you where to spend your money."

"You have every right. I'm giving you every fucking right over my whole damn life, Lenika," Ethic stated.

"Is that baby yours?" she asked, voice cracking. She couldn't even think the thought. He could tell she had been thinking about it for two days straight. He could tell that YaYa's baby reminded her of Love.

Ethic hung his head, leaning forward onto his knees. His hands massaged the back of his head. "I don't know."

A tear fell, and she chased it away, quickly, with one hand.

"Maybe we did move too fast. We're fighting. We're fighting bad, baby, and Morgan isn't even settled yet. The argument between us is weighing on me. The one between the two of you is even heavier. Maybe we need more time…maybe we can try this again, down the line, after the baby comes…"

She nodded her head in agreement, but only to save face. Every word out of his mouth sucked the life from her. "Yeah," she said, as she stood. "Maybe."

Ethic watched her walk out of his life, and for the first time since meeting her, he didn't give chase.

CHAPTER 14

Bella climbed out the car, her eyes scanning the block, as she held her hands up to her face to block the sun. A group of neighborhood boys hung out in the middle of the street, directly in front of Nannie's house, engrossed in a game of basketball on a rollaway rim.

Bella watched, as Hendrix shook every player on the opposite team, lacing the ball through his legs and breaking ankles until he went up for a shot. All net. The ball bounced into the yard, rolling all the way over to her feet, and Bella bent down to pick it up.

"What up? You gon' toss my ball back?" he yelled, holding up his hands.

Bella frowned. "Not if that's how you're going to ask me," she said.

Bella took him in. She drank him in, like she was thirsty and he could hydrate her. His eyes were dark, penetrating, but they confused her, because when he came up off the curb and into the yard, squinting at her, she swore she saw sparks of amber in them. His lanky arms and chicken legs had the nerve to have tattoos on them, and the hair on top of his head was pulled into a bun, while his sides and back were tapered low. The beginnings of a mustache and goatee was colored sparsely on his face.

"Yo, Pretty Girl. I need the ball, so I can finish shaking these niggas," he said.

"Bella, get your behind in this house, before your daddy kill every little boy on this block," Nannie said, coming out onto the porch.

"Hendrix, get off my grass, you know better," Nannie fussed.

"My bad, Ms. Pat," he said, holding up hands of surrender, as he backed up to the sidewalk.

"Don't my bad me, boy! I'm not one of your little friends," Nannie continued, pointing at him with a warning finger.

"I'm sorry, Ms. Pat," he corrected.

Bella turned to the house, cradling the ball between her arm and her hip.

"Aye, Pretty Girl, you're killing me," he said. "What I'm supposed to do without the ball?"

She shrugged. "Stop playing," Bella said, as she tossed the ball into the air again and again as she climbed the steps. "And stop calling me that. You know my name."

"Nah, that's what everybody else call you," he said, as he backpedaled back into the street.

"Game's over. Pretty Girl told a nigga he got to get to work. I'm tryna work for that. That's gon' be all me one day. A nigga just got to get his weight up, you heard me?" He slapped hands with another kid in the middle of the street and then glanced back at the house, where Bella sat on the ledge, with his ball sitting pretty in her lap.

It's not going to be easy, she thought, but the sight of him made her feel sick inside. She had seen Hendrix around, hugging corners, playing ball, and hanging out around the block. Every time she had come to Nannie's house, her eyes went searching for him like a magnet to metal. Thanks to him, she was eating Hot Cheetos and drinking quarter waters on a regular. He just pulled another side out of her…a daring side…an inquisitive side, and she wanted another moment with him to store in her mind. She loved Nannie, but he was the reason she was so insistent about spending time there over the summer. He made the boys at her school seem like knock-offs. He had never paid her any attention, until now, and just something as simple as him calling her pretty had her smiling from ear to ear.

"Bella, get in this house!"

She stood and rushed into the house because she knew if she stayed outside a minute longer, she would be pushing her luck.

Messiah sat in the leather chair, eyes closed, head leaned back, as he felt the poison enter his body. His chest prickled, like he had a thousand ants crawling inside him, as they administered the solution. They said it was keeping him alive, but it was killing him, he could feel it.

"You doing pretty good?" the nurse asked, as she came over to check the drips hanging from the pole above him.

He didn't answer. He just kept breathing, kept thinking, focusing on the face inside the depths of his mind. It was a private party in his head and the guest of honor was Morgan Atkins. She was smiling. They were laying in her bed and she was up under his arm. The way she looked up at him made him feel like Morgan just very well could be a gift from God. The way he felt when he was with her. It had to be a glimpse of heaven. He questioned if he had ever really had her at all. Or was she a manifestation of what he thought the afterlife was like? Had he been diagnosed and then hallucinated the rest? After he was gone, would he go back to that place, where his heart was light, and nothing else mattered. Heaven. His time with her had been heaven; and he just wanted to repent, so he could guarantee he would get back to that place. A tear wet his cheek and he sniffed, clearing his throat to regain his composure. He missed her terribly. Wondering what she was doing…how she was doing…if she missed him…it was torture.

"I'm so sorry I'm late! There was an accident on the highway. I was stuck in traffic on I-75 for hours," Bleu whispered, as she entered the infusion room. Only then did he open his eyes. Bleu's long, box braids were mixed with white thread and metal energy beads. The bullring she rarely wore in her nose was present today and her face was bare. He knew she had done that on purpose because all she did was cry around him. It never failed. With each visit, Bleu had to excuse herself for a few minutes to go pray in the hospital chapel and cry. He knew, because when she returned, her eyes would be red, and her makeup ruined.

"You got my food, nigga?" he asked.

"I got 'em, boy. Flint tacos from La Familia," she said.

"I wanted you to cook 'em, B. I wanted yo' tacos," he protested. "It's Tuesday, B. You breaking code like a mu'fucka."

Taco Tuesdays was a ritual in Bleu's house. She made them every week and the crew slid through every time. They sat at her kitchen table for hours, eating, talking shit, and playing with Saviour for hours before they would get ghost in the streets.

"Next Tuesday, I'll cook them. I promise," she said.

"I can't taste the shit anyway," he stated.

She sat down in the chair across from him.

"You look good. Really good, Messiah. You don't look sick. The chemo might be working. How do you feel?" she asked.

"I look better than I feel, B. Looking sick ain't the problem. I've never looked sick. I feel like shit," Messiah shot back. "Every fucking hour they in here poking me with some shit. Niggas checking my piss, B! The food is ass, the fucking TV ain't got shit on it, my fucking Netflix won't stream in this bitch, not one nurse in this bitch with a fat ass, and the whole damn hospital smell like burnt rubber."

Bleu turned to the nurse that lingered in the room. "Burnt rubber?" she asked the woman.

"It's a side effect of the treatment," the woman said.

"I'm just tired of all this shit. I got life left in me and I'm stuck in this fucking room. I'm still here but I'm not out there, B. Motherfucking time is moving without me and I got breath in my body." His words broke a bit and he leaned forward. Elbows to knees, trigger fingers rubbing, head bowed, as he sniffed. "Shit is fucked up. Shit ain't never been fair."

Bleu watched, as the nurse removed the drips from the attachment.

"Just hit the button if you need anything, Mr. Williams. Would you like me to bring you some ice water? I know you said the medication makes your mouth dry and taste weird," the nurse said.

"I just want to get the fuck outta here, man," Messiah said, as he stood and sat on the edge of the bed.

"We're fine. If he needs anything, I'll come get you," Bleu answered more politely.

Bleu stood and lifted the blanket, as Messiah swung his legs beneath it.

"Do you need your bucket?" she whispered.

"Nah, I'm good right now," Messiah said. "It's cold as fuck in here, B."

"That's just the chemo, Messiah," Bleu said, as she crossed the room to get a second blanket out of the closet. She spread it out over him and then climbed up into his bed. "Scoot your mean-ass over." Messiah made room for her and Bleu pulled out her phone. "Your Netflix don't work cuz your ghetto-ass got Sprint. Ol' trap-phone-having-ass," she said, smiling.

A stubborn snicker left his mouth, as she held up the phone. The app opened but then froze.

"Who got the trap phone now?" he asked, laughing. "I told you this shit is a prison. Only thing missing is the bars."

Bleu sat up in the bed. "Okay, well, let's break you out."

"Fuck you talking about, B?" Messiah said.

"We're leaving. Get up," Bleu said, with urgency, as she hurried to grab him some clothes from his duffel bag. She tossed them at him. "Get dressed."

"B, I just had chemo. I'll be throwing up by morning," he said.

"And we'll be back by then; but right now, we're getting some fresh air," she stated. She turned toward the door. "Now, get dressed."

Five minutes later, Bleu led the way down the hallway, as Messiah walked behind her, black hoodie pulled over his head, as they made their way to the elevator. Bleu dipped down the stairwell.

"We'll catch the elevator on the next floor," she said.

"Mr. Williams! Hey!" Messiah paused and looked up the stairwell to see his nurse. "Mr. Williams, you shouldn't..."

"Go! Go!" Messiah said, as he and Bleu took off down the stairs. They skipped a few floors before taking the elevator to the lobby.

"Be cool," Messiah said, as they stepped onto the main floor. He grabbed her hand and took the lead, pulling her toward the exit.

"Maybe we should go back. What if you get sick? What if something happens," Bleu rambled, suddenly changing her mind.

"Nigga, don't bitch up now. We out this mu'fucka," Messiah said, pushing through the revolving door. "Where'd you park?"

Bleu removed her keys and tossed them to Messiah and the pair took off toward the lot. She ran around to the passenger side of her Jeep Cherokee and Messiah hopped behind the wheel. He peeled out of the parking lot.

"Are you sure you're good?" Bleu asked, laughing.

"A day ain't gon' kill me, B. I'm good," he said.

"Where to?" she asked.

"Just ride, Bleu," he said. "Don't try to control. Don't even think about shit. All I got is a day. All I got is you and one day. I know you smart as fuck, but turn your brain off for the next twenty-four hours." Bleu stared at the side of his face, as he glanced over at her. She nodded, pushing out a breath of anxiety.

"Okay," she answered. He reached for her radio and turned it up.

If you're looking to find
A love that will stand 'til the end of time
Baby, relax your mind
That love is hereee, yeahhhh
I'll do everything I swear
Take the pain and the hurt
You won't know it's there
Your wants would be nothing
Put that on everything

Messiah would normally detest the idea of riding to something so smooth, but the lyrics touched him right behind his rib cage, causing a lump to form in his throat. His eyes prickled, and he sniffed, blinking them away, as he ate up the highway. Bleu put the Brandy song on repeat. It was something about the words, about the meaning. She had been listening to it on her way to the hospital. Crying, and listening to this song, as she drove the three hours to come see him. He would never be able to show her how much he appreciated her time. She had an entire family and she refused to let him die alone, even though he would prefer to, even though he had left town so that he wouldn't burden others with the slow death…Bleu wouldn't go away. She put it on everything; and if Bleu was nothing else, she was solid. They rode down the highway with the windows down and the sunroof lifted until Messiah saw water and rollercoasters rising in the distance.

"Cedar Point?" Bleu asked, frowning. "You get 24 hours and you want to spend it here? At an amusement park?"

"I've never been," he said. "If I got to check up out of here, don't you think I should ride a rollercoaster first? Ain't that what regular mu'fuckas do as kids? I ain't never get that, B. I just want to be a kid for a day."

They were through the gates within a half hour and surrounded by thousands of people.

"What first?" Bleu asked.

"Shit is crazy. I ain't been around this many people without being strapped… ever. I don't even remember the last time," Messiah said, a bit unnerved, as he looked around.

"It's not needed today," Bleu said. "Come on. First things first. Henna."

"Henna? That fake tattoo shit? I'm not getting that," Messiah protested.

"Yes, you are," Bleu countered. She walked over to the stand that was setup and began looking through the designs. The woman working the cart turned to her.

"Can I help you choose something?" she said.

"Yes, we want matching henna. Something that represents friendship and eternal life. He's my best friend. I want something that will show him that this thing is forever. Even when I can't see him, can't hear him anymore..."

Bleu's voice faded, and she closed her eyes, sucking in a deep breath.

"Ayo, B," he said. Bleu's teary eyes met his and he nodded across the walkway. "Forever mean forever. You down?"

"A tattoo?"

"Come on, BFF," he teased, as he wrapped an arm around her shoulder and pulled her toward the shop.

"I'm not a fan of tats, Messiah. They hurttt," Bleu whined, as they walked through the door.

"They aren't that bad," the artist in the shop said.

"After the shit we've both been through, the pain we've felt, this shit will be a breeze. Ain't no backing out," Messiah pushed. "She's going first. We gon' get this one."

Bleu cut her eyes at him and snatched the book from him. "Since yo' ass ain't gon' be here to live with this decision, I'm picking, cancer boy," she said.

Messiah paused, looking at her in shock, before bursting into laughter.

"That's cold, B," he snickered.

She laughed and stuck up her middle finger at him, refusing to look at him. He didn't care that she was mad.

He was insistent. Tattoos. Proof that he had been here when he was gone. He knew she wouldn't need it, but it still felt necessary.

"This one," she said, pointing down at the book.

"A half of an angel wing?" the tattoo artist asked. "I can make that real dope. Put one wing on your thumb and draw it out over the 'U' part of your hand. Then, I'll do the other half of the wing on yours, bro. If you place your thumbs side by side, it'll look like a full set of an angel's wings. I take it you've got cancer?"

Messiah nodded.

"I'm sorry to hear that, bro. This is a good tat to represent you. What you think?"

"Yeah, that's dope. Let's do it."

Bleu sat in the artist's chair first, and as soon as the needle hit her skin, she gritted her teeth and squeezed her eyes tightly. "I swear, I'm smacking you as soon as he's done," she threatened. "Owww, Messiah! This shit hurts!"

"You act like you ain't never did this before. Tough that shit out, B," Messiah said.

Bleu felt every prickle of the needle, but she sat still for two hours until it was done. Messiah took his without a problem; and when both were done, Messiah held his hand up. Bleu leaned her head on his shoulder and held hers up too.

"Even when the breath leave me, B," he said.

"And we're going to fight for more. You've got to fight, Messiah, for every, single breath," she said. "Come on. Let's go ride these damn rides before I change my mind."

Messiah snickered, and Bleu paid for the tattoos, before following him out. They stayed inside the gates of the park until it closed, and they rode every ride that Messiah felt would make his heart beat harder. He was desperate to live, fraught for exhilaration, anxious to feel like he was still six feet above the ground. Bleu could barely keep up; and despite her fear of heights, she didn't back out. She rode every ride with him, screaming in terror, and hanging onto his forearm for dear life, but she did it. She lived with him. She gave him a carefree day of living. He almost forgot he was sick. Messiah detoured out of the gate's perimeter.

"Where are you going?" Bleu asked.

"To the beach," he answered.

"How do you know it's a beach?" she wondered.

"You don't hear the water, B?" Messiah asked. "I can feel it. I don't know how, but I just want to be near it."

Bleu was stunned to silence, as she followed Messiah. The pavement turned to grass, as they walked further away from the lights and noise of the park. Then, the grass turned to sand and Bleu heard the water.

"Lake Erie," Messiah said.

It was pitch black and there wasn't another soul in sight, but the sound of the waves washing ashore was beautiful. Messiah took a seat on the sand.

"Messiah, I have on white. I'm not…"

Before she could finish her sentence, he yanked her down.

White dress in the brown sand because Messiah said so. King Ssiah.

Bleu sighed, as he planted his hands behind him and looked up.

"I'm scared, Bleu," Messiah whispered. He pulled his hands forward and dusted them off, as he wrapped his hands around his knees. He hung his head and sniffed, as he bit his lip to stop it from quivering.

Bleu sat, Indian-style, and gazed down the beach because she wanted to give him a moment to himself. She knew him well enough to know he wasn't crying because he trusted her with his tears, but because he couldn't hold them. Hers fell freely and she didn't want him to think she pitied him. She didn't. She pitied the world. A world without Messiah Williams was a shitty-ass world. It would never be the same. She wiped her nose with her wrist, trying to restore a bit of composure; and when she turned to him, his lips were on hers. Aggressive, angry, needy, strong. Everything he was, was wrapped up in this kiss. Messiah gripped her braids so tightly it hurt, as he stole her tongue. He was crying. His face was wet, mixing with the mess that was her emotions, because they were spilling down her face as she kissed him too. Her heart raced and exploded every time his lips touched hers, but she pulled back.

"Messiah," Bleu whispered. She placed both hands on his face. "Stop." He kissed her anyway. Earnestly. Like someone had a stopwatch and he was racing against a clock. In a way, someone did. God had put him on a countdown. Messiah was the roughest of them all, the toughest out the bunch, and God had tapped his soldier and sat him down.

"Messiah!" Bleu protested.

Messiah stopped, pressing his forehead to Bleu's, squeezing his eyes closed, as a sob forced itself to the surface. Bleu's chest heaved, as her tears dripped into the sand. He was kissing her, and she knew he was just trying to feel something, trying to close his eyes and will his mind to convince him that her lips were the ones he craved. They weren't. She wasn't Morgan.

"You don't want me," she whispered. "You want Morgan."

Messiah's lip quivered, and he closed his eyes, pressing his forehead against Bleu's harder, gritting his teeth, almost growling, before full-blown sobs broke through his lips. He broke. Right there in her arms, as Bleu wrapped him tightly in her embrace.

"I know," she whispered, as silent tears streamed down her face. He sniffed away his pain and pulled back from her, taking her face in one hand. He gripped her like she owed him money. "Shorty Doo-Wop, you got to let me feel something else. I'm dying, man. I don't wanna feel this, B. Make me feel anything else," he whispered, softening his touch, as he finessed one side of her face, before he kissed her, again. Messiah took her down to the sand, lips on hers, hands sliding her panties down; and then she sucked in air, because whatever life he had left was now inside of her.

Bleu knew she should stop this, but she couldn't. They were like a runaway train on a downhill track. You just had to let it go. To try to stop it would be catastrophic. He was so rough with her. She felt his anger… every bit of it. He had carried it with him his entire life, and he was infecting her with it. It was so potent, it was tangible inside her body. No wonder he was so violent, so tortured, so bellicose. He was so full of self-destruction that he couldn't even give out pleasure without pain. He had been with women who felt lucky to have him. He had made them feel like the king had chosen to gift his time with them, in the past. Anybody he had ever taken to bed had felt like he was the catch. Even Morgan had been willing to take him in any form. She had accepted whatever energy he gave off, just to have him, just to call herself his girl. Morgan had been willing to endure the hurt that came with the love, because yes, the love was worth it. Bleu felt the love, but she didn't ignore the pain. He wouldn't punish her for all he'd been through. She wouldn't let him. She had been through shit too; and if he couldn't find bliss in the gift she was sharing with him, then they didn't need to be doing this. She reached up for him, tangling her fingers in his locs.

"Messiah," she whispered. Her eyes glistened with tears. "Don't do me like that. I don't want it if it has to hurt. If I have to take it, give it to me, Messiah. Give me you."

Messiah's entire body went still, as he hovered over her, filling her but not moving, as he stared in her eyes. Shock shone in his stare, and then she saw respect, then lust, then behind it all, she identified love. Bleu pulled her hand from his locs and one came out in her grasp, breaking her heart. She held it in her hand, gripping the weakest link of his crown. When her eyes met his, she saw fear this time. Bleu sat up, using all her weight to put him on his back. Bleu's body moved so slowly that he felt like she was casting a spell.

Like he had smoked some good-ass weed and was floating. Her sex was like a drug.

"Damn," he groaned.

Sand dug into her knees, as she rode his wave and he gripped her hips, his fingers digging into her sides.

Seeing Bleu under this night sky, with the moon and the stars as her backdrop, made her look like a queen, made her seem like a goddess, and he was merely human. It was like Bleu had the power to make him live forever and she was deciding right there, in the sand, whether he was worth it. Messiah gripped her ass with one hand and wrapped the other arm around her thin waist, pulling her down. Chest to chest, the tips of their noses touched, as Bleu worked him, calling his bluff, like he was all bark and no bite, like she scoffed at his aggression. Like she wanted to boss up on him and yell, "cap now, nigga." In the battle between Bleu and Messiah, Bleu was winning. Everything from the way she moved, to the way she breathed, to the way she moaned, blew Messiah's mind.

"Messiahhh," she whispered.

He tensed into her, splitting her further. She was soaking him, pulsing for him. The inside of her vibrating his dick so good it made him groan out loud. "B, shit," he whispered, as he tilted his chin down to see what she was doing down there, because no woman had ever done the shit before. "Fuck."

He kissed her to stop himself from crying. Bleu was turning him into a bitch. He didn't know what the fuck she was working with down there. All the crystals in her braids, the beads and shit, they had to be magical, because this wasn't normal pussy. His toes curled, ass tightened, and he called her name. "Bleu, fuckkkkk." Yup, he was a whole bitch. Messiah might as well have asked her if she was going to call him afterwards. He now knew why Iman was hanging around after all these years, waiting for another shot at it. This was once-in-a-lifetime pussy.

Messiah had been with a lot of women. Not even Morgan had been better. He had never felt anything this good. It felt so good, he forgot he felt bad, forgot he was supposed to be dying, because right now, he was living in the present with Bleu. She was a present. Her presence. Not pre-sent to him before he needed her. She elevated their connection exactly when he needed her to most. When he needed the lines to blur a little. She was a gift. His best friend, and he knew that despite how bad he was, Bleu loved him. She cared for him deeper than people's understanding. Deeper than the definition of what friendship was supposed to be. Because this was extra. This was out of bounds of what she was obligated to give him. He had seen her turn down more worthy men, and here she was, giving him the discount just because he'd asked. Just because he had come short on emotion and she had more than enough empathy to share. Bleu was beautiful, and he appreciated her. He loved her. It wasn't like what he had with Mo. Nothing burned as hot as his love for Morgan Atkins. He wasn't in love with Bleu, not in lust, not head over heels, make his heart stop at one glance, but he was learning that love came in different forms. His soft spot for Bleu Montclair had always been present throughout their friendship, but never acknowledged; because when you've never loved, you don't know what it looks like. Bleu and Messiah were beyond some trivial woman and man shit. That wasn't what they shared. She was just lovely. A lovely fucking woman, who had grown and learned from her mistakes. A woman unashamed of her past, of her flaws. It was with those wise eyes that she looked at him and saw fit to love him, despite all his ill intentions. She wasn't Morgan, but she wasn't on the outside with everyone else either. At this very moment, she was inside his heart. If he had to choose someone to die in front of, it would be her. He couldn't put the burden on Morgan. She wasn't strong enough to handle it. Bleu could. Bleu would. Even though he knew she didn't want to, she would because she was a phenomenal human being. The best friend he could ever have. He wasn't worthy of her. He didn't even deserve this; and still, she rained all over him. Bleu's face twisted in pleasure and Messiah sat up, her in his lap, he pulled her braids and her head tilted back, exposing her neck. He kissed her skin, as she rode him in circles.

Messiah's body shuddered, as he buried his face in the groove of her neck. He came inside her because it felt too damn good to pull out, and he wasn't ready to withdraw from this moment. Bleu came too, breathing heavy, as they stared at one another.

"Thank you," he whispered.

Bleu blushed so hard her skin heated, as she wrapped her arms around his neck, looking over his shoulder at the lights of the amusement park in the distance.

"I would have fallen apart years ago if it weren't for you, Messiah," she whispered. She pulled back to look him in the eyes. "Thank you."

She stood and pulled down her dress. She turned her back to him, as she grabbed her panties and placed them inside her crossbody handbag. She expected things to be awkward. Sex always complicated things; but oddly, Bleu felt nothing but peace. As Messiah adjusted himself, he stood and dusted himself off. Bleu began to walk off and Messiah grabbed her hand gently, forcing her to face him.

"When I'm gone, don't slide back, B. No drugs," he said.

"I won't," she promised, a tear traversing the cavern of her nose and falling onto her lip. Messiah kissed that tear. A peck to her lips. Then, her cheek, as he wrapped her in his arms.

"I love you, Bleu." It was a huge step for Messiah Williams. Expressing emotions to another human being, someone other than Morgan.

"I love you too, Messiah," Bleu sobbed. He held her until she got it all out, and then he took her hand, tattoos locking in place, as they began to walk across the beach. Bleu stopped.

"You know what I've never done?" she asked.

"What's that, B?" Messiah asked.

"I've never slept on the beach under the stars, and I think we should. We should do that and whatever else you haven't done. A bucket list."

"A fuck it list, cuz I wouldn't do no corny shit like that if I wasn't dying; so, fuck it. I'm with it," he snickered. They made their way to the life guard station and climbed up. Messiah sat against the wooden station and Bleu rested her head on his shoulder, hands still locked, tattoos expressing more about their friendship than words ever could.

It was the perfect end to an imperfect day for an imperfect man who'd led an imperfect life.

CHAPTER 15

"Yo, Bougie! I'm headed to Gundry Park," Lyric called, as she stepped out onto her porch. "You want to go?"

"I've got to ask Nannie," Bella shouted back. "Who's all there?"

"Everybody up there," Lyric answered. "Go see what she say."

"If you ask her, she'll say yes," Bella said, lowering her voice. "She's gonna tell me no."

Lyric skipped down the steps to her porch and came up to meet Bella, as they stepped inside Nannie's home. The smell of moth balls greeted them, and Bella's feet sank into the pokey side of the plastic runners that lined the front door as she kicked them up.

"Ow," she winced, as she straightened it the right way, before making her way inside to the kitchen where Nannie sat with Mr. Larry.

"Heyyy, Ms. Pat," Lyric greeted. "Hi, Mr. Larry."

"Hey, Lyric, baby," Nannie returned, as she puffed on her cigarette, flicking ashes in the metal ashtray, as she wrote numbers in a 3-subject notebook.

"You got your mama numbers?" Nannie asked.

"No, ma'am. She not done with them yet. She'll probably send Trey over here with them before the midday hit," Lyric answered. "I'm going to the park with my friends. Can Bella come?"

"Ain't nobody at that park but boys. No."

Bella turned, in surprise, when she heard Alani's voice behind her.

"I thought you were home!" Bella said, in shock. "When did you get here?"

"Late last night," Alani answered. "I just want to do some more work on one of the houses. I have a new tenant moving in this week," Alani lied. She didn't want to put Bella in the middle of her fight with Ethic. She didn't want to alarm her, despite the alarm she felt in her soul.

"And no, you're not going to the park," Alani finished.

"Well, can we go around the corner to Bianca's house?" Lyric asked.

"No further than Bianca's house, Bella," Alani said. All it took was one look from Alani. Bella nodded. "Be back on this block before the street lights come on."

"I promise," Bella said.

"And when I call your phone, you answer," Alani added.

"I will. Promise," Bella said, extending her pinky to Alani. Alani locked hers against Bella's and then wrapped her arms around her. "I love you," Bella said.

"I love you too, B," Alani said.

Bella walked out with Lyric.

As soon as they bent the block, Bella removed her jacket and tied it around her waist, revealing the cropped, Fendi, baby t-shirt she wore beneath.

Bianca's house sat one street over on the corner and Bianca sat outside on the porch, a cell phone was attached to her face, as she cradled it between her shoulder and cheek. The tips of her fingers were red from the Hot Cheetos she ate, and short, denim shorts were folded even higher on her skinny thighs.

"We on our way to the park now, boy," Bianca said into the phone, as Bella and Lyric walked up.

"We got to chill here. Bella can't go to the park," Lyric said.

"What that got to do with us?" Bianca asked.

"Just tell them to come around here," Lyric stated.

Bianca rolled her eyes. "Yo, Dee. Y'all want to pull up at my house instead?" she asked. A pause. "Okay, cool, but wait like thirty minutes. My mama about to go to work."

She hung up.

"You gon' have to get your lie game together, B. Ain't nobody gon' be sitting on the porch the whole summer just because you on lock," Bianca said.

"I can just go home. I'm not really pressed, either way," Bella responded.

"Ain't nobody said they want you to go home, Bougie," Lyric stated. "But we definitely have to figure out a way to work around Alani strict-ass because summertime on the Northside is lit."

The screen door opened and a dark woman with big hips and a long, sleek, ponytail emerged from the house. She wore scrubs and Crocs. "I'm working a double, Bianca. I want them dishes washed before I get home, and take out them pork chops tonight, so they'll be thawed by the time

I get home in the morning. It's a load in the dryer I want folded too, and don't have nobody in my house."

"What about them, Ma?" Bianca asked.

"You know I don't care about Lyric being in my house. I don't even know this girl. Who you, baby?"

"I'm Bella," she answered.

"This is Alani's boyfriend's daughter," Bianca said.

Her mother's eyebrows lifted. "Oh, your daddy the one be coming through here in that Range Rover, sniffing behind Alani's mean-ass?"

Bella snickered. "Yes, ma'am," she answered.

"You tell him when Alani mess that up, to come around the block," the woman said.

"She won't mess it up. He better hope he doesn't mess it up," Bella defended.

Bianca's mother put her hand on her hip and snaked her neck back, in surprise. She pointed to Bianca. "Your ass better defend me like that when I'm not around!"

Bella laughed.

"These two and that's it, Bianca. Don't have nobody else over here," the woman warned.

"Okayyyy, Ma," Bianca whined.

"Bye, Ms. Wanda," Lyric called out. No sooner did Bianca's mom turn the block did Bella hear the engines coming up the block.

"There they go," Bianca called out.

The engines of motorcycles and four wheelers rang out, as Hendrix came flying up the block, black t-shirt bubbling from the wind whipping around him. He lifted on his back wheel. Bella's eyes followed him up the block. She was in awe but fought the smile that threatened to erupt on her pretty face.

When Hendrix and his crew pulled up in the driveway, he nodded to Bella.

"Get on," he instructed.

Bella looked back at Lyric and Bianca. She knew she shouldn't dare. She knew Alani would kill her, but the pounding of her heart and the giddiness inside her pushed her forward anyway.

"Where are we going?" she asked.

"If you got to ask questions, maybe you should just stay here," he stated.

Bella paused. The look in his eyes dared her. He was challenging her to break the rules, to take a risk on him...to put her trust in him. She climbed on back.

"What am I supposed to tell Alani?" Lyric called after her.

"I'll be back way before dark," Bella shouted.

Hendrix took off. Bella squeezed her eyes tightly. She was so afraid, her hands shook. She knew if she opened her eyes she would ask him to stop, so she just let the wind whip through her hair and trusted him, as he took the streets at what felt like dangerous speeds. She didn't know how Morgan rode on the back of Messiah's bike. She was terrified.

God, please.

She was filled with relief when she felt Hendrix let up on the throttle and the motorcycle slowed. She finally opened her eyes to see they were pulling up to Mott Park. Bella's entire body tensed, as the sound of gunshots echoed in her mind.

"Let me off!" she shouted.

She remembered. The day that changed all their lives. This was the same park. Almost the exact spot where Raven Atkins had been gunned down.

"Hendrix, let me off!" Bella panicked and threw Hendrix off balance, sending the bike skidding across the pavement.

Bella hit the ground hard, as the blaring horn from an approaching car sounded out. Hendrix hopped up from the ground, injured, but not bad enough to stop him from banging on the trunk of the passing car.

"Bitch-ass-nigga, who the fuck you blowing at?!" he barked. The bike was on one side of the street and Bella was on the other. He looked down at his skinned leg and winced, gritting his teeth, as he rushed to her side.

"Ow!" she groaned, as she scurried backward until she was sitting on the curb.

She peeled up her now tattered pant leg and revealed a nasty burn from her leg skidding against the cement.

"You okay? Tell me what hurts." Hendrix instructed.

"I'm okay," she said. "It's just my leg."

She tried to stand. "Just hold up," Hendrix said, leaning her against a parked car. He jogged toward the motorcycle and picked it up from the middle of the street, wheeling it over and parking it.

"Yo, the big homie gon' fuck me up," he mumbled, as he put the stand down and bent to look at the scratched body. He turned to Bella.

"I'm sorry," she whispered. "I freaked. This is where it happened."

"Where what happened?" he asked.

She shook her head. "Nothing," she answered.

Bella folded her arms across her chest and turned her head to look toward the playground, so he wouldn't see her tears. She could hide her face, but she couldn't hide the fact that she was trembling. Those gunshots were still going off in her head.

"You're pretty as hell, man. Like, for real. Shit's crazy," he stated, shaking his head.

Bella frowned. "I know," she answered.

"You're wild, Pretty Girl. A nigga tell you that you look good and you tell me you already know? I think you meant to say thank you."

"Why would I thank you? You're not responsible for my pretty and I'm not being arrogant or anything, I just already know that. My daddy tells me that every day; so, yes, I know I'm pretty," she said, smiling.

"So, I got to tell you something you ain't never heard? Okay. Got it," he answered. "Can you walk? Like, are you good or you want to go back?"

Bella reached down, wincing, as she rolled down her pant leg. "It hurts but I'm okay," she said. He grabbed her hand.

"Come on. I'ma show you something, so you can show me something," he said.

"I hope you not getting fly, boy, because it's not anything out here you can show me that will make me show you that," she said.

"Man, I know you a good girl. I'm not talking about that," he said. "You a baby out here. You ain't ready, anyway."

"Glad you know," she answered, as she followed him down the hill that led to the park. They walked by the empty play area, bypassing tennis courts, and across a field until the ground dipped lower and she saw a tunnel.

The shadows hid the inside and Bella's feet stopped moving.

"You scared?" he asked.

She looked at him, skeptically, brow bent, and she blew out a breath of unease and followed him inside.

Graffiti and moss covered the brick walls.

"What is this place?" she asked.

A camping tent sat in the middle of the tunnel and Hendrix unzipped it and held it open for her.

Bella, hesitantly, climbed inside.

A lantern, a sleeping bag, pillow, and Footlocker bags were strewn about, inside.

"Hendrix..." she whispered. "Do you live here?"

"Coming through the hood to slum it don't seem so fun now, do it, Pretty Girl?" he asked.

Bella felt like someone was squeezing her heart.

"How did this happen? Where are your parents? Didn't you say you have a brother?"

"My bro on his own grind. He got a new baby. I ain't tryna shake up his situation."

"And your mom?" Bella pried.

"My mama around. She ain't shit, though. She put me out a week ago. Her bitch-ass boyfriend stole my stash and I stabbed his ass. He told her to put me out, so she did. So, I sleep here. It's cool. I got to work out the hole and pay off my debt to the big homie…"

"Who is the big homie?" she asked.

Hendrix chuckled. "You can tell you from the burbs, Pretty Girl. You ask questions like you working for the police."

Bella laughed. "I'm sorry," she answered.

"It's all good. I trust you," he replied. He stared at her and Bella looked away.

"You don't know him. I move work for Merrill Gang," Hendrix said. "Once I pay them back what I lost, I'ma come up and get up out of here. Get a little, one bedroom somewhere. Grab one of these crackheads and get them to put it in their name and I'll be straight. This just temporary. A nigga gon' come up. Anybody ever slept on me woke they ass up real quick."

Bella's heart was bleeding, but she knew better than to make him think she looked down on him. She looked around and noticed a book sitting on a pile of clothes.

"So, you read?" she asked.

"When I'm not hustling," he said. "It's not a big deal." He reached for the book, but Bella snatched it out of his reach.

"The business of profit and loss?" She read. She frowned. "This is like homework." She held up the book, in confusion, nose turned up. "Why not read literature? Fiction. Something to take your mind to another place."

"Fiction can't show me how to flip this money when I get enough to go legit."

She sat down on the sleeping bag and pulled the lantern close to her. "Okay, so teach me something."

"Mannn, you tryna clown a nigga," Hendrix said.

"Noooo," Bella said. She came up on her knees and grabbed his hand, pulling him to the ground with her. He was bashful, as he wrapped his arms around his knees and hooked one hand to the opposite wrist.

"That ain't a game to me, Pretty Girl. That's my way out," he said. "Everybody around me get sent up outta here. I got potnahs getting locked up like grown-ass men, and I got niggas that's in the dirt. I don't want to walk through either one of them doors." Hendrix pointed to the book in her hands. "That's my door. That's my exit. You never had to make it through that door because you were born on the other side of it, so you don't understand."

"I want to understand," she said. "I don't know you that well, but I believe that you'll get everything you want one day."

"Yeah?" Hendrix asked.

"Yeah," Bella nodded. "I believe in you."

Hendrix had to bite his bottom lip to stop himself from turning into a whole bitch. Those words. That simple show of support. He had never heard them before. No one had ever had faith in him like that before. She didn't even know him, and she had spoken confidence into him. She made him feel like maybe, just maybe, he would make it one day. "So, what you gon' do with all your money when you make it? What's on the other side of the door?" Bella continued.

"You, Pretty Girl. You're on the other side of that door, and I can't even shoot my shot until I'm on the other side too," he said.

"You can shoot it. You might miss, but you can practice your shot," Bella said, blushing.

"Nah, yo' mu'fuckin' pops making sure niggas ain't scuffing up the floors in the gym until they own it. I'ma play my part right now, until I'm ready."

"Your part?" Bella asked.

"I'ma be ya dawg, Pretty Girl. Ya killer. You say get 'em and a nigga gon' get 'em," Hendrix said.

"I don't want you to do any of that. I just want you to reach the door one day," she said. She giggled, looking away from him, as he stroked the peach fuzz on his chin and frowned a bit. Baby Bella had him feeling like a sucker. "To have a house and a bed one day. Maybe, to read these types of books in college one day... Maybe, have your own business or something..."

Hendrix scoffed.

"Why are you laughing?"

"College ain't for people like me," he said.

"Well, that's what's on the other side of that door. College and family, pledging a fraternity, because I'm for sure pledging a sorority, and backpacking across Europe...maybe Asia, one day."

Hendrix shook his head, in disbelief. The things she talked about were so different. He'd never even fathomed college. He, for damn sure, couldn't see himself pledging anything. "Yeah, you living in outer space. Ain't none of that for me. I'm just trying to live to see eighteen. That'll be a win for me."

Bella didn't know what to say to that. The thought of not making it to adulthood, of not going to college, of not having a warm place to sleep, was so foreign to her that she didn't know how to respond. They were truly from two, different worlds. Things that he had to worry about, she never had - and never would. It made her sad. It made her feel like she couldn't breathe. How could he survive with that much worry on his mind? How could he focus in school if he didn't have a home to take the homework to? *Does he even go to school?* Sitting in this tent with him felt so unfair. An awkward silence filled the space between them. He stood to his feet, dusting off his clothes.

"You ready to get back?" he asked.

Bella wanted to stay. She wanted to stay zipped up in this tent with him, so he could look at her like he always looked at her, and make her feel like she was going to melt, so he could remember the door. So he could stay focused on getting to the door and not dying in the streets before he even knew how dope it could be to plan a backpacking trip through Europe. He was worth more than the R.I.P. vigil the neighborhood had planned for him. Her plans were better…greater…and she wanted him to experience them. Bella's goals were clear. They were painted out in her pretty, little head; all she had to do was wait for the time to pass, so she could achieve them. The pit in her stomach that came with the thought of Hendrix dying before he ever really got to live made her want to stay down with him, to slum it a little, until he came up…it made her want to push him to the top, but she couldn't stay. She had to return to her world, before anyone noticed she was missing.

"Yeah," she whispered, as she stood.

"Don't tell nobody about this, a'ight?" he asked.

"I won't," she replied. "Are you sure you're okay out here? I have money. I can take money out the ATM, if you…"

"Nah, Pretty Girl. I'ma take care of you one day. You ain't never gon' have to take care of me. I'ma be straight," he said. "You can let me call you, though."

"My dad checks my line, so you can't call me past ten," she said.

"Pretty Girl got rules, a nigga got to follow rules," he answered. She followed him from the tent and they walked the path back toward the bike.

She pulled her hand from his grasp, when she saw the spot where Raven had died.

"I showed you something I never showed anybody. How I'm living. You want to tell me why you keep freezing up?" he asked.

"I just saw somebody die here when I was little girl," she whispered. "It freaks me out being back here."

"So, we won't come back here," he said.

"I have to. This is where you are," Bella said.

He climbed on the bike and Bella hopped on the back, without caring that she had just hurt herself on it an hour before.

"Back to Bianca crib, right?" he asked.

She nodded, and he kicked off the stand. It was time for them to go back to their separate worlds, but each of them couldn't deny that they liked the feeling that they produced when they merged them. They were so different.

The deepest contrast between two things. Black and white. Up and down. Hot and cold. They were polar opposites. All they needed was time to grow. Bella only hoped that he was worth the risk she was ready to take.

CHAPTER 16

Hendrix took the long way back to Bianca's house and Bella held on tightly, trusting him completely, as he hit wheelies and sped through the city streets. Her heart raced, as the wind whipped through her hair. She wasn't even afraid. She knew she should have been, but somehow with Hendrix, he had made risk seem worth it. Every nerve ending in her body was alive. She felt everything and nothing at all, when she was with him. Her father didn't even exist. She didn't care what punishment was waiting when she got home, as long as she got to fill her day with Hendrix. Bella had never been in love before, she didn't even know if this was that; but whatever it was, she liked it. Her young heart dipped when Hendrix pulled up to Bianca's house. The girls were still sitting on the porch, only a few more random faces were present now. Bella hopped off the bike.

Hendrix held the brake and twisted the throttle. The bike came alive, pipes smoking, engine growling, back tire spinning, as he grinned at her.

"When I'ma see you again?" he asked.

She shrugged. "I don't know."

"When you can get away, you call me, a'ight? I'll come scoop you, wherever you are," he said.

She nodded. "I'll DM you my number. What's your IG?" she asked, pulling out her phone.

"Hennythingispossible," he said. "Get at me, Pretty Girl."

He pulled off, flying down the street, as Lyric came off the porch.

"Bitttccchhh, where y'all go?!" Lyric exclaimed.

"First, don't call me that," Bella stated.

"It's just how I talk, girl. My bad, Bougie, dang," Lyric stated. "Stop stalling. I'm your girl, give me the tea! I heard he got his own apartment and everything! Did he take you there, and what happened to your leg?"

Bella looked down; and it was like, suddenly, she felt the pain from the fall. "I just fell off his bike; and nothing happened, we just talked. Did Alani come looking for me?"

"Nope, you good; but when she sees that leg, she's going to definitely ask what happened," Lyric said. "You better start thinking of your lie now."

"How did this happen, Bella? This is really bad," Alani asked, as she dipped a large towel in a bowl of water and peroxide, before putting it to Bella's leg. Bella winced.

"Ow, ow, ow," she whispered.

"Bella, what the hell happened?" Alani asked. "This looks like a burn or something."

"I just fell," she lied. "Bianca has one of those mini dirt bikes and I tried to ride it and fell off. It's no big deal."

"Since when Bianca mama got the money to buy one of those bikes?" Alani asked.

Bella opened her mouth to form another lie, when a heavy knock interrupted her. Timing had saved her. As soon as Ethic's voice greeted Nannie in the next room, Alani had transformed into a ball of nerves.

Ethic entered the room and Bella's stomach filled with knots. If he pressed her hard enough for answers, Bella knew she would fold. Ethic had always been able to elicit truth from her.

"Baby girl, how did this happen?" Ethic asked, as he pulled out a chair and then placed his hand over Alani's, removing the towel she held. He dipped it in the sterile water and then placed it on Bella's leg. The injury bubbled with white fizz, as the peroxide went to work.

"She says she fell off Bianca's little dirt bike thingy, but I ain't never known Bianca to have a dirt bike," Alani said, folding her arms across her chest.

"This is kind of bad," Ethic said, grimacing at the way his daughter's leg was skinned down to the white meat. "Can you walk?" he asked.

Bella hobbled to stand. "It's fine, Daddy, it doesn't even hurt that badly," she said. It hurt like hell, but Bella wanted the focus off her injury because she dreaded explaining how she'd gotten it. It seemed the more time that passed, the worse the pain got.

"She didn't even come back when it happened. It's been

like that for hours. It could get infected, Ethic," Alani said.

"I'm going to take her to the emergency room, just to be safe," Ethic stated. "The shit looks like a burn. Are you sure Bianca doesn't have a dirt bike?" He whispered the last part, as Bella made her way to the door.

"I mean, I just know those things cost a little money and her mama struggling like the rest of us. I've never seen her with a dirt bike," Alani whispered. "I should have never let her go around the corner. I'm sorry."

"She's about to be a teenager. Shouldn't have to keep eyes on her every second. This ain't your fault. I'm just trying to figure out what she could have been doing to take the skin off half her leg," he said, forehead wrinkled, in concern.

His stare lingered on her for a while and Alani couldn't quite catch air.

"Ride with us?" he asked. He was so close that his lips touched hers, as he spoke. "Come home with me."

She shook her head, taking a step back.

"Maybe Bella should stay from around here for a little while," Alani whispered. "I know her, and she's leaving something out of the story. Plus, this…" Alani paused, as he touched the side of her face. "Seeing you. I can't. I can't do this."

"You want to tell her that? She's going to be where you are. You know that," Ethic stated. "You're the love of our lives. She's going to come to you, Lenika. I can ban her. I can say no, and she's coming anyway. If you really don't want her here…if she's not welcome…"

Alani sighed. "Of course, she's welcome, Ezra. She's my person..." Alani swept her hand through her hair, in frustration. "I just don't want to see you."

"What I got to do to make it right? Just tell me and I'll do it."

"I told you what you had to do, and you didn't do it," Alani shot back. "Instead, you sent thousands of dollars to a woman I told you to cut off. So, don't try to accommodate me now. You moved how you wanted to move, now I'm going to move how I need to move. You put me out, Ethic."

"I never did that. You left. You walked out of my house in the middle of the night because we had a disagreement," Ethic stated. "

"You told me you wanted to try again after Morgan's baby comes, Ethic," Alani huffed. "You want to press pause on me, while you continue to send five thousand-dollar checks to the next bitch. Was I supposed to go back to your bed after that?"

"Stop bringing that up like it matters. Five thousand dollars might as well be five dollars. It's nothing. It's fucking petty. It's not even close to what I give you," Ethic stated. "You got a hundred thousand coming to you every month. Fuck you stressing over five fucking thousand dollars? I'll roll down my window and hand that shit to a bum on the street. The shit's nothing."

"What?" Alani frowned. "What are you talking about? I've never asked you for anything."

"And you'll never have to ask me or anybody else on this Earth for anything. Since the day Love died, you've gotten twenty percent of all the residuals from my businesses and investments. Every month. I used to split it four ways. Now, it's split five. It's piling up in an account in your name."

"Keep it. I don't want it," Alani said, stubbornly. She tried to walk around him, but Ethic gripped her elbow and pulled her back. With her back against the wall and him blocking her path, she was trapped. It was the loveliest trap she had ever been in. Her breathing labored, as her lip quivered.

"This fight with you is on me, Lenika. It's weighing me down. I got a whole house but no you. It's a daddy and three kids there, but no mama." Ethic feathered her cheek with the lightest touch. It felt like he was putting her in a trance. "We want our mama home, baby."

"Better call the bitch that uses your last name. Disaya Okafor." Alani thought about the shit and pushed him hard. "Disaya Okafor? Do you know what that does to me? What am I supposed to do with you? I can't trust you. No way do you love me like I love you, because all I see is you. The things I sacrifice daily to love you." Alani shook her head, scoffing, as she turned her head to the side, just to break the intensity of his stare. She needed him to stop touching her. His touch made her weak and those eyes boring into hers made her forget why she was mad in the first place. "I asked you to end whatever it was you had with her. You didn't. That's fine, but you can't have both. This, between us...it's over. It's time that we both just come to terms with that. I'm done with you."

"That will never be the case," he said.

"You said we were forcing it. So, stop forcing it. Leave me

alone. Let me go. Let me find someone who loves me and only me. Someone who doesn't send money to other women behind my back. Let someone else have me."

"No," Ethic stated. He was done entertaining the conversation. She was too emotional and anything other than logic frustrated the hell out of Ethic.

"Whyyyy?" Alani whined.

"Because I said so," he stated. His tone was so callous it silenced her. He flicked his nose, in irritation. "Play with a nigga life out here if you want to."

"Bella's waiting on you," she whispered, tears clouding her eyes. "Don't come back here, Ethic. Don't call, don't come by. If the kids want to visit, they can call me. They know my number. I'll send Mr. Larry for them," Alani said, forcing herself to go cold…putting her heart in a box that she planned to hide. She had done it before, she could do it again. She could compartmentalize what she felt for him. Deny herself of him. Be without him. Her heart was already breaking.

I'm going to die without him.

He was angry. She could feel it, and when he picked her up, sweeping everything on the countertop to the floor as his lips took hers, she absorbed it…the hostility.

"What are you doing?" she gasped. "Ethic…"

"What's all that noise in there?" Nannie yelled from the next room. The entire dish rack, and every dish in it, was now on the floor.

Bella walked into the kitchen, just as Ethic slid Alani's panties from beneath her dress.

"Oh my god! Daddy! Nannie, they being nasty on your kitchen counters!" Bella shouted, as she covered her eyes and rushed from the room.

"Ethic!" Alani hissed, in protest, as he lowered to his knees, pulling her hips to the edge of the counter until he was face to face with her weakness.

Bitch, don't fucking fold.

Ethic pulled her clit into his mouth, sucking hard and long. Alani knocked the damn toaster to the floor, she jerked so hard.

"Get y'all asses off my counter!" Nannie hollered, from the living room.

Alani looked down at the top of his head and saw his long eyelashes lower as he closed his eyes. He ate pussy like it was a delicacy. So appreciative.

He planted one more kiss to her middle, before lifting.

Alani's head hit his chest and he held the back of her neck.

"You ain't fed me, baby. You know what I need from you. How I like to eat it twice a day," he whispered in her ear, as he slid his hand up her thigh and played with it, flicking it, rubbing it. Alani's mouth fell open in pure pleasure. He was so goddamn nasty. So mannish. "I'm tired of bullshitting, Lenika. Come with me."

Alani wanted to. She wanted to be a fool for this man; because, if there was ever a man to be a fool for, surely it was him. But she couldn't. The letter from YaYa had just given her the courage to do the inevitable. Leave. Leave the dream land that they had created from the day she'd walked into his shop. Ethic Land. They had been living in Ethic Land

and the real world judged their connection. She felt it every time Morgan spoke. Every time Morgan looked at her in disgust. Alani had avoided mirrors for months because she was ashamed of the reflection. What the hell were they even doing together? How dare they even try?

"There's just too much in the way," she whispered. "It's not even just about the letter. Morgan's suffering is…she's suffering, Ethic." He removed his hand because now the conversation was serious. He would never allow YaYa to get in the way of he and Alani, but he knew that Morgan could, and he saw no way around that. "Sometimes, I see her come out of it, you know…like I see a glimpse of life in her, and then she looks at me and she dies a little. I don't belong in her life. If there was ever a reason to leave it alone, our children should be a good enough reason. If us being together hurts any of them, we have to let it go, and all I see is hurt on that girl."

Her words were a harsh reality, and he took a step back, while finessing his lips. He pulled them into his mouth and then shook his head.

"Loving you…" He shook his head. "…the shit is like prayer for me, Lenika. You know how you get down on your knees and you talk to God when you're indecisive about something? Or when you're worried or scared? You pray. When I feel any of that, I just look at you, and I mean, really look at you. I study you. How many seconds pass before you blink, how your throat sinks in when you swallow, how you bite your nails when you watch TV, just the minor shit, but it ain't minor. It's major. Your beauty is in your details, Lenika.

The moles on your face. The fucking corn on your pinky toe that you try to hide…"

"Nigga, I KNOW YOU FUCKING LYING," she shouted. "I don't have corns, Ezra!"

"I watch you, baby. I pay attention. When you're asleep, or cooking, or fussing at one of my babies, I take a minute and I look at you. Then, I touch you, and like fucking magic, whatever the problem was is gone. I find so much clarity when I look at you. The thought of not being able to look at you…" Ethic blew out a heavy breath and rubbed both hands down his wavy head. "The shit has been a privilege, Lenika. Loving you. A fucking honor, yo," he said.

Ethic brought his lips to her forehead and she closed her eyes, leaking tears, leaking fears, because she was afraid of what life after this moment would look like.

When he pulled back, Alani had to force herself to keep her eyes closed because she couldn't witness his exit. The slamming of the old, rickety screen door made her breakdown. She turned her face to the side, kissing her shoulder, as she sobbed. He was gone, and she had to be okay with that. Only she wasn't. She never would be.

CHAPTER 17

Morgan sat in the chair across from Nyair's desk. She was silent. Stubborn. She wasn't in the mood to talk to anyone and it showed.

"You know, this don't work unless you talk to a nigga," Nyair said.

"You talk so reckless to be a pastor," Morgan said, smirking, as she crossed her arms and legs. Her body language spoke volumes. She would never speak the words, but Morgan was giving "fuck you" vibes to Nyair.

"I speak from the heart, Morgan. When I'm feeling godly, I speak God's word. When I'm feeling my flesh, you get a different man," he said.

Morgan's brow dipped in intrigue, as she squinted, trying to figure him out.

"Are you married, Nyair?" Morgan asked.

"I'm not," he said.

"Never met a pastor who didn't have a first lady," she said. "What's wrong with you?"

Nyair smiled and Morgan focused on the deep dimples in his cheeks. He was a stunning man. Charming, handsome, hood, and fucking holy. She eyed the tattoos on his arms and neck. His position and his credentials didn't match.

"There's something wrong with me because I don't have a lady?"

"I mean..." Morgan shrugged. "I would just expect you to have someone."

"I had someone. I lost her. I had two someones in my lifetime. Things don't always work out the way we plan, and we have to learn to be okay with that," he said.

Morgan broke their gaze.

"Have you thought about hurting yourself again?" Nyair asked.

"Every day," she admitted.

Nyair didn't flinch. "To get whose attention?"

Morgan's eyes burned. "You don't know me," she responded.

"I know that you're sending smoke signals. You want help, but you only want it from one person in particular. Who is it?"

Morgan's eyes filled to the brim. "Is it Ethic?" Nyair asked. You want his attention?"

Morgan was silent.

"You don't like Alani, do you?" Nyair asked.

"Finally, something you get right," she whispered. She was being so defiant, so rude, but it didn't bother Nyair. He finessed the hair on his chin and smirked. "Because Ethic gives her attention?"

"He shouldn't even be with her," Morgan whispered.

"If not her, then who? Who would you want Ethic with? Because you love him, and certainly you want him with someone who loves him and loves his children. You say it ain't her...who is it?"

Morgan couldn't answer that, because in her eyes, no one would ever be good enough to fill her sister's shoes. No one was good enough for Ethic's love. The way he did it, the way he gave his all…the way he covered his woman under an umbrella of complete love, was a thing of beauty. It was like watching a sunset. Seeing Ethic love Alani was like watching the sun go down over the Grand Canyon. It took Morgan's breath away. It made her angry that people couldn't see love when they looked at her…because Messiah loved her in the dark. His love was a shadow. It made theirs feel cheap. It made Mo feel unworthy; and every time Alani smiled, Morgan felt jealous because Ethic had taught her that a woman's smile reflected the man she chose. Morgan wasn't smiling these days.

"You? You want him to love you like that?"

"He does love me like that," Morgan said. "Ethic doesn't love anyone more than me."

And there it was. The unhealthy attachment. The ownership Morgan felt she had over Ethic's affections. She said it so matter-of-factly that it made Nyair's brow raise in stun.

"You know you can't be everything to him, Morgan. You do know that, right? That there is a difference in the way he loves you and the way he loves Alani? He's a man. He loves you beautifully and wholeheartedly. I see it when he looks at you, but he has limits with you, Morgan. A man has needs that only a woman can fill. You can't be that for him. That's not your role. Why are you uncomfortable allowing someone else into his life?"

"Because it's always just been us. She doesn't deserve to be a part of that. He's so good and she's…"

"The one who makes him happy, but you're not happy and you're used to him being unhappy with you. You're used to finding solace in his sadness."

"He's the only one who felt my pain," Morgan whispered. "We both lost Raven. We're the only two people who know what it feels like to miss her."

"And you think he doesn't miss her anymore?" Nyair frowned. "He will always miss her, always love her, but he can't die with her. You can't die with her. Half living is dying, Morgan. You've been sad for a long time. That shit has to get heavy."

"You just sinning all over this church, huh?" Morgan asked, finding a light spot in their heavy conversation. She didn't even realize that he had her right where he wanted her.

"I've done worse things under this roof. Words are just words," he stated, smiling, mischievously.

Morgan took in all of him. With skin the color of brown sugar, he had to taste good. His eyes peered through her. His smile warmed her. His football player's frame was big, like she could climb him. Nyair was fine, and those damn dimples. She blushed just from the thoughts that ran through her mind.

"I can imagine," she said. "On top of this desk, probably. Fake-ass pastor." She snickered.

"You looking for trouble," he stated, shaking his head.

Morgan held up two hands, in surrender. "Definitely don't want any trouble."

"Throw some holy water on your ass," he snickered.

Morgan hollered. She giggled so much that her stomach hurt. A good hurt. One that released a little of the pain.

"Young-ass," he said, shaking his head. "I'd ruin you, little Morgan, and then Ethic would kill a man of God. Let's not even go down that road. Let's not make it cliché. I don't hit everything moving. You shouldn't either. What looks good to you ain't always good for you. I want to be able to talk to you without crossing the line. I want you to hear me. I want to hear you. I can't counsel you if there are innuendos hanging in the air. Can we keep it cool and just try to get to the root of you? I don't know you that well, but I'd like to. Maybe I can reach some understanding that'll tell me what made such a beautiful girl want to die."

"Yeah," Morgan said, as she peered at him. Nyair had a way of disarming, a way of eliciting trust. She didn't know why she felt like she could talk to him, but she felt like pouring out her heart. He didn't see her for just her looks. He wasn't even phased by her. He wanted to hear her voice. Like Messiah. Messiah had heard her voice.

"Yeah, we can keep it cool. I'm sorry," she said, as a tear slid down her face. "For being extra." Morgan tended to act out, to seek attention, when things weren't going her way. It often worked but Nyair wasn't fazed. "I don't know why I do that. Try to make other people uncomfortable to avoid talking about what makes me uncomfortable."

"Growth is uncomfortable," Nyair said. "So, tell me the real, so we can start growing…so you can shed this cocoon you're stuck in and take off, butterfly," Nyair said.

"Butterfly, huh?" she asked, eyes twinkling in approval. Something about that analysis felt accurate.

"I'm expecting a baby by a snake, and you know I should be calling him that because he's related to the man who destroyed my entire family. He's related to Raven's old boyfriend..."

"Mizan," Nyair finished.

Morgan's eyes widened, in recognition. Even her heart went tender, as anxiety built in her. Even knowing he was dead and gone; even still, she felt fear when his name was mentioned.

"You knew him?" Morgan asked.

"Yeah, I saw him around. He was a bad dude. Saw your sister around too. She's still the prettiest girl I've ever seen," Nyair said.

Morgan smiled. "Yeah, she was." Her voice was low, as she ran pictures of Raven through her mind. "Messiah is Mizan's brother, and it's crazy because I still want to love him. I still want him. I need him. I don't even care who he's related to. I'm not even mad about that part. I mean, I am, but I could get over that, you know? I could forgive that because I know Messiah, at least the boy I think I know must have had a really good reason to lie. But the way he left. The things he said to me before he left. It was like he never really even loved me at all."

"And that's what made you get in that car that day?" Nyair asked.

"Living isn't living without him," Morgan answered.

"So, because you felt he didn't love you, you didn't love you anymore? You hear how that sounds? Do you know how inconsistent other people are? Look at you, Morgan. You can't even hold yourself down. Can't even love yourself right. What if someone out there was depending on your love to keep them alive? What if Bella needed your love to breathe? Or Eazy? You messing up loving yourself, but something so valuable...their lives depend on you loving them. They'd be dead. You never let another person value you more than you value yourself. People come into our lives and we're lucky to have them while they choose to stay. We enjoy the time they're here, but when they leave, they leave, and you must be okay with it being just you again because nothing's promised. No moment, besides the present, is guaranteed. If you only got to love him for one day, you should appreciate that day. If you only felt his love for a second, you got to sit back and think, damn, that was a glorious second and I'm grateful for the time we had. You don't discount the value in the moments afterward when you're alone, because you have to love the time you spend with you just as much. You've got to love you more than anyone else loves you. Shit is wild that you can't see what other people see when they look at you."

"What do you see?" she asked, a face full of tears staring at him.

"You ever see a piece of glass crushed against the concrete?" he asked.

"Umm... no," Morgan said. "What does that have to do with..."

Nyair pushed back from his desk. Dark denim and a button-down shirt was his attire. A sleeveless puffer jacket rested over it. Two, diamond chains around his neck. VVS, because Morgan knew a thing or two about fine jewelry, and a fitted 810 cap. He was definitely not your everyday pastor.

"Come on," he said. He grabbed a crystal decanter from his desk and led the way outside.

When they stood in the empty parking lot, he tossed the decanter to Morgan.

"Whoa!" she shouted, as she caught it. She hadn't expected him to toss it. "What are you doing?"

"Don't fumble," he said. He clapped his hands together and Morgan tossed it back. Nyair caught it out of midair, effortlessly. His large hands wrapped around the decanter like it was made of pig skin.

"You played football, clearly," she said, smiling.

"Thirty million-dollar hands," he stated, winking.

Thirty million-dollar ass, Morgan thought, smirking. Nyair was built solid, like he ran touchdowns for a living. *So fine.*

He tossed the decanter to her, again, but Morgan wasn't athletic at all. It slipped through her fingers and crashed against the pavement.

"Nyair! I'm so sorry. I really didn't mean to. It-"

"Slipped," he interrupted. "You slipped up. Fumbled… kinda like your man fumbled you. He probably didn't intend to, probably didn't want to, but he fumbled you. He broke you, but look down at the pieces."

Morgan looked at the shards of glass glistening under the sunlight against the black, tarred pavement. They shined like diamonds with colors dancing in the pieces.

"You asked what I see when I look at you."

Morgan looked up at him, in awe.

"I see a broken girl. I see pieces of you that are shattered because a man dropped you, but the pieces shine. They're really beautiful."

Morgan sucked in air, as she wiped away a tear that fell from her eyes.

"You can't leave your pieces all over the floor, Mo. You pick your shit up. You put your shit back together and you live to love another day. We don't always get the explanations or apologies we deserve. People don't always love you right. The only thing you can control is how you love yourself. Love you, Morgan. Love yourself hard. Over-love you and don't apologize for it. That way, when someone is under-loving you, when they're not serving you, when they're not giving you the same amount of love you give yourself, you'll recognize it and stop accepting less than what you're worth. Cuz you're worth a lot."

Morgan looked off in the distance. "I am, huh?"

"You are," Nyair stated.

"You really are a pastor," Morgan said, smiling and laughing through tears.

"On a good day," Nyair said, brow bent and smile wide. "On a bad day, I'm just a man trying to find his way. I ain't perfect, but I'm trying to do my part to make sure I'm giving off God's love. I want you to feel that from me. I want Ethic and everybody I come across to feel that from me, cuz I've given out a lot of bullshit in my day."

"I feel that from you. Authenticity. You're not stuffy and that helps me hear you better. Thank you for not judging and for seeing me."

Nyair nodded. "Anytime. I'm here when you want to talk. Even if it's early. Even when you think it's too late. You can call. You can drop by. I'll be here; and do me a favor, take it easy on Alani. Give her a chance."

"She told you to tell me that?" Morgan asked, folding her arms across her chest.

"Nah, but somebody needed to," he said. "Mean just like your sister was."

She laughed, as they walked back towards the entrance. "She was mean, wasn't she?"

They laughed and reminisced on the legend of Raven Atkins, as they headed inside; and for the first time in a long time, Morgan felt normal, like maybe she could survive without Messiah.

CHAPTER 18

Alani drew in a sharp breath, as she hooked the diamond necklace around her neck. Her stomach knotted, as she fingered the stone that hung against her clavicle. It was so elegant. It was perfect. Just like the little guy that had given it to her. Eazy's face filled her thoughts and Alani scoffed and then released a sad smile. She and Ethic weren't together, but Alani made sure she kept the promise she had made to Eazy. He needed her 'mama magic' and she had promised him that she would be there to give it to him every day for the rest of the school year. Alani woke up every morning and drove the twenty minutes to Eazy's school, just so she could be there when he got off the school bus. The five minutes she spent hugging him and speaking life into him before he walked through the doors each morning was important. She was a woman of her word, but it was hard to maintain when she and Ethic were falling apart. She missed being home with Eazy. The brief interaction wasn't nearly enough. She missed all of them. Those Okafors, but she had decided…she and Ethic had decided to do what was best for everyone. There was too much going on. YaYa wasn't even the biggest factor. She was an issue, but if they were both honest, her letter just happened to be the straw that broke the camel's back. It was Morgan. They couldn't be together right now if they wanted to. Sure, Morgan said it was okay for Ethic and Alani to date, but the suicide attempt...the depression. It was too heavy not to take heed. They had to be the adults, they had to make the sacrifice. What was best for Morgan just happened to be the thing that gutted Alani.

"We want our mama home, baby."

His last words haunted her. It had been two weeks of no contact...two weeks of unbelievable yearning. Alani wanted him, Morgan needed him. She bowed out with grace.

Alani looked at the two dresses that laid out across her bedspread. One red, one black. It felt disrespectful to choose the black. She would never wear black for another man again. Her little, black dresses were reserved for the one she couldn't have, not for business meetings with professors turned literary agents.

She slipped into her undergarment, hoping it sucked everything into its right place. Yoga had tightened her up nicely, but two babies had done a number on her stomach. It just wouldn't tone up for the life of her. *Thank God for Spanx.* She struggled into the material, hopping and jumping, until the black fabric covered her thick thighs and turned her flab into an hour glass, and then she slipped into the red dress. By the time she had it all on, she was hot as fuck and fanning her hairline, so her silk press didn't start to curl up. It was center parted and sleek; her makeup was done to perfection. She felt like a woman tonight…not like a mother with two dead babies, but a beautiful woman who had every right to take a spin on the town. As she slid into her high heels, her heart begged her to cancel. Netflix and her new bedspread were calling her name. That was the perfect Friday night to her. Curling up with a bottle of red and five seasons of any show was a sure way to keep her content. She would drown in the drama of a fake television world in a heartbeat to forget her own, but it was too late to cancel. Alex was already on his way to the restaurant; and according to him, they had important deal points to discuss. *It'll be rude to cancel so last minute.*

She slipped into a pair of nude heels and grabbed her nude clutch, before hurrying down the stairs.

"Where you going looking like you selling it?" Nannie asked. Alani looked up at Nannie who sat in the living room with Mr. Larry, watching judge shows.

"Nannie, don't start," she said. "It's just a business dinner."

"Business is handled in the daytime," Nannie said. "Ethic know you going out in a red dress to this business dinner?"

"I told you, Ethic and I decided not to see one another," Alani whispered. Her voice cracked.

"And I still don't understand why!" Nannie shouted. "You don't let kids run you, you run the kids. That oldest daughter of his…"

"Morgan," Alani corrected.

"Well, *Morgan* needs mothering more than Eazy and Bella. You parent her, you don't run from her. You acting like you was raised by a white woman. When have you ever let a child tell you how things are going to go? When you turned eighteen and acted a fool, what did I do?"

"Showed me you could act a bigger fool," Alani said, chuckling at the ways Nannie had brought her down to Earth when she had thought she was grown all those years ago.

"You better show that girl who's the mama and who's the child and go get your man back," Nannie said.

"It's different with Morgan," Alani defended. "She's fragile. Even before what Lucas did to her. She's lost a lot. Ethic is all she has. I just don't belong there."

"Did he say that, or did you say that? That sounds a lot like you and none of him. That man wants you," Nannie said.

"Needs outweigh wants," Alani whispered, feeling her chest go tender. She hated talking about it. She hated thinking about it. "His daughter comes first. She shouldn't have to be uncomfortable so that two adults can be happy. It's decided, anyway. Just stay out of it."

"Well, go sell it to your professor, because this ain't no damn business dinner," Nannie snapped. Alani knew she was in a mood. She was partial to Ethic. They had developed a friendship, one that Alani envied. No matter how many times Alani explained that she and Ethic weren't communicating, Nannie refused to cut him off. They spoke daily, prayed together on the phone every morning. Her dinner with Alex, particularly, put Nannie in bad spirits.

"I won't be late," Alani said, leaning down to kiss Nannie's cheek, despite her ill temper. "Bye, Mr. Larry."

"Bye, La," he said. "Have a good dinner."

"Thank you. At least someone is being supportive!"

"Supportive my ass, that man wants in your..."

Alani was out the door before she could even hear the rest. She grabbed the key to her Tesla, the car Ethic had refused to take back, and made a quick fifteen minutes of the trip to the restaurant. She parked valet and exited her car, quick-stepping to stop her hair from getting ruined by the rain.

Alex stood at the hostess's desk, hands tucked into the pockets of an expensive, perfectly-tailored suit. His eyes shone brightly when they met Alani's.

"Hi," she greeted, plastering on a half-smile, a fake smile, because that's where she was in life...back to fake smiling. She did a lot of that lately, to make people think she was okay...to convince herself that she could survive without Ethic...that she could survive without her babies and stay standing tall without him to hold her steady. The smile was painful; it was so forced, but just like everyone else, he didn't notice. *Ethic would have noticed.*

"The table is this way," he said, placing a hand to the small of her back. His hand in such an intimate place made her feel like ants were crawling up her back. They sat at the white, linen-covered table and Alani placed the cloth napkin in her lap.

"This seems like a lot. Dinner wasn't necessary. I could have come by your office, Alex," she said.

"I thought we should get to know one another outside of the university setting. This book will have us working in a different capacity. There'll be a lot of long nights, book tours...we might as well get to know one another more intimately."

The word *intimately* snatched Alani's eyes from her menu and her heart stalled. It wasn't that he wasn't attractive. He was. He was successful and cultured and refined and a great catch for some other woman…a woman who hadn't experienced the Ethic Effect.

"Oh, um, I guess we should become friends," she said, trying to establish a zone where he existed, and he knew the limitations of their relationship. *Keep your ass right in the friend zone.*

"You look beautiful," he complimented.

Alani gave a tight-lipped smile and a flat, "thanks."

"So, the deal points? What did the publishers say?" she asked. Alani was desperate to get to the business. Discussing deals and contracts prevented him the opportunity to muddle the purpose of this dinner…it steered him away from *you're beautiful* sentiments and broaching the subject of intimacy.

"We have time for that. Let's eat first. I'll order a bottle of wine," Alex said. "Do you prefer red or white?"

Alani stood. "Umm… red. I'll be right back. I'm going to visit the ladies' room."

She pushed back from the table and blew out an exasperated breath. She hurried toward the back of the restaurant and pulled out her cell phone. Her fingers danced on the screen, as she pulled up Nannie's contact. She needed her to call in ten minutes, so she could fake an emergency and cut the night short. She could get the deal details later… in the daylight…and on campus. Alani's face was buried in her phone and she bumped right into the corner of one of the tables, knocking a wine glass into the lap of a beautiful woman sitting there. Just Alani's luck, the woman wore all white and was now covered in red wine that Alani had spilled.

"I'm so sorry," she said. "My God, your dress!"

"It's fine…it's fine!" the woman responded, pushing back from the table, standing and blotting at the stains on the expensive fabric.

"Lenika…"

Alani's entire frame stiffened. His baritone. His scent. His presence. She felt it in her bones. She turned to find Ethic emerging from the hallway that led to the restroom. Her heart plummeted, when she saw Eazy trailing behind him. Her boys. Her Okafor men were here…Alani rolled eyes back to the woman…with her? They were here with another woman.

"Alani!" Eazy shouted, without care that his voice carried throughout the entire restaurant. He rushed her…all boy and no finesse. Just the way Alani liked it, giving her a rough hug, wrapping his arms around her waist. Alani wrapped one arm around Eazy, but her eyes were stuck on Ethic. Her eyes were glued to him like little, five-year-old hands had cut them from paper and placed Elmer's on the back before attaching them to Ethic. He took in the scene in seconds. Alani's stare bounced from him to the woman, then to him, and then to the woman. She recoiled, her mouth falling slightly agape to push out the scoff of disbelief…the insult…the invisible slap in the face that discovering him had delivered.

She didn't have time to wonder where Bella was. She came waltzing down the hallway with Morgan next.

"Alani!" Bella said, wearing her shock, and then giving Alani a broad smile and rushing in for a hug. Of course, they were here, at this restaurant, at this time…Alani wasn't there to make dinner for them any longer and this was the finest restaurant in the city. Ethic didn't eat bullshit. Food or pussy. He preferred the best...the best cuts…the most delicate pieces. Alani's heart ached. *Like her. God, has she fed him?*

Alani had given Lily Friday nights off, during her short tenure in the Okafor household. *Family Night Fridays*. That's what she had planned to make it, and Lily deserved to spend hers with her family. So, Ethic ended up here. Feeding his kids with this beautiful dinner companion on a Friday night. *Fuck Nigga Friday*. How had it become that? Alani wanted to scream. Morgan didn't speak, but at least her babies were loyal…at least they were excited to see her. Alani took in the entire scene. It was a blow straight to her soul, as she put two and two together. The woman was beautiful. Chocolate skin that looked edible, jet black, short cut, and a body to die for. Expensive everything. High-class everything. He was on a date, two weeks after ending things with her. Had this woman always been in the picture? Was she always in the background, waiting for her turn, playing her role, like Dolce? Was she important or was she one of many? Was Dolce back in the picture too? Was Green Eyes? How many bitches did he have? How much competition did *she* have? Clearly, his women were familiar with his children. Dolce had been around them, YaYa had popped up out the blue for Eazy's birthday, and now this one. Alani's fingertips graced the table for balance, as she placed one hand over her stomach. Sickness filled her. She kissed the top of Eazy's head and hugged Bella tightly. At least they were loyal. Her minions. Her babies.

"I'm sorry about the dress," she whispered, before bumping pass Ethic and rushing down the hallway. The bathroom was her solace. It was the perfect place to hide… to get control of her emotions, because no fucking way was she letting him make her cry. If he could move on after two weeks, fine. Let him. Fuck him. *She's probably going to fuck my man!!!* Alani snatched paper towel out of the holder and dabbed at the corner of her eyes. Her lip quivered, and she gripped the countertop, bending over, in misery, but she forced herself to pull it together. She sniffed away her feelings. They were shattered, but she couldn't lose it. She couldn't fold in front of Ethic and his black Barbie. She had to walk out of this restaurant with her head held high. When she got to her car, she could lose it, because that much was inevitable…she was going to lose her shit. *Just not here.* Alani closed both eyes because the tears were wetting her mascara, threatening to make it run. She rolled desperate eyes to the sky and blew out a breath, and then closed them again, pulling in deep breaths until the burning subsided. She was shaking, she was so distraught. *I've got to get out of here.*

Alani dabbed her inner eye with the paper towel, washed her hands, and then pulled open the door. One step and she froze. Ethic stood, leaning against the wall, rubbing both hands over the top of his head, like he was stressed, like he was worried.

"Lenika..."

Alani went to move by him, but he captured her wrist and pulled her back to him. His hands were in her hair. The scent of his cologne was hypnotic, but her feelings were too crushed to fall for the charm. Lies. She was falling...but she was too hurt to like it.

"Ethic, no," she whispered. Her tears fell.

"Yes," he countered, peering down the bridge of his nose at her, as one hand slid up her thigh. "Say yes, baby. You don't even know how much I've missed you."

"No." She withered in his embrace, but she pulled back anyway. He didn't relent. He pulled her ass right back, into his body, no space between them, trapping her chin between the 'U' shape of one hand.

"It's only been two weeks and you..." Before she could even finish...

"Alani, sweetheart, is everything okay?"

Her world moved in slow motion, as she turned toward Alex.

Sweetheart?

With misted eyes and hollow insides, she felt frozen. She felt her face move, as Ethic turned her back toward him. Those eyes went dark...and she knew...she knew he had flipped that switch. She saw his anger resonate through his entire body, as his hold on her stiffened...the intent behind his touch changed.

"Sweetheart..." Ethic repeated the word like it was the crudest flavor on his tongue. Like it left a bad aftertaste in his mouth.

Alani took a step back and turned her gaze to Alex, and then back to Ethic, who stood there, fingers pinching pursed lips, one hand in the pocket of expensive slacks…forehead wrinkled in deep thought. That tattooed hand traveled to the bridge of his nose where he pinched, before he finessed his wrinkled forehead with his pointer finger. She could see him debating. *Who is he going to kill first? Me or Alex? Alex or me? Eenie, meenie, miney, mo.* She felt like she had been caught cheating and an explanation rested on the tip of her tongue, until she remembered that she had caught him first. Technically, it wasn't cheating. They weren't together. They had decided, but that made no never mind. He was here with his family…with what was supposed to be *her* family… only her seat was filled by another woman.

"Alani, is everything okay?"

Alani's heart quickened. She had corrected him before. Why was he still calling her that? She was Lenika to him. She was Lenika to everybody. Their relationship was strictly professional, but that name on his tongue made it sound oh so personal. Why did he insist on crossing lines she had clearly drawn out for him?

Ethic scoffed, and then came off that wall. Alani's feet had never moved faster. She stepped in front of him and placed a yielding hand on Ethic's chest. "He's my professor," she whispered. "My agent," she stammered, correcting.

"Her date… Alex," Alex added, extending his hand.

Alani snapped her neck toward Alex, with astonished eyes.

"Yo, my man. Let me rap with you for a minute," Ethic stated. Nicety didn't live in his tone.

"Ethic..."

It was like she was no longer even in the room. Ethic didn't even acknowledge her. He was zeroed in on Alex.

"Yeah, uh, sure," Alex stuttered.

Ethic and Alex stepped out of earshot. Alani was a bit grateful that they were in the line of sight of not only her but the other patrons in the restaurant. Ethic couldn't kill the man with his children and a hundred witnesses watching. Still, her stomach was tight, like she was watching her father interrogate a boy she was dating. His face was tight, stressed, and she could see the pieces of pain that dwelled in him, as he stood with his shoulders squared and hands tucked away in his pockets, while speaking to Alex.

Alex did a lot of nodding and his lips were moving fast. *He's explaining...* Alani paced that small hallway for what felt like forever, until Ethic released her agent. He didn't even return to her. He went back to his table and Alex came to her side.

"Nice guy," he said. "Shall we?" he extended a palm for her to walk first.

Alani's eyes widened. *Nice guy? Did this nigga just give him permission to see me? He should be flipping tables in this bitch. Oh, he got life so fucked up right now.*

Alani walked back out to the main dining room. Her heart sank even further to her stomach when she saw Ethic re-seated at the candle-lit table with the wine-covered woman and his children.

Alani was trying to hold her composure. She was trying to not let her emotions get the best of her, but she was losing.

"Alex, you'll have to send me the details for this deal via email. Oh, and please don't call me Alani again. I asked nicely before. Do it again, and I'll be finding new representation for my book," she said. "I'll expect your email on Monday." She left him standing in the middle of the restaurant, and then approached Ethic's table, not caring that she was interrupting.

"Bella, baby, can you take Eazy to the dessert station? I think you guys deserve to eat dessert before dinner. Don't you, Big Man?" Alani asked, smiling. Her heart fluttered. Just setting eyes on them made her bleed emotion. They were her babies and she had missed them terribly. The no-contact order she and Ethic had set was torture; especially, where the kids were concerned.

"Yes!" Eazy shouted.

"Inside voice, Big Man," Alani reminded. "And walking feet, please." She smiled, because she knew it took everything in Eazy not to run.

Bella and Eazy lifted from their seats, and Morgan looked on in astonishment, as Alani placed her palms on the white tablecloth. The woman looked up at her, in stun, and then over at Ethic.

"I know, sis. You're wondering who the crazy woman is that's interrupting your dinner and spilling red wine all over your thousand-dollar dress. I know. I apologize, that was a mistake, and I'm sure Ezra will cover the damages."

"Lenika..."

She put up a finger, halting Ethic, as she looked the woman in the eyes, smiling nicely, before continuing.

"As of two weeks ago... I was his girlfriend and not in the *'it's a cute title but we have no real commitment'* type of way. In the *'I will beat a bitch ass for even breathing in his direction'* type of way..."

"Lenika," Ethic said, his voice calm.

"Umm... Alani..." Morgan added.

There she was, with that finger, again...taking a note right out of the book of Ethic, second installment, seventy-second page, third verse. She was in charge. This was her show and she had no time for interruptions. She needed her message to be heard loud and clear, because this could go one of two ways...this black Barbie in her all white and red wine accents could go peacefully, or Alani could take it left and slap fire from her ass. Alani had no preferences. She was with the shits, no matter which way the wind blew.

"Now see, I love him, and I mean, love his dirty drawers, do anything for, to, and with him type of love. Then, these three..." she pointed from Morgan, to across the room where Bella and Eazy were eying the confections through the open glass. "I love them too. Even though this one here can't really stand me, but apparently, new girlfriends in white dresses and expensive shoes seem to be okay with her."

"Baby..."

Alani marked Ethic with her wounded eyes, and the amusement playing on his lips and dancing in his stare made her frown in confusion. Her lips parted just enough to let out a scoff of disbelief and she shook her head. *He's unbelievable. He thinks this shit is funny.*

"This is Carmen..."

"I don't need no introductions because the bitch is not staying, mmmkay? You're about to call an Uber and send her on her way because my patience is about this thin." She pinched her pointer finger and thumb together until they were almost touching. "And I'm trying to be a lady about this shit, but I'm two seconds off her ass."

Nika was back. Ethic's dick jumped.

This fucking crazy shit is so fucking sexy.

"It's been two weeks, Ezra. Two weeks and you have her out with the kids like one, big, happy family. Like I never even mattered..."

"She's Eazy's therapist," Ethic stated, sitting back in his chair and dead-panning on her, one finger resting on his temple, while his thumb held up his chin.

Alani's mouth snapped closed. Her eyes rolled across the room to Eazy who had his nose pressed to the glass of the dessert counter.

"His what?"

"Carmen, this is my..."

"Girlfriend, understood," Carmen finished, holding up her hands in defense, while smiling. "I can't say I blame you." Carmen winked at Alani, who lowered her head in the palms of her hands. She was mortified. She looked up at Ethic, and then at Carmen.

"I'm so sorry..."

Morgan sat there, eyebrows lifted, and snickering slightly, as she shook her head in disbelief.

"Wait," Alani said. "Therapist?"

"The school is trying to diagnosis him with ADHD," Ethic informed.

"What?" Alani felt fire consume her entire body. "Why didn't you call me? Why didn't you tell me? My poor baby. You don't tell him that. Please, tell me you haven't told him that?" Alani's legs felt weak and her stomach went missing, her head spun with dizziness, as she sat in the chair Eazy had occupied.

"He thinks she is an old friend," Ethic said.

"Carmen is the best in the state. She wanted to evaluate him in a public setting. Where rules apply. Where he would be expected to sit still," Ethic explained.

Carmen nodded. "You have a very good handle on him. He's run everywhere all night, until you showed up," Carmen said.

Alani's eyes prickled, as emotion shown in them. "Teachers aren't supposed to diagnosis students with anything." Alani pointed one, nude-painted fingertip into the table, sternly, as she spoke. "They're not doctors. It's illegal. ADHD is one of the most misdiagnosed conditions in black boys. No way are we there yet. No way does he need therapy or even a formal diagnosis yet. You're not putting him on medication...he's a boy...he's seven years old. He's not supposed to be a robot." Alani's heart was broken. So many stigmas were already placed on Eazy, simply because of the color of his skin and his gender. He was a young, black boy...he would grow into a black man...the most feared species on Earth and already people were trying to tranquilize him. "You will not send my baby to a fucking therapist once a week for a problem that isn't a problem. They're trying to institutionalize him. He will not be lying on the end of anybody's couch, discussing issues he doesn't have. No." She looked to Ethic. "No, Ethic." She was so upset that her voice shook. "Half the problem is that fucking white-ass school you have him in. He won't be going there anymore." She barked that shit like she had a say. "It's the end of the school year. No way should teachers be planning and communicating from year to year about how to deal with him. Maybe he's bored in class. He's super smart. Brilliant, in fact. If they aren't challenging him, of course he's distracted, of course he can't sit still. They also are not of his culture. They can't compare Eazy to the little white children, or Indian children, or Asian or whatever other type of child that they feel is the norm. Black children need to see a representation of themselves in the classroom. I bet there isn't one black teacher in the school. The upbringing is different. The tolerance. The expectation for obedience. All of it. Why didn't you call me? I swear to God I'ma beat the brakes off his fucking teacher." She was so passionate. So upset. She stared Ethic in the eyes, emotion building in her gaze, and he felt his entire soul stir. He hadn't slept right since receiving this call. Seeing her investment in his son, her uproar over his mistreatment, made him emotional.

"You're absolutely right," Carmen spoke up. "Everything you're saying is correct. I don't want to diagnose him at seven and I have no intentions of putting him on medication..."

"Good, because that's not an option," Alani said. She said it like it was her choice to make, with conviction, like she was offended that it had even been a topic of conversation...like she had birthed Eazy and they were discussing her child. She may not have birthed him, but he had certainly re-birthed her. Eazy and Bella had given her new life in one of her toughest times. She would always go to bat for them.

"I just want to be an advocate for the two of you, his parents, because teachers do tend to put this disorder on African American boys at an alarming rate. The way you interact with Eazy is perfect. Using terms like walking feet and getting him to slow down. Teach him to control his body and not be so impulsive. Make him have times of extreme focus, like reading or completing puzzles. He'll always need an outlet for the energy, if we discover this is what he suffers from. So, sports, or some type of activity where he exerts energy will help. Let's just approach this in that sense."

Alani nodded. "I like that," she said. She looked at Ethic. "Right? I'm sorry. I know this isn't my place."

She swiped away a tear that had escaped her. This was crushing her. This judgement of such a pure, little boy... this misunderstanding of his energy...an energy so rare that it was worth something. This little boy was worthy of understanding...of compassion. She wanted to kill his teacher. "They're just trying to make it seem like something's wrong with him. There's nothing wrong with him. He's perfection, Ezra."

Ethic leaned across the table and swiped at another runaway tear that rested on her face. He laced his fingers into a bawled fist and placed elbows to the table. He nodded. "Yeah, that approach sounds best."

Carmen nodded and pushed back from the table. "Well, let's stay in contact, maybe bi-weekly sessions. We'll keep it in public places, so he doesn't become institutionalized. He's too young to be seeing the inside of my office right now. It was nice to meet you, Lenika. I'm very confident that Eazy has two people who love him very much, and no matter where this goes, whether he has ADHD or not, he is going to be just fine."

"I'm really sorry about the dress and for being so rude..."

Carmen put up a hand of dismissal. "Trust me. If I had that...I would be the same way. The bill for the dress will be attached to the first statement, though," she said, with a wink. Alani smiled, and Carmen walked away.

Ethic motioned for Bella and Eazy with his hand. They came rushing back over with two, huge helpings of assorted desserts.

Alani stood. "I'm going to go, but I want to know about this part. It's important to me," she whispered. "I know we decided that we can't." She paused because she didn't want to talk about their reasons for not being together. "Just don't shut me out of this part, Ezra. I care." He stood too.

"I'll walk you out," he stated.

"No, it's fine. Stay here with them. Enjoy your dinner. Goodnight, guys." Her voice was drowned in solemn. Alani couldn't let him walk her out because she didn't know if she would be able to hold her sorrow in the entire way. Alani walked away. The distance of every step she took felt like miles. She had never loved anyone the way she loved this man. Being apart was torture. Being away from his kids…ugh…worse than death itself. She handed the valet her ticket.

"Miss, are you okay?" the young man asked. Alani nodded, but a sob escaped her.

"She's fine."

Alani sucked in air, when she felt his hand wrap around her waist.

"You're fine," he whispered, moving her hair aside to kiss the nape of her neck. She nodded. She turned to him and the tension in his face caused her to cry harder.

"I'm trying real hard to stay away from you, baby, but you got to let me know you're okay. Are you?" he asked.

She nodded and lowered her head into his chest. He kissed the top of her head, and when she lifted eyes to him, he took her lips. Alani melted. She felt this everywhere.

"Ethic, stop. We can't," she whispered, breathlessly, as she reached up to cup his face in her hands. He held onto her wrists and kissed the inside of one.

"You're like a fucking drug, Lenika," he groaned. "I want to fuck you, baby. I need to fuck you. Lenika, damn. You in this dress for another man. I could have killed him."

How she came from his words alone, she didn't know, but her body shuddered.

"Cum for me, baby," he whispered. Her eyes widened in stun, slightly, because no way should he know…How the hell did he know what had just happened with her body? He slid a finger up her inner thigh, right past those Spanx, and finessed her swollen clit, discreetly. "You're dripping." He pulled that finger back and rubbed it on his bottom lip like he was putting on ChapStick. He pulled his full lip into his mouth and sucked on her, then pulled her face to his, with aggression, bullying his Alani-flavored tongue into her mouth.

This nigga here. Whew, chile. Alani was suffocating in Ezra. Dying slowly. The most peaceful way to go. Drowning in a love so strong she didn't want to survive after him.

He released her, and she took a half step back to gather herself. The valet returned with her car and it saddened her because it meant their time had once again expired.

"You'll keep me updated about Eazy?" she asked. "We don't have to talk."

"I want to talk. I want to do more than talk. I just...I don't know how to put you first and put her first."

"How is she? Is she doing better at least?" Alani asked. "Tell me we're apart for a reason."

The doors to the restaurant clanged open and Morgan came bursting out.

"You might as well stay," Morgan shouted.

Both Alani and Ethic looked at Morgan, in shock.

"It's fine," she said, rolling her eyes. "You love him. So, stay." Morgan was so stubborn she couldn't fix her face or her tone, but she was yielding a bit and Alani was grateful. "And her dress was ugly anyway. I wouldn't have liked her either," Mo added.

Alani snickered at that and Alani handed her keys back to the valet. She walked to Ethic and he pulled her in close.

"I fucking missed the shit out of you," he groaned in her ear.

"What did you say to Alex?" she whispered.

"Told him to keep his black suit handy. He might need it soon," Ethic stated.

Alani's entire body tingled. "Stop risking niggas' lives out here," he warned. He nipped her ear with his teeth and pecked her cheek.

"Okay, I said she could stay. Don't nobody want to see all that," Morgan said. Alani blushed, and he took her hand, before leading her back inside, with her family. They were a woman and man in love, with two, small children and an unruly teenager. It didn't get more normal than that. Alani prayed it lasted.

CHAPTER 19

I just have a guttt feeling
Don't know why, I don't know what it wasss really
But the more we touch, the more, it starrrts, killing
Killing me

Ella Mai sung the story of Morgan's life, as she laid in the darkened room, shades drawn, submerged in the dark, as tears soaked the pillow she hugged tightly. She couldn't understand how she hadn't seen this coming…how she had missed the signs…how her intuition had failed to detect Messiah's lies. She needed answers. She needed her man, but her man wasn't her man anymore. He was someone she didn't know…someone who had the potential to harm her, who had planned to harm her, and that fact was rotting inside her brain. She should have been all cried out. She had been doing it for weeks, but Morgan couldn't shake this feeling. She had overdosed on Messiah, and now that he was gone, she was in withdrawal. Forcing herself to go back to the place where she knew how to make it through a twenty-four-hour period without seeing him, without touching him, or hearing his voice…it was excruciating. He was like oxygen. Without him, she would die. She was dying…slowly.

The door to her room flew open, without warning, and Aria flew into the room.

"Mo, get your ass up. We aren't doing this another day. Crying over a nigga and what not... No, ma'am! Get up!" Aria said, as she pulled the covers off Morgan.

"I can't, Aria," Morgan whispered.

"Bitch, you're pregnant, not dying. Get up. We don't even have to go anywhere special, but you're not sitting up in this room another second. Not on my watch. We can just go for a walk. Let some sun hit that ashy-ass face. You look washed," Aria pushed.

Morgan sat up, throwing her feet over the side of the bed, and closing her eyes to try to calm her queasy stomach. She licked her lips, and then folded them inside her mouth, as she took a deep breath.

"I don't know why they call this morning sickness if it lasts all day," Morgan whispered.

"Is it that bad?" Aria asked, frowning sympathetically.

"It's miserable," Morgan admitted. "I don't know. Maybe if my heart didn't hurt so bad, if I had someone here holding my hand and rubbing my feet, it wouldn't be so bad, but doing it alone..." Morgan stopped because her words were breaking, and she didn't want to cry. She had been crying for a week straight and it never made her feel any better. She had never been so broken. Even when she had lost her family, even when Raven had died... because she knew she held no blame in what had happened to them. In this scenario, she held guilt, she felt treasonous for loving Messiah. It was torture.

"I can reach out to Isa, Mo. I don't think his number's the same, but I follow him on IG. A nigga stay liking my pics and shit, but I blocked him after that snake shit Messiah pulled, but I'll take a L for the team, sis. You know he's with Messiah, so if you need me to pillow talk his ass to get to Messiah, I will. You should tell him about this baby, Morgan. This is bigger than both of you," Aria said.

"He hasn't reached out, Aria. He picked up and left town without even thinking twice. I didn't mean anything to him. He was setting my family up the entire time. My last name makes me a trophy, some kind of prize for hood niggas with bad intentions. He wanted to smear my name. He wanted to fuck up my father's legacy. It will forever be fuck him. I don't owe Messiah anything, especially not an explanation. I don't trust him. My baby will have Atkins' blood in his veins, and his family has a history of destroying mine. I'm surprised he didn't kill me when he had the chance."

"Mo..."

"Just stay out of it, Aria. I know you've got whatever you've got going on with Isa. I'm not asking you to cut that off or stay away from him. I don't care if you unblock him, just don't talk about me. My business is my business. Isa can't find out about this baby either," Mo insisted.

Aria raised her hands, surrendering, but skepticism lived in her eyes.

"And don't look at me like that. He's no victim," Morgan whispered.

"Okay, Mo, I got you. You don't want him to know. I think it's fucked up, but it's not my place to tell it," Aria said.

Morgan climbed from the bed. Reluctance filled her every step, as Aria waited patiently.

Morgan grabbed a hoodie and jean shorts and then slipped into flip flops. A quick ponytail was the remedy for her hair, before following Aria downstairs to the first floor.

The sight of Ethic laid out on the oversized couch with Alani tucked in front of him made Morgan pause. She was trying to be more understanding, when it came to Alani, but it was hard to see him this comfortable with a woman that wasn't her sister. They sat up when Morgan entered the living room and Alani pointed the remote to the TV. The volume of the movie that had been playing ceased. Morgan had never seen Ethic so relaxed in the middle of the day.

"You're up?" Alani said, in surprise, standing to her feet. "Do you feel better?"

Morgan let an extra beat linger, birthing an awkward energy in the room. She wasn't an easy win like his other children. Morgan just couldn't jump on the Alani bandwagon. She was a reminder that Raven was no longer the most important woman in Ethic's life. "Not really, but I could use some air. I'll be back later."

"Your locations on?" Ethic asked.

"They're on," Morgan responded.

"Stay out of the city," Ethic instructed. "Keep your phone nearby." Ethic pulled Alani back down onto the couch, but Alani simply sat, instead of stretching out like she had before. She didn't want to make Mo uncomfortable.

Morgan nodded. "You know what? I think I'll stay the weekend at Aria's. I'm going to pack a bag."

"Mo..." Ethic sat up.

She knew he would protest, but she was going anyway. "I need to get back to living, Ethic. I think it's time for me to go back to my place. I can take summer courses, or go to Europe, or go on tour with my friends...anything is better than sitting around here all summer crying over things nobody can change."

"You gon' do all that pregnant, Mo? I know you're used to things revolving around you, but time's up for that. You've got more than you to think about now," Ethic said.

"Yeah, I've thought about it. I don't know if that's going to work out for me. I'm not like y'all. I don't want to try to find love through mountains of pain. The two of you shouldn't even be together. All that pain. All that hurting each other, deceiving each other, and now you're lying on the couch watching a movie like none of it ever happened, but I know she still hates you. She must, because I can't ever imagine not hating Messiah. She's pretending, you're pretending, like you're better, but it's not going to get better. I'm never going to not feel this, and I don't want to have a baby with someone I'm always going to hate. I'll make the appointment. I don't need you there to hold my hand. I can do it myself, I'm not a little girl."

"Then stop acting like one, Morgan."

Everyone in the room looked at Alani in surprise. "Aria, Morgan will be out in a bit," Alani said, dismissing Aria from the house. She didn't even look at Ethic, as she continued. "Ethic, could you give us a minute?"

Ethic looked at Morgan, who appeared less than enthused about this private conversation Alani wanted to have, but he didn't know what to do. Her entire aura was entitled and rude and disrespectful. She was filled with animosity and hurt. She had always been spoiled. He had always had to pour a little extra into her to make her happy because of what he was trying to compensate for - the loss of her parents. Somehow, all that doting, all that extra, had turned her into a person with little regard for how her words and actions affected others, affected him, Alani, even Messiah. Morgan Atkins only worried about Morgan Atkins, and disappointment filled him, as he stood from the couch. His first instinct was to save her from Alani, but he trusted her to handle it. This was something Morgan needed a woman for. Something Ethic had prayed for a woman to come into their lives for; to handle these delicate moments, these difficult moods that Morgan went through; because although the circumstances varied, her reactions...her mood swings...her tantrums and acts of rebellion, were not new at all. Mo was too old to take on a motherly figure, but he hoped Alani could do what he couldn't...get through to Morgan. Ethic knew she was about to deliver some tough love. He left the room, kissing the side of Morgan's head on his way out.

"Morgan, can you sit, please?" Alani asked. She placed fingers to her temple and rubbed because she felt the headache threatening to blind her.

Morgan sighed but moved stubborn feet over to the couch, sitting beside Alani, with plenty of distance between them.

"I'm not my brother, Mo," Alani started. Morgan's entire body stiffened. "I know that's what you see when you look at me. I can't even begin to tell you how sorry I am for what he did to you. He wasn't raised like that. He knew better. I taught him better. Nannie taught him better," she whispered. "I'm sorry…so sorry. You will never know how much shame I feel over what he did to you. I can't imagine how hard that is for you, or how terrified you must have been that night. I know Messiah made you feel safe. I can tell that you're afraid without him. The Morgan I saw at the ball and at Eazy's pool party is like day and night to the girl that's in front of me right now. You had Messiah then, and he made you feel powerful because you knew he would always have your back. You don't have him now, and you're angry and hurt and broken and confused and your pieces are all spread out. You don't even know how to begin picking them up."

Morgan was silent, but the grief she stifled escaped through the tear ducts of her eyes. She was stubborn and trying to wipe them away, but they kept coming. "I know what that feels like. Ethic made me feel that way, and I made some really bad decisions out of anger, out of shame for loving someone I felt I shouldn't. My baby suffered. He died right inside of me, Mo, and I live with that…" Alani paused, because she was crying now. She cleared her throat and cleared the tears. "I live with that, Morgan. Dead babies that weigh on my soul so heavy sometimes it feels like I'm suffocating. If you don't want this baby because you're young and you don't think you're ready, that's one thing; but if you don't want it because you're angry at Messiah and you're trying to hurt him in some way, then that's selfish. It's not right. If you loved him once, you love him still; and if you make a rash decision off temporary emotions, it'll haunt you for the rest of your life. We all just want to help you, Mo. I know you're angry and you're taking it out on everyone around you, but we just want to help. Even if that means helping you raise this baby, while you finish school or go dancing around the world. We'll do that. We're here. I'm here, and I know you don't like it, but I'm not going anywhere. I can't go anywhere, Morgan, because as bad as you think our love is, it's real. It's realer than anything I've ever felt. Just like you, I love the man I'm supposed to hate, but I don't hate him. I love him with my whole soul; and if I continued to make my choices out of spite, I would be lonely right now. I would be miserable. I might even be dead, because again, just like you, I thought about ending everything. Let us help you."

Morgan sniffed and stood from the couch. She began to walk out the room but stopped and turned toward Alani.

"You know the difference between your situation and mine?" Morgan asked. "Ethic wanted you. He chased you. He could barely function, knowing that he had hurt you. He couldn't stay away. You shot him, and he still couldn't live without you. The thought of being without you ate away at him for months. Where's Messiah?"

Alani's eyes filled, as she stared at Morgan in sympathy. She had never known anyone lonelier. Morgan had a need that could only be filled by one man.

"He left me, Alani. Him being able to just up and leave, without calling me, without thinking about me, that's even worse than him being Mizan's brother. I'll never forgive him for that."

"That baby is a part of him, Morgan. You should think about if you want to get rid of the last piece of him that is still here," Alani whispered.

Morgan stood there, squaring off with Alani. She turned toward the door and paused, without looking back. "I know you're not your brother. I still see him, though, when I look at you and it's hard. Everything is just always so hard."

Morgan shook her head and then stormed out the front door. She rushed to Aria's car.

"Get me out of here," she said. Aria, her ride or die, took off, without asking one question.

CHAPTER 20

"Soooo, I was thinking, I could have my birthday party at Nannie's this year." Bella suggested.

"Nannie's?" Ethic asked, looking across the kitchen table at Bella.

"Yeah! I mean, I have friends over there," Bella explained. "If I have it all the way out here by us, they won't come. My friends here can come to the block, if they want to go. If not, oh well."

"The block, huh?" Ethic asked, snickering. "What you know about the block, baby girl?"

"That I own it, so it should be perfectly fine to have my party there, right?" Bella asked.

"Oh, *you* own it?" Alani asked, smiling.

"I meannnn, kinda, sorta, through affiliation. My parents own it, so they kind of mine too," she laughed.

Alani's heart fluttered. "I see no lies, B," she said, winking at her.

"So, can I? Like, make it a really big deal? I'm turning thirteen, Daddy. I'm a teenager. I want like a huge party," Bella said.

"We could throw a block party," Alani suggested.

Ethic swept a hand down his head, wrinkles filling his

forehead. "Can't control a block party, B. I don't know about that. If it gets out of hand..."

"It won't, Daddy, please? You already warned everybody on the street. That would be so dope! We can get a DJ and a photo booth, and I want one of those blow-up things with the Sumo suits and a henna artist...

"We can do a bounce house for the little ones on the street, right in the front yard. That way, Eazy and the other babies will be right in our line of sight. Mr. Larry can grill, and I'll do sides for the entire neighborhood, so you don't have to pay anyone to cook."

"And Super Soakers, B. You got to get water balloons and Super Soakers, so we can have a water fight!" Eazy chimed in.

"I'm not getting my hair wet, Eazy," Bella stated. "This isn't a kiddie party."

"Oh my god, a dunk tank would be the cutest, though, Bella. Like, throw a whole, little carnival," Alani added, as she placed dishes full of home-cooked food in the center of the table. It was only lunchtime, but Alani cooked three times a day. She lived in the kitchen. His kitchen was a chef's dream, and she put it to good use.

"No, that's too childish. I just want a turn up with my friends," Bella protested.

"But Daddy can be in it, B! We can dunk, Daddy!" Eazy yelled.

"Inside voice, Big Man," Alani reminded. She could see him getting excited. His little body was dancing with excitement. "Can you please grab glasses from the cabinet, Eazy?" Redirection. She needed to redirect that energy. Give him a task. Steer his focus and give him something to do with all that energy. "Putting your father in the tank is a great idea," she said to Bella. She paused to grip the back of Bella's chair and propped one hand on her hip.

"I'm not sitting in a dunk tank," Ethic stated. "I haven't even said yes. I ain't feeling it. Tell me some other options, B. I don't know about the block party."

Alani moved to the counter to grab another dish and placed it on the table. She stood behind Ethic's chair, this time, rubbing his shoulders.

"Write down all the things you want to do; okay, B? Some other ideas," she said aloud, but behind Ethic's back, she mouthed the words, "We're having a block party."

Bella smiled, as Eazy celebrated in his seat.

"We're not having a block party," Ethic stated, not even having to see Alani to know she was plotting against him.

"Who said we were?" Alani asked, as she leaned down to his ear. She kissed his neck. She nodded to the kids. "We're having a block party," she mouthed.

Ethic grabbed her, suddenly, pulling her into his lap, and Alani hollered in laughter as Eazy hopped up from his seat.

"Hey! Get off her!" Eazy said, pushing Ethic.

Ethic laughed, as Eazy tried to defend Alani. He stuck his hand in the bowl of mashed potatoes Alani had just placed on the table and smashed a handful in Eazy's face.

"Shut up, homie, this my woman," he said.

"Daddy! That was so childish," Bella hollered, snickering.

"Ethic! Get yo' damn hands out my food!" Alani shouted.

He had her sideways over his lap, like she was a child, spanking that ass so hard it stung a little bit.

"Ow! Ethic!" Alani laughed.

Eazy reached for the potatoes and tossed some at Ethic.

"Oh, y'all want war? Daddy been winning wars since '95, homie." He released Alani, but not before giving her a face full of sweet potato pie.

"Ezra!" Alani shouted. She stood, wiping filling from her eyes. He had mashed it so good in her face that she had it coming out her nose.

"War!" Eazy shouted. All four of them reached for a dish on the table and tossed it.

"Agh!" Bella shouted. "Wait! Don't get it in my hair!" She was certainly becoming a teenager. Every day, Bella grew more and more finicky about clothes and hair. Alani had even had a few lipsticks come up missing, and she was sure Bella had helped herself to them. She was blossoming before their eyes.

Laughter filled the kitchen, as they waged war across the dinner table.

"Okay, okay, man, fucking block party it is," Ethic grumbled, giving in, hands raised in surrender. He picked Eazy up and he hung sideways across his body, like a guitar, as he roughhoused with him. "Now, who's going to clean all this up?"

"You started it," Bella said. "I'm going to call my friends and tell them about my party." She hurried out of the kitchen and Ethic put Eazy down. He hightailed it out next.

"I'll order Chinese or something!" Alani shouted after them. "Get cleaned up!"

"Okay!" Bella shouted back.

"I'm not hungry!" Eazy answered.

"You're eating, Eazy!" Alani hollered.

"Aww, man!"

His reply made her laugh. Ethic looked around the kitchen. "I'll call Lily over to clean this up. You don't have to."

"Baby, this is my home. My kitchen. I'll clean it," she said. "I can keep this house just fine without Lily, Ethic. You don't have to keep paying her. I'm here now."

He pulled her into his arms, running his tongue up her neck where pie stuck to her skin.

"Lily being here gives you time to fulfill other needs," Ethic whispered. He picked her up, her ass in his hands, and put her on the kitchen table. "Cuz a nigga got needs, Lenika."

He slid between her legs and hovered over her, taking her lips.

"Ethic, I'm a mess. The kids are right upstairs, and they're awake, boy," she said, hopping up from the table and easing by him. He grabbed her hand and pulled her through the house. "What are you doing? I need to clean up..."

He pulled her into the coat closet and filled her mouth with his tongue. Alani's protests became moans, as he moved down her body. Sliding silk panties aside, he attacked her clit.

Alani was a victim of assault and she couldn't even scream. She reached out to hold onto something and brought the whole damn coatrack down, sending her crashing to the bottom of the closet. Christmas ornaments and old knickknacks came raining down around them.

She screamed, in surprise, as she landed on top of him.

Ethic laughed harder than she had ever heard him laugh, and it only caused her to giggle. He was so tickled. So easygoing, and it delighted her to see such a hard man soften so. Alani peeled herself up, sitting up in the closet. She pushed him.

"It's not funny, Ezra!" she shouted, but she couldn't stop laughing either. They were ridiculous the way they snuck kisses and feels, like teenagers, who were afraid to get caught. This time had backfired.

"Alani, are you okay?!"

Eazy's voice floated through the door and Alani adjusted her clothes before pushing open the door.

"What are you guys doing in there?" Eazy asked, as he looked at the adults in his life sitting on the floor in the closet.

"Playing hide and go get it," Ethic answered.

"Ethic!" Alani screamed, covering his mouth with one hand, to stop him from saying anything more.

"What's hide and go get it?" Eazy asked, frowning.

"Don't listen to your daddy, Big Man, come on," she said, climbing out the closet and steering him toward the kitchen.

"What is it? Did you win, Dad?" Eazy asked.

"Not yet, E, but Daddy definitely gon' get it," Ethic snickered.

"You're so horrible," Alani said, smiling, and shaking her head.

"If Daddy don't get it, ain't no block party going down," Ethic stated. "Canceling everything," he said, running his hand across his neck.

"Just give him some pie, Alani!" Bella screamed from upstairs. "Cuz I already called everybody! Eazy, get up here and let grown people be grown!"

Ethic's eyes widened, as Eazy ran by him. "Bye, Dad! Go get it!" he shouted. "Bella, what Daddy about to get?!" he asked, as he flew up the stairs.

Alani and Ethic laughed until their stomachs hurt.

"Sooo, apparently, it's time to have a talk with Bella," Alani said, eyes lifted in astonishment.

She tossed a dish towel at Ethic.

Ethic sighed a heavy sigh. "I'm about to have a 13-year-old," he said. "I don't think I'm ready for this a second time."

"Well, this time, you're not doing it alone," Alani said, eyes sparkling in pure joy, as she began to sweep the floor. They spent the evening cleaning up a mess. Even the most mundane tasks were intimate with them. With Alani and her 90's music that was a necessity whenever she cleaned, she spent an hour, scrubbing the kitchen, dancing with her man, freaking him, but not too much; Alani was an old bitch, and she didn't have Stiletto Gang stamina. If she popped that thang too hard or dropped it too low, she might not be able to bring it back up. They were the oldest 30-something-year-old couple in the world, and it felt amazing. It felt like a routine, as Ethic assisted, but mostly distracted her with the soft kisses he kept planting to the back of her neck. Their love was so pure, the hardest thing either of them had ever done, but so rewarding. They had earned it, and they relished in it - when things were going right. They hung that shit up on a nail and admired it, like it was art, because they had taken their time to perfect every detail. Ethic's phone chimed, disrupting the moment, and he pulled it from his pocket. His entire body went rigid, when he read the name on his phone.

Alani noticed his mood change, and she rounded the kitchen island, finishing the last bit of cleaning.

"Everything okay?" she asked.

Ethic slid his phone in his pocket.

"Everything's fine. I just need to step out for a little bit, go handle something," he stated.

"Is this something female?" she asked, brow bent. She knew it was mistrust from her past causing her to question him. His body language knocked on the door to her intuition and Alani wasn't the type to be passive about her shit.

"You don't got to worry about basic nigga shit with me. You fucking with the plug, ain't nothing boyish about my intentions with you. We don't ask each other shit like that. If we even need to ask questions like that, we shouldn't be doing this."

Alani paused, and her hand hit her hip, as she analyzed him. Any other man and she would have called bullshit and accused them of deflection, but Ethic was right. He was her exception. Every rule she had ever set for herself, he broke. He kissed her. A peck. "Wait up for me?" he asked.

She nodded and folded the dish towel and hung it from the faucet. "Of course," she said. "I'm gonna go get cleaned up. You sure you're okay?"

"I'm good. I need to shower and then step out for a minute. I won't be late. Is that cool?" he asked.

"Of course," she answered. "We'll be here."

"So many men take shit like that for granted. A woman that's home with his kids…that's happy to be home, taking care of his kids. Someone faithful. Loyal. I never will. I want you to know that. I ain't a perfect man, but I'ma put my all into giving you everything you need. I took a lot from you, baby. I just want to give you something real. Something true."

Alani couldn't meet his gaze because her eyes were betraying her. She hated when he talked about it…where they had started…what she'd lost… it was a sensitive subject for her. It always made her feel guilty. Foolish. Like she was putting a man over her child, and Alani wasn't the type of woman to ever do that. She knew women like that. She had judged women like that, and now here she was in his bed, loving someone who should have been unlovable. Alani struggled so badly with that. It weighed on her every second of every day, but she couldn't help how she felt. She couldn't not be here. She couldn't un-love Ezra. She had tried, and it had almost killed her. Now, nothing mattered but this, and she knew it was selfish to feel this way, to be this way; but if she couldn't have him, what would she have? He was water. Without him, nothing else could function. Her heart, her lungs, her brain, it would all just dry out. She would die, and Alani wanted to live. She wanted to have food fights with his kids, get fucked on countertops, and suck dick in closets. She wanted to do yoga with him, and restore neighborhoods, and tame wild horses. Alani wanted life with him - an entire life. She wanted to create memories that outweighed the horrific event that had brought them together. She would never forget it, could never, because her daughter was rooted in her womb. She could still remember the feel of her kicks from the inside, but Ethic was there too. In her womb. Through Love. She felt those kicks too, so she was at an impasse. Stuck in Ethic Land, with Mr. Okafor.

"This is real," Alani whispered, as he closed the small distance. He towered over her, taking her face in his palms, stroking her skin with his thumbs. Alani's heart pounded, and she was almost afraid to look up at him. He pinched her chin and tilted it, forcing her eyes to meet his. Staring in his eyes felt like an orgasm. All types of shit detonated within her. This type of love couldn't be healthy. It was the kind that wouldn't allow her to ever witness him giving the same thing to another. She was a prisoner. Those eyes on her, penetrating her, were like chains. She couldn't even breathe until he reminded her to.

"Exhale, Lenika," he whispered.

Alani blushed, as she sighed. The type of power he had over her was terrifying. Thank God he was a real man, a whole man, a loving man, because if he was abusive in the slightest way, she would be a victim because there was no escaping this.

Ethic licked his lips, not letting up on his stare. She saw the amusement in his eyes.

"You like that you make me feel like this? Don't you?" she whispered. Her neck rolled right, and she grabbed the hand he caressed her face with, kissing it and closing her eyes to absorb the moment.

"I like that you allow me to make you feel this. I dig the vulnerability. You weren't always this way. I had to earn it. A nigga earned it, so I'ma spend it."

"I love you so much. I can't even explain. I don't even like saying it because it doesn't describe how I feel. Like, everyone says they love someone. It's a bunch of people saying it and not meaning it, which dilutes the purpose of those three words. How I feel about you isn't diluted, it's potent. It's more than what any woman has ever felt for any man. It's…"

"It's what?" Ethic asked.

"I don't know," Alani whispered, laughing a little.

"You know. What is it?" he asked. "You think it's devilish."

Ethic knew. He knew he was drawn to her in ways that made it unholy. Ways that made him idolize her. Made it a sin because she was worshipped by him. He didn't care, but he knew she did.

"Nooo," she whispered. "Baby, no" she answered, closing her eyes and pressing into him, so that their noses touched. Her hands caressed the back of his neck. They fit together like puzzle pieces. Like his face had been designed by a grand architect to merge with hers.

"It's like you *are* me. Like we're the same person. Like we share the same thoughts. Sometimes, you speak, and I swear you've pulled the words out my head. When you're asleep at night, you breathe like me, like to the same rhythm. Like, even now. My stomach hurts a little bit because I know your shit is tore up because I fried the chicken instead of baking it. It's like I feel everything you feel. Like I'm you. Loving you is teaching me to love me. Like I love myself more because I love you; and you clearly love me, so how can I not love me? I don't know," she said, shrugging, getting frustrated because she knew she was rambling. "I probably sound crazy, but I am you."

"And me you, Lenika," he whispered. He knew exactly what she felt. The explanation wasn't even needed. "I am you."

Ethic walked into the diner and scanned the restaurant, before deciding on a booth in the corner, all the way to the back. He slid into the seat and a waitress approached.

"Welcome, handsome," she greeted.

"Thanks. Can I just get a coffee, black, no sugar," he ordered.

"That's it?"

"That's it," Ethic confirmed. The woman grabbed a coffee cup from the bar and snatched the pot of coffee up and poured him a cup before walking away.

"You okay, darling?" She asked the woman sitting directly behind Ethic,

"Perfect, thank you," the woman replied. They were back to back and her sweet voice made Ethic scoff.

"You really should eat something, Ethic. Or is that new girlfriend of yours filling you up quite nicely?" the woman asked.

Amusement played on Ethic's face. "She never sends me out the house without the taste of something good on my tongue," he stated.

"Smart girl," she said, smiling wide. "Hi, Ethic."

"Zya Miller, theeee Zya Miller," Ethic said. He never turned around and neither did she. To anybody watching, they were just two strangers eating alone.

"I hear you're really happy these days," Zya said. "Heard she's a little plain, but then again, my source is a little extra, so I guess her perception isn't always reality."

Ethic knew YaYa had gotten word back to Zya about Alani. He chuckled, knowing YaYa was bothered by Alani.

"She's not up for discussion," Ethic answered. "But if she was, I'd tell you she's the shit niggas dream about. Much too good for me."

"You don't give yourself enough credit, Ethic," Zya answered.

"You got something for me?" he asked.

"I have nothing. I've checked every state database, put

ears to every hood in Michigan, and even searched morgue records in every metropolitan area in this shitty-ass state. He's like a ghost, Ethic. Messiah Williams almost doesn't exist. I did find something very interesting, though."

"What's that?"

"You said he and Mizan were brothers, right?" she shot back.

"That was the purpose of his entire plot. To avenge his brother's death and his father's," Ethic said.

"Only he isn't Mizan's brother," Zya said. "Mizan's father isn't Bookie. Bookie was his lover," Zya informed.

"Fuck you just say to me?" Ethic asked.

"Bookie's name is not on his birth certificate, Ethic. I also have hotel footage showing they were intimate. Bookie might have started off molesting Mizan. I believe there was a relationship between Bookie and Mizan's mother, at a point. There are pictures to support that. It probably started as abuse, but the photos I have of Bookie and Mizan... The relationship continued well into adulthood for Mizan."

"When he was with Raven?" Ethic asked.

"I believe so," Zya confirmed.

So many haunting thoughts ran rampant in his mind. So much heartache over the ways Mizan had abused Raven. He had exposed her to more than heartache. He had exposed her sexually. If Mizan was still active with Bookie and Bookie was molesting Messiah, there was no telling what other men Bookie had been with. Ethic was sick. His poor Raven. He carried so much blame on his shoulders because he should have never left town without her all those years ago. He should have put Mizan down and taken

Raven and Morgan with him much sooner than he had. She would still be alive if he had.

"And Messiah? How is he tied up in this?" Ethic asked.

"He doesn't know that Mizan isn't Bookie's son. That's the only thing I can gather. Word is, Mizan used to beat Messiah real bad. I'm not sure if Mizan abused him sexually, but there are files from social workers. Bruises, broken bones, a busted spleen, cracked ribs. My sources say those beatings came from Mizan, and this is just speculation, but I think Bookie was controlling Mizan. He knew Messiah was running to Mizan for help and Mizan was keeping Messiah from telling. It's really fucking sick."

Ethic was seeing red. Both men were dead now, at his hand, but somehow it didn't seem like enough.

"So, Messiah's riding for a nigga that's not even his bloodline and a father that abused him?" Ethic asked.

"It's one of the worst stories of manipulation I've ever heard, Ethic. That boy never had a chance. He probably wishes you had just put a bullet in his head. The suffering he must have survived..." Zya paused. "Let's just say I think he's been through enough."

"And now I can't fucking find him. I taught him how to keep men off his scent and now I can't sniff him out. Morgan's carrying his baby. I need to bring him back here," Ethic stated. "He's going to miss the birth of something that will make every single moment of his past no longer matter. It'll no longer shape who he thinks he is. Becoming a father will change him," Ethic stated.

“I’m sorry I couldn’t be more helpful,” Zya said, standing. “If I hear anything about Messiah’s whereabouts, I’ll make sure I let you know. It’s always good seeing you, Ethic. That girl you got at home… She’s lifted a weight off you. I saw it when you walked through the door. I’m relieved about that. I worry about you. Until next time, handsome.”

She stood, and Ethic didn’t turn around until he heard the chime of the bell above the door. By the time his eyes searched for her, she was gone. It was like she had never actually come at all, but the feeling of dread and regret that swirled in him reminded him that she had…and with her, she had brought a truth so ugly, it was impossible to forget. He could only imagine how hard it was for Messiah to live with. A hurt-filled boy had transformed into a dangerous man. Ethic could relate.

CHAPTER 21

What is this? A tailgate?" Mo asked, as they pulled onto campus. Every fraternity and sorority was out in full effect, repping their sets. The entire quad was alive, the parking lot too, and Morgan climbed from the car in curiosity.

She had missed this vibe. She had been so wrapped up in Messiah that she often ran off campus as soon as classes were over, hopping into his snow-white BMW and putting miles of highway between her and the action. She had loved that. The seclusion, the intimacy of the world he had created for her. It had been just the two of them in a world of their own. She was trapped behind walls Messiah had built around their love. She had understood the privacy, the need to connect in secret; but now he was gone, and she was behind those walls alone…they felt like a prison.

"Nah, a fundraiser. The Greek counsel is trying to raise money for the Flint Water Crisis," Aria added. "Stiletto Gang isn't Greek, but we bought a table."

The pair climbed out the car and Morgan felt sadness course through her. She had given all this up. The carefree lifestyle of a college student. She was pregnant by a man who had gotten ghost on her and she felt foolish. "Almost every student organization on campus is supporting, trying to raise funds."

She walked through the crowd and up to their table.

"BITCH! Where have you been?" White Boy Nick shouted, in excitement, as soon as he laid eyes on her.

It was hard to be somber around him.

"I'm around," she said, with a small smile.

"You dancing?" he asked. "We live-streaming it and telling people to donate if they like it."

Morgan shook her head. "Nah, I ain't feeling too good," Morgan lied.

"Come on, Mo. All of us combined could stream a dance and won't get the donations you would. Just do half a song," Nick said.

Morgan mugged him with the full bitch face, but she said, "Fine." She hoped she didn't throw up. Morning sickness had been insufferable. She handed Nick her phone.

"You not gon' take your hoodie off?" he asked.

"Look, I can just say no," Morgan said, losing patience. No way could she lift her shirt. It was like, now that she knew she was pregnant, what she had assumed was thickness, now looked like pregnancy weight to her.

"Okay, okay," Nick said. "So sensitive."

Aria laughed. "You sure you're good?" she asked.

Morgan nodded. "Yeah, come on, go live," Mo said.

"Yo, it's your boy, White Boy Nick, taking over Mo Money's Instagram account. We're live at the Fli City fundraiser at MSU, repping for Stiletto Gang. Mo is about to show out for y'all. If you like what you see, click the link in the bio to donate. All funds will go toward the residents of Flint, suffering from the Flint Water Crisis," he said.

Aria pressed play on the Beats Pill.

Let me see it (Let me see it)
Let me see it (Let me see it)
Let me see it (Let me see it)
Bend over, let me see it

Messiah smirked, as Instagram live-streamed in front of him. Morgan stayed showing the fuck out and his jealousy seared him.

I see you living, shorty. Wit' ya fast-ass, he thought, as he watched Morgan on his phone screen. He sat back in the leather chair and shook his head, watching the crowd around Mo go crazy in excitement. She was a star. She always had been, and he was missing her shine. Sadness squeezed at his heart because he knew he would never see her again. He couldn't go back. Ethic wasn't even his main concern, although a concern, but he just couldn't face Mo. He had told so many lies, kept so many secrets. He knew she was hurt… damaged by him, and Messiah would die with that on his heart. Her disappointment.

"If you just tell her, you won't have to stalk her on IG."

Messiah clicked out of the video and placed irritated eyes on Bleu.

"Nigga, don't look at me like that," she said, with a raised eyebrow. "You know it's true. I'm the only one who knows. Isa and Ahmeek don't even know. Ethic doesn't know. This is a heavy secret to keep, Messiah. You need people here with you. It's getting bad, Messiah. Where is Meek and Isa?"

"Meek's in Michigan, overseeing the business there. We got money up at the school that need collecting. Isa's collecting the bread in Chicago. The money don't stop just because I can't get to it. They still conducting business as usual."

"Meek's at Michigan State? Why don't you just call him and have him bring Morgan here," Bleu argued. "You know she'll come. She'll be pissed, but she'll come."

"Because I don't want her to see me like this, Bleu. Hooked up to fucking IV's and radiation and shit," Messiah barked. "Hair falling out. I'm dropping weight because of this shit." He motioned to the tube running into his right arm, and his face was riddled with anger. "I'm not letting the girl I love watch me die. Meek either. Isa ass either. This is weak. Nobody respects you when you're hooked up to this shit. Nobody fears you. I don't want nobody to see this shit," Messiah said.

"You're naming people who never feared you, Messiah. They love you. We all love you, and they'll be here for you through this," Bleu said, pleading with him to see things her way. "Especially, Morgan."

"Don't say her name no more, B. I don't want her here. You're all I got now. I understand, if you don't want to watch it either. I'm good. I can do it alone."

Bleu's lip quivered, as she reached for Messiah's hand. This was their date. Once a month had turned to twice a week. Bleu was making the drive, as often as she could, because she didn't want him to be alone. Lunch, a game of Monopoly, and a side of chemotherapy with radiation treatments for dessert. It was the date that she would make sure she never missed because it was his last chance at staying alive. Their one escape to the beach had passed them by, as if it had never happened at all. When the sun came up the next morning, they didn't speak of it again. It was like a joint dream they had shared; and when it was over, it had been wiped from their memory. Bleu didn't mention it and neither did he. They fell right back into their normal routine.

"This was a bad-ass Christmas gift, B. Fucking cancer treatment," Messiah mumbled.

"It's better than not doing anything," Bleu said. "It's the best treatment in the Midwest, these are the very best doctors, Messiah. I'm glad you finally accepted it."

"I'ma get your ass a vacuum for Christmas, or a washing machine, some real bullshit, because that's what this is… bullshit. Even if it works… what kind of life I got left? The shit that might keep me alive stops me from making life, from making babies, B. The fucking bullshit makes you sterile. As a matter of fact, I'm getting your ass a fucking mammogram for Christmas…this bullshit," Messiah snapped. She could see the anger in him. He was so angry that he was dying. Lymphoma. When he had first found out about his diagnosis, he had been fine with dying. He had been fine with his days being numbered, until Mo. Morgan had made him want to live. Morgan had made him want to grow old, and now he was livid with everyone because it was unlikely that he would. As the days crept into weeks, and weeks crept into months, he felt it more and more. Her absence and his departure. His body was breaking down a bit more each day.

"It could help, Messiah. Just keep trying. You promised," she whispered. "I made you a promise that I would stay clean and I've kept it. I need you to keep your word."

Messiah's jaw locked in emotion and he sniffed away devastation, as he looked back to his phone screen.

"Pretty-ass," he mumbled, as he hit like. It was the first time he'd ever liked one of her posts on social media, but the account he used, MURDERKING810, wasn't an account she could trace. His profile pic was a butterfly because that's what Morgan was to him. Her sister had been a moth; destructive, and fated for disaster, fated to fly into a flame. Morgan was different. She would fly, but she would fly free, floating through life, from experience to experience, letting everyone admire her beauty from the bottom because she would always be on top. A queen on her throne. Soaring high. A fucking butterfly.

He squeezed the bridge of his nose, swiping a tear that was trying to turn him into a bitch.

"Yo, B. You'll tell her? After it's over? That I loved her. You'll tell her, right? You'll make sure she knows?" he asked. He repeated this to her daily.

"Messiah, stop talking like..."

The look he gave her shut Bleu right up.

"Yes, Messiah. I'll make sure she knows." Bleu went into her handbag and pulled out her journal. She handed it to Messiah. "Why don't you just write it down. What *you* want to say to her. You're going to hurt her, Messiah. She won't understand. She already doesn't understand why you've done what you've done. She should hear it from you. In your words. Write it down and I'll make sure she gets it when…" Bleu's words broke, and her lip quivered. "She'll want to hear it from you." She sat the journal on the stand beside his chair.

Messiah nodded and leaned his head back against the leather chair, closing his eyes, with images of Morgan playing in his head.

CHAPTER 22

Morgan smiled on the outside, trying her hardest to blend in and make her happiness seem believable. The sting that threatened her eyes and the slight haze in them was hard to stop. Everything was forced. Her smile, her laugh, even the dancing. It all took so much cffort.

She stood and tucked her hands into the front of her hoodie. "I'm gonna go," she said.

"What? Mo? Come on?" Aria said. "You're supposed to be having fun. The fresh air is good for you."

"I came," Morgan said, holding up both hands and shrugging. "That should count for something. My place isn't too far from here. I'm going to just walk."

"Girl, I'll take you," Aria stated, grabbing her bag.

Morgan shook her head. "No. I just need some space, boo. I'm fine."

Aria gave her a worried look, a skeptical look, the same look that Ethic and Alani, even Bella, had been giving her for weeks. Everyone was just waiting for her to do something crazy, again. It was overwhelming, it was embarrassing. "I'll call you."

Morgan flipped the hoodie over her head and headed

across campus. She was halfway to her place, when she heard the car horn beep behind her. Morgan turned to find Bash's Jeep slowing to a stop. She halted, as he rolled down his window.

"Hey, Morgan! Can I take you somewhere?" he asked.

"I'm just up the block," she said.

"Hop in, I'll drive you anyway," he offered.

Morgan sighed and walked over to his car and climbed in.

Bash pulled away from the curb. "I'm about a mile down. The apartments will be on your right-hand side," Morgan said. "Thanks."

"You look good. It's been a minute since you've been around," Bash said.

"I've been busy," Morgan answered, as she looked out her window.

"You look sad. It's a shame."

Morgan turned her head toward him. "What do you want from me, Bash?" Her eyes were slits of suspicion, as she waited for a response. "I mean, you have to want something. All men want something. They're never interested for the reasons they say they are. They lie their way in, and then get what they want, and leave me in pieces. So, just be straight up with me. You want to fuck me? You want to date me? What do you want? Let's just cut to the chase, because I really don't feel like doing this dance with anyone else."

"I'd like to marry you, Morgan Atkins," Bash said, as he gripped the steering wheel with one hand and glanced at her. "One day, I'd very much like to do that," he said.

She scoffed and shook her head. "You don't even know me, Bash."

"You don't seem to be interested in the good guys right now. You're young. You're into the bad boy thing. When he breaks your heart..."

"He already did," Morgan whispered, looking back out the window. "So, what? This is the part where you swoop in? Make me feel better? Become my man?" Morgan asked. The car stopped in front of her building. "Because if I can't have *that* man, I don't want no man. If you not *that* man, you're not even a man to me. You're a boy, because nobody is man enough to measure up to him. So, just don't...don't play defense and try to get the rebound. I'm not the same girl you met in philosophy class, Bash. I would take your soul just because I can."

Bash scoffed. "You should miss that girl from philosophy class. The one who believed in love. She was dope."

Morgan pushed open the car door, then shut it, and walked up the stairs to her place. When she was tucked safely inside, she removed her clothes and pulled open the drawer where Messiah's belongings were housed. She took out a basketball jersey and slipped it onto her frame, and then grabbed a bottle of his cologne and sprayed it on her wrists. She climbed into bed, pulled the covers up to her chin, and with only his scent to comfort her, she cried herself to sleep.

CHAPTER 23

Bella felt the vibration of her phone beneath her pillow. She groaned, as she rolled over with it in her hand.

Bella's eyes could barely focus on the screen, it was so bright. The house was still but she could smell the scent of coffee. Lily had arrived for her shift and it was always the first thing she did every morning.

Henny
You coming to the hood today?

Bella frowned and sat up in bed.

Bella
If you're going to text me this early, that's not the first thing you should send.

Bella saw bubbles dance on her screen and then stop. She waited a minute and rolled her eyes, before putting her phone face down on her nightstand. She laid back down. The phone vibrated against the wood. She snatched it up, and when she opened her messages, she saw a video. She grabbed her headphones and connected the Bluetooth, before pressing play.

Can we tallkkkkk for minute? Girl, I want to know your nameee
Can we tallllkkkkkkk for a minute? Girl, I want to know your nameee

Bella's attitude disappeared, as she watched the video of Hendrix singing his heart out. Flutters made her heart feel like it would beat out of her chest. She had never seen a boy cuter. Hendrix was rugged and thuggin'. She would have never expected him to be able to sing. Rap, maybe, because what boy from the hood didn't think he could rap? The singing was a pleasant surprise; and if Bella hadn't wanted him before, she did now. Bella's smile was a mile wide across her pretty face, as the sound of his adolescent tone filled her ears. He was amazing, and he had Bella from the moment he had taken that potato chip off her plate.

Bella

I don't know that song, but I love it.

Henny

How don't you know that? Every ghetto mama played that song every Saturday night, while playing Spades. It's a classic.

Bella

Never heard it. Sing something I know.

There was another long pause and Bella waited; this time, patiently. The smile never left her face. When the video came through, she pressed play.

Yoooo, tell me, fellas, have you seen her
It was about five minutes agoooo
When I seen the hottest chick that a youngin' ever seen beforeeee

Her entire heart ached, as he crooned to her. Bella loved Chris Brown. She had written down every lyric to every, single hit song he had ever made. There were posters of him all over her room, and she wondered how Hendrix knew that this song was her favorite.

Bella replayed the video twice, before typing her response.

Bella

You should have never let me know you could sing. I'll want a song every day. LOL.

Henny

LOL. I got you. Now, you coming through the hood or what?

Bella

I can't today. I have cheerleading tryouts for the Fall. That'll be all day. I'll try to get Alani to bring me tomorrow.

Hendrix didn't answer, and after a few minutes of waiting, she knew he wasn't going to. Bella saved the video and then logged into YouTube and posted a video of the cover of the song to her account. Her father didn't check her YouTube, so she didn't worry about him seeing it, but Hendrix was too good not to share.

Eazy pushed open her bedroom door.

"Knock, Eazy!" She shouted.

"Daddy said, as long as he's paying the bills, I don't have to knock!" Eazy said, as he ran to her bed and jumped in beside her. "Who's that?" he asked, looking at her phone screen. Bella clicked out of it.

"Mind your business, Eazy," she stated. She kicked out of the covers and traveled across her bedroom.

"Hey! Who is that guy?!" Eazy shouted after her.

"What guy, Big Man?"

Bella's blood froze in her veins, when she saw her father step into the room.

"Nobody, Daddy," she lied. "Just a guy who does covers online. I was listening to them and Eazy wanted to see."

Ethic kissed the top of Bella's head and then rustled Eazy's, before turning toward his room.

"Lenika's not feeling well," he said. "Don't wake her. Lily will take you to cheer tryouts. I'm going to go check on Mo."

"K," Bella answered, tucking her phone in the pocket of her pajama pants. She felt it vibrate and her heart skipped a beat. "Hey, Daddy, can I go to Nannie's after? I want to show Lyric and them my uniform."

"You haven't made the team yet, B," Ethic said, chuckling.

"Daddy, I'm gonna make the team," she answered. Bella wasn't short on confidence. There wasn't much that intimidated her.

"I'll call her to see if she's busy. If not, I'll tell Lily to drop you off afterwards," he said. "I love you. Good luck."

"Big Man, you want to roll with me? Or stick with B?" Ethic asked. "Lenika isn't up for a lot of roughhousing today."

"I want to go with you," Eazy answered.

"What's wrong with her?" Bella asked.

"She just says she's ill, B. I want her to rest," Ethic answered. "Call me and let me know how tryouts go."

When Ethic was out of sight, Bella pushed Eazy hard. "Stay out of my room!" she shouted, slamming her door. She opened the message. A selfie of Hendrix, sneering, gold grill on his bottom row and straight whites, smiling at her at the top. Bella swooned. She had never felt like this about anyone before, but she knew better than to let it show. She wasn't only hiding the feeling from her father, but from Hendrix as well. He'd never know how much she lost it when he looked at her. She had watched Morgan over the years. She was always the one to love hardest, and in return, she hurt the most. Bella would make sure that she had the upper hand in everything. Her friendships. With boys. She would never put herself in a position to break, if someone walked away from her. So, instead of putting a heart on the picture like she wanted to, she simply put her phone on DND, limiting Hendrix's ability to contact her for the rest of the day. She needed to focus. She had tryouts; and only when she was ready to extend her attention would she respond.

Alani laid in the darkness, hugging the pillow tightly, eyes clenched so tightly, even her tears couldn't escape, as she listened to the world outside the bedroom door. Eazy's voice brought so much emotion out of her that Alani had to fold her lips in to catch the sobs that were threatening her. Bella's laughs and Ethic's instructions were next. They were hers. Her new family. Her new normal, and they had no idea that she was dying inside this room. She just wanted them to leave…to hurry and walk out of the door, to leave her behind, and drive away, but she knew that he would double-back. She knew Ethic wouldn't cross the threshold of his castle without coming back to check on his queen. She wasn't even surprised when she heard the door creak open.

"Hey, I brought you some soup, baby," he whispered. His tone. Concerned. Caring. As if he was taking care of one the kids instead of a grown woman.

"I don't want it, Ethic," she whispered. "I'm fine."

Ethic sat the tray down on the nightstand, and then got on his knees beside the bed. He stroked her hair, and still Alani didn't move, didn't look at him. If she opened her eyes, she would bawl.

"Breathe," he whispered.

She didn't even realize she hadn't been, until he reminded her to.

"What hurts, Lenika? It's like I feel the shit but don't know what's wrong. You got to tell me, so I can make it better," he said. The strokes to her hair were so light and comforting. She wanted him to stay. Wanted to tell him what hurt, but she couldn't.

"I just want to rest. I just don't feel good, Ethic. I'll be okay. I just need a few hours alone," she whispered.

Ethic felt something stir in him. Her voice quivered, pulling at him.

"Look at me," he said.

"I can't, Ethic, please, just leave," she whispered. "I'm not mad at you. We're okay. The sun just hurts. I have the worst headache, baby. I just want to keep my eyes closed and go back to sleep."

She felt him kiss her lips, and she wanted to pull him under the covers with her and cry on his chest. "Feel better. I'll try to make it quick. If you need anything, you call. I'll come home," he promised.

"Okay," she whispered.

She felt him, as he departed. She felt his love getting farther and farther away. She waited until the entire house was still, until she was sure that everyone was gone, before she opened her eyes. Her cheeks wet instantly, as emotion flooded her. Alani placed bare toes to wood and lifted out of the bed, dreading each step, as she leaked blood across the floor.

She sobbed, as she held onto the corner of the dresser, steadying weak legs, as she doubled over in pain. A miscarriage. Another one. Alani knew exactly what it was, the moment she'd opened her eyes when Ethic touched her that morning. She hadn't even realized she was pregnant. She hadn't missed a period, but there was no mistaking this pain. She had been through this too many times not to know. She was losing life. Bit by bit. Blood drop by blood drop. She was losing another child.

The pain jolted through her like lightning and Alani's body jerked, as she gripped the wood. She hurried to the bathroom and sat on the toilet.

Alani was a broken woman. Ethic knew about the parts of her that needed repair. Her heart and soul were already tarnished in his eyes. She couldn't tell him that her body was useless as well. They had already lost so much. Love had been her fault. *If he finds out I can't replace Love, he'll never forgive me. He won't want me.*

Alani felt like half of a woman. What was a woman good for, if not to create life? If not to renew life? Recycle the Earth? Alani was damaged, and she could never let Ethic know how much. He deserved so much more than she could give him, and she would try to make up for it in every other way. Alani had been through this so many times, she didn't even need a doctor. She couldn't have been that far along. She would put this in the back of her mind, with her daughter, with Love, with the three miscarriages she had been through before, behind the bad memories of her mother, next to the devastating abandonment of her father. Alani had an entire history of hurt to hide this one behind. She only hoped Ethic never discovered it, because they couldn't survive anymore losses.

Threw away your love letters... Iiii
Thought it'd make me feel better... Iiiii
Finally got you out my bed, but Iii, still can't get you out my head

Morgan sat, Indian-style, at the foot of her bed, scrolling through old messages in her phone. It was mind-blowing to her that all she had left of the man she loved was old words he'd left behind.

Messiah

I know this shit sounds crazy, shorty, but you make me want to just drop bodies out here. Just kill niggas before they even get the opportunity to step to you. I'm not normal, Mo. Over you, I go crazy every time.

Messiah

I love you even when it feels like I don't. That'll always be true.

Messiah

I bet you pretty than a mu'fucka right now.

Messiah

A nigga hungry, shorty. Come put that shit on my plate. I'm outside.

Messiah

I'm high as fuck, shorty, but I'm just thinking. You're bad for me, Mo. I ain't cried in a long time. Since I was a kid. Ain't been a victim since then, shorty. 'Til you. I'm your victim, Morgan, cuz you're killing me, and when you're there and I'm here, a nigga cry. You're fucking me up, Mo. I ain't even the same nigga no more because of you. I just want to get the shit right, but I'm so fucking wrong. Ain't shit good about me but you.

Morgan went through deleting every, single one, but it didn't matter, because she remembered the words by heart. There were hundreds more. In her thread. Fossils of the love Messiah had left behind. Relics of what she had thought would last forever. It would take her days to delete them all. The way her heart ached every time one disappeared, she knew she didn't want to delete them at all. His words, reading them, seeing them, was all she had left. She dialed his number. She didn't know why she was even trying, because the calls always went to voicemail and the box was full. This time was no different. It ate away at her, each time. To her surprise, she didn't cry. She was sick, but she could control it. She was learning to deal with pain… to compartmentalize it so it didn't swallow her whole. She never thought he would be the one to do it, to make her resilient. He was supposed to be the one she could be vulnerable for; instead, he was hardening her. Making her angry and bitter and cold…so unlike the young woman he had claimed to love. She called, again. She tried to stop herself, but she called, again.

Her breath caught in her chest, when the call connected after one ring.

"Messiah?" she called his name like she was injured, like she was so weak she could barely say it. "Ssiah, please. I miss you. Come home. Just come back. I don't care about anything else but you. Come home, Messiah."

"Yo, that ass looking a'ight today…"

Morgan's stomach plummeted, as she pulled back to look at the phone. He hadn't meant to answer. He wasn't even on the other end, but Morgan heard him. His voice. It was the closest she'd been to him in months. *Is he with someone else?* Morgan could barely breathe.

"Messiah!"

"Look back at it, boy." She heard the soft voice and there was laughter in the woman's tone.

"I'm just saying, you getting thick as fuck. Waist slim, ass fat. Whatever you doing, keep doing exactly that."

Morgan was sick.

He's with someone else. He's with some other bitch and I'm here pregnant with his baby!

Morgan couldn't breathe. She was so shattered. How could he just move on? How could he not call her? She was too hurt to hang up the phone, because she knew she might not ever hear his voice again. So, she listened. She closed her eyes and listened to the voice of the man she loved.

"A nigga hate sharing his space but you ain't so bad. I can get used to you."

Morgan died a little more with every word Messiah spoke. She heard the line go silent, and then she heard breathing, heavy breathing, like it was close to the phone.

"Messiah?"

She heard his breath catch.

"Come back to me," she whispered.

There was a long moment of silence.

CLICK.

She blinked away her stun, as her body went numb. She wondered if Messiah realized that his love was tied to her self-worth. Every time he re-injured her, Morgan wanted to stop breathing. *I'm going to die without him. I don't even want to do this, if he isn't here. Any of it. He's killing me. This will kill me.*

"Aghhh!" Morgan screamed, as she tossed her phone across the room, causing it to break against the wall. Messiah was driving her crazy. Her hormones were all over the place. The baby, the heartbreak, the loneliness, the abandonment, it was all too much. Her bottom lip trembled, and Morgan covered her mouth with both hands to quiet her cries. He hadn't said one word, but his soul screamed to her. It had been so loud, so potent. He was a drug. She was addicted to his connection, yet she had never felt so disconnected. Like, they hadn't paid the bill and service had been revoked. She was suffering immensely. *I can't take this. I can't. I can't. I can't do this.* Morgan stood and rushed to the bathroom, snatching open her medicine cabinet. Shaky hands knocked things out of place, until she came across a razor. She cracked the plastic from around the blade and then stared at the blade. She closed her eyes.

"Love yourself so much you don't let another person come short ever again."

"I am woman. My crown is not his to repossess."

Morgan repeated the mantras, as she cried. Ethic had told her. Nyair had told her. She knew how to survive without Messiah. She was in pieces, but they were beautiful. She remembered. She was trying her hardest to believe it. "I don't need him. I don't. I don't." She whispered the affirmations, desperately, as she held the blade tightly in one hand. "Love yourself, love yourself. Love yourself. He can't take my crown. Love yourself, love yourself more than you love him. Love yourself. Don't do this. Love yourself. I am woman." Morgan was trembling. Her fingers opened, and the blade fell to the floor.

She leaned forward over the sink and vomited, sobbing, as she gripped the edges of the sink.

The knock at her door drew her to it like a magnet, because she was grateful for the interruption. She needed whoever was on the other side. She needed eyes on her so that she wouldn't let the burden overwhelm her again. Morgan could hear her heart pounding in her ears and her insides revolted, as she made her way to the door. As soon as she pulled it open, the sight of Ethic caused her to sob harder. She didn't know where he had come from or why, but the relief she felt flooded her. He had to have felt her. He had to have known she needed him. Like CPR, he revived her, because Morgan couldn't guarantee that she would have been able to breathe on her own after hearing Messiah's voice.

"He's never coming back for us. I'm here with his baby and he doesn't want me," she cried.

Eazy stood next to Ethic's side.

"I want you, Mo, and the baby. I won't ever leave," Eazy said, wrapping his arms around Morgan's waist. They stood there. The three of them, embracing, as Ethic kissed the top of Mo's head and Eazy rubbed her barely-there baby bump. Morgan fell apart in the arms of her family. She wished she could see solace in Messiah, but he wasn't coming back. It seemed that he was determined to make her suffer, and all she wanted to know was why, because even through all the pain, Morgan still loved him so.

"You okay over there, roomie?"

Messiah looked over at the seventy-year-old woman who occupied the bed next to his. His face frowned, in devastation, and his heart ached, as he stared at Morgan's number on his screen. He had been lying on his phone and mistakenly answered her call. His name on her lips. Messiah. Those zz's. They cut through him like glass.

"I'm good," he whispered. His words didn't match his tone. His entire temperament had changed. The old woman's room had flooded, and she had been put in his private room for a few days. She had been like a breath of fresh air, joking, and talking with him all hours of the day. She was good company and he had enjoyed soaking up her wisdom, but after hearing Morgan's voice, he just wanted to be alone. *Why the fuck you hang up on her?* He scolded himself. Fear had stopped him from speaking. It had been so long since they had talked, he didn't know what to say. Casualties didn't seem appropriate. Morgan would want an explanation and Messiah didn't want to tell more lies. The truth he could never give. He was afraid to tell her his truth. His reasons why, but damn her voice had been so pretty. It had been soothing to every part of his body, which was inflamed with pain, a hangover from his treatments. He dialed her back, but it went to voicemail. Anxiety tightened him, as he called three more times. Voicemail. Voicemail. Voicemail. He wanted her so damn bad. He missed the hell out of her. His girl. Such a beautiful fucking girl. He pulled the curtain closed that separated the beds and felt his reserve give out, as he pulled the hospital gown over his face, lifted eyes to the ceiling, and broke. Every hard piece of him crumbled, as his face contorted, and he tried to stifle the pain. Her voice. The one she had gifted to him first, was like the key that unlocked the box to his undoing. *God, take care of her for me, Man. Just let my shorty be good.*

Messiah had no idea the way his absence was tearing Morgan apart. Hearing her voice made him want to hop out the hospital bed and rush to her.

Come back to me.
Come back to me.
Come back to me.

Her voice, so delicate with a hint of rasp. His name. Those zz's. On her lips. He could see the pout they made in his head. Messiah climbed out the bed, snatching the IV from his arm. As soon as his feet hit the cold, tile floor, his legs gave out. The chemo and radiation treatments he had endured earlier that day had snatched the strength from his body. Messiah leaned balled fists onto the mattress, as his stomach went missing and bile built in his throat.

Messiah gritted his teeth and closed his eyes.

Fuck this. Get to yo' fucking girl, nigga.

Messiah practically growled, as tears filled his eyes, and he took a step away from the bed. His legs buckled, and Messiah's eyes burned with determination, as he turned back to the bed. He flipped the whole fucking mattress off the bed, as he hollered in agony.

He wanted her. He wanted her more than anything in this moment.

"Nurse! Nurse!" the old woman called from behind the curtain.

A woman rushed into the room.

"Mr. Williams, what's wrong?" she asked. "We have to get you back in bed."

"Get your hands off me," he stated, voice so deadly that the nurse froze. "I'm getting the fuck out of here."

"You can't leave," she said.

"I have to, man! She needs me, and I can't even take two steps out of this fucking bed!" Messiah lowered his chin to his chest, as his entire chin quivered. He was trying to let her go. He was trying not to put the grief of watching him die on her soul. Damn, he was trying so hard, but her voice was ringing in his head. Over and over. Messiah wasn't sane enough for this. He had a few screws loose that only Mo could tighten. He was going to kill somebody in this hospital, if he didn't see her face, but he knew he couldn't. He was no good to himself. *You're a burden. Let her go.*

He gripped the railing to the bed, in anguish, and then turned to sit on the frame of the bed.

"How much longer? Until it's over?" he asked the nurse.

"There is no concrete..." The nurse stopped to gather herself and she sucked in a deep breath. She was visibly shaken by this outburst. "Your fight isn't over," she stammered. "The moment your mind and heart give up, your body will too. You should try to be optimistic."

"Shit ain't even worth fighting for without her," Messiah said.

Messiah laid in the dark for hours, thinking about Mo. He had messed things up with her so badly that he didn't even know how to make it right. Leaving felt as right as wrong would allow. He picked up his phone and called Bleu. It was late. Too late to be calling, but tonight an exception was necessary.

"Messiah?" she answered, voice heavy with exhaustion, groggy, and deeper than usual.

"I just wanted to hear you, B. Just to say thank you, you know? I ain't shit and you stuck with an ain't shit nigga. I just needed to hear your voice."

"Messiah? Is everything okay? It's four in the morning. What's wrong?"

Messiah sniffed away overwhelming emotion and cleared his throat, because he felt like a bitch. If he had to go out, it wasn't going to be on his knees.

"Nah, B, more like what's right?" he answered.

There was a pause on the other end. "Messiah? You're not making sense. You're worrying me. You're making me anxious, and you know what that does to me. Tell me you're okay," she whispered.

"You're the shit, B. Go back to sleep." He hung up the phone and climbed out of the bed. He leaned all his weight onto the metal pole, where bags of medication, steroids, and antibiotics, hung. The bags were connected to tubes that ran right into his IV. Bullshit. They were filling him with bullshit, just to keep him breathing. Messiah was a man. A dominant, alpha-male, with ego and pride, and he couldn't even hold his own weight. He struggled all the way to his bag and unzipped it, removing the chrome .9mm pistol that was tucked in the bottom. He was never unprotected, even in the hospital. He stayed strapped. Everywhere. His gun was like his dick. He couldn't go anywhere without it, and the bigger the better. He went into the bathroom and shut the door. The reflection in the mirror, he didn't even recognize. He had lost so much weight, but that wasn't what made him appear different. It was his eyes. In them, he saw a soul, a soul that Morgan Atkins had put there. It was because of her that he felt everything. He had learned to numb the pain over the years. He had trained himself to need no one. To depend on no one. Then, she had peeled the scab from his wounds and he was bleeding. He was infected with her love. He couldn't live with this. The separation. And he was tired of dying slowly. Tired of missing her…tired of fearing the next treatment…tired of wondering what day would be his last. Morgan and Messiah shared a love so strong that if they couldn't have one another, they'd rather have nothing at all. Some would call him weak, but he knew better, they knew better too, because niggas would never call him anything but his name to his face. King Ssiah. Messiah MF Williams. There was just so much pain and Messiah was ready for it to end. Messiah gritted his teeth harder and then opened his mouth…

Ssiah, no!

He heard the voice so clearly, he had to pull the door to the bathroom open to make sure she wasn't there with him.

He heaved, as his chest rose and fell, as adrenaline coursed through him. In his head, her voice reverberated, stopping him.

I'm begging you, please, Messiah!

"Ssiah, no!" Morgan sat up in bed, drenched in a cold sweat, as she called out his name. Morgan reached for the lamp next to her bed, causing light to flood her old room. She was at Ethic's, but her mind… her mind was still stuck in the nightmare she had just awoken from. The dream where he was standing alone with a gun to his head, finger to the trigger. "God, please no," she whispered. It took her some time to steady her breathing. The panic that locked up her chest was hard to shake. "It was just a dream. That's it." She told herself; but damn if it didn't feel like so much more.

Morgan and Messiah had created a bond that transcended space. She had no idea just how real her dreams were, but as she pulled the cover up over her shoulder, she took a deep breath and whispered, "Bring yo' ass home…"

"I can't, shorty."

Morgan flipped the covers off her, suddenly, because she heard that shit. She felt it, and suddenly, everything he had ever told her played back in her head. "Something's wrong…" she whispered, as tears came to her eyes. "Oh my god, Messiah. Where are you?"

TO BE CONTINUED...

Guyssss! These people are killlinggggggg me. So, here we are, two books past the finale I announced in Part 4, and I have no excuse except for the characters aren't done with me yet. Ethic isn't done with me. Alani, my sweet Alani, is not done. Morgan and Messiah are just so lost. They still need me. The conclusion to this series is breathtaking. It transcends life and death. It's not even about who lives or dies anymore. It's about connection. It's about love between people who have no other choice but to submit to the bonds they feel because they truly can't help who they love. These people are going to love until they're forced to let go. Let's see who has the endurance to hold on. We're almost there…the end. There's no need to rush, but the finish to this literary journey you've joined me on is up ahead. I can see it. I can feel it, and it'll be worth every painful flip of the page. I promise. Ethic's journey will end in the next book, but let's appreciate it while we're in it. There's no point in rushing through art, if you don't understand what's being conveyed. Go there with me. If you're reading this, you've already held on tightly for five books. Give me one more. I promise, this series will forever change the way you read AND love. It has definitely changed every fiber of me. Thank you for letting me bleed this story. Part 6 pre-order is available now at www.asharmy.com.

-xoxo-

Ashley Antoinette